The Sweet Spot

Also by Heather Heyford

An Oregon Wine Country Romance

Kisses Sweeter Than Wine

Intoxicating

The Crush

The Napa Wine Heiresses

A Taste of Sake

A Taste of Sauvignon

A Taste of Merlot

A Taste of Chardonnay

The Sweet Spot

A Willamette Valley Romance

Heather Heyford

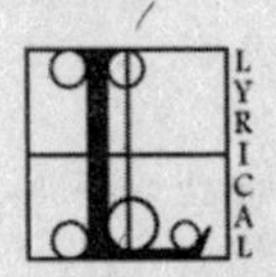

LYRICAL PRESS
Kensington Publishing Corp.
www.kensingtonbooks.com

LYRICAL PRESS BOOKS are published by

Kensington Publishing Corp.
119 West 40th Street
New York, NY 10018

All Kensington titles, imprints, and distributed lines are available at special quantity discounts for bulk purchases for sales promotion, premiums, fund-raising, educational, or institutional use.

Special book excerpts or customized printings can also be created to fit specific needs. For details, write or phone the office of the Kensington Sales Manager: Attn.: Sales Department. Kensington Publishing Corp., 119 West 40th Street, New York, NY 10018. Phone: 1-800-221-2647.

First Printing: March 2018
ISBN-13: 978-1-5161-0256-3
ISBN-10: 1-5161-0256-8

First Electronic Edition: March 2018
eISBN-13: 978-1-5161-0259-4
eISBN-10: 1-5161-0259-2

10 9 8 7 6 5 4 3 2 1

Printed in the United States of America

This book is dedicated to Esi Sogah, with gratitude for your patience, faith, and wisdom.

Chapter One

Oregon's wine country

Hank Friestatt eased off the accelerator as his SUV bore down on a compact car traveling well below the posted speed limit. He skimmed his rearview mirror and then rechecked the straight stretch ahead, but theirs were the only two vehicles around. No cops with radar guns hid along side streets. No oncoming traffic barreled down in the opposite lane. So what was the holdup?

He lowered the window and craned his neck out to look around the car ahead, only to pull up sharply when its brake lights blinked red. Inside the rear window heads turned and fingers pointed across miles of carefully tended vineyards toward a stunning, white-capped peak in the distance.

The snow atop Mt. Hood was just another reminder of Hank's past life . . . endless, carefree days spent on the ski slopes and dreaming of becoming a pilot, before he'd become tied to the family business the way a grapevine is tied to a trellis—secured with a double knot, allowing enough room to grow, but not enough to move out of place.

The scene was so pastoral, so harmonious, it was easy to forget that Mt. Hood might erupt again at any moment, just as it had in 1865, the year Hank's family immigrated to Oregon.

He rubbed his aching temples. That's what he got for staying too long at the White Horse last night. But it was well worth it to spend a few stolen hours with his few friends who had nothing to do with the wine business. They got his mind off work. Then again, none of them had to get up at five to mow, and then pay the mountains of monthly bills racked up by an established vineyard estate that included a working winery.

Just as he'd thought. A rental, full of the season's first tourists. His eyes flickered impatiently over the dashboard, rapidly recalculating his ETA to the airport.

Most of the visitors to his family's resort arrived on Sunday afternoons. When there were stragglers—people who didn't care to rent a car, workaholics, type A's who couldn't manage even a complete week's vacation—Nelson typically went for them. But Nelson was in an ankle cast after taking a tumble down the back steps of the inn last Friday night.

It would be simple to swerve around those slowpokes and be on his way. But there was a double yellow line prohibiting passing. And in driving, as in life, Hank tended to follow the rules, even when odds were he wouldn't get caught.

He tossed his ball cap onto the passenger seat, turned on the radio, and slung his wrist over the steering wheel.

"When I find your house, I'm gonna rip that door off its hinges . . ."

There were love songs, and then there were scorchers that could knock a woman up all by themselves. He'd only heard this one a few times before and didn't know all the lyrics yet, but those he did know poked at his insides, urging him to explore their meaning and conversely, warning him to leave well enough alone.

He cranked it up and sang along, picking up a new line here and there. What else did he have to do, stuck here behind those rubberneckers?

Grandma Ellie said what he needed was a good woman, as if that were the answer to his restless spirit. But no woman had ever incited that kind of passion in him. Then again, who felt like that in real life? It was just a stupid song.

He jabbed the station button repeatedly, in search of something else. What, he didn't know. He was going to be late. That's all that was eating him. That, and the fact that right now he ought to be supervising the vine-thinning and shoot-repositioning instead of wasting time driving to Portland.

Finally he turned into the Arrivals lane of Portland International Airport. Checking his watch yet again, he rolled to a stop at the Delta sign, slapped his cap back on, and jumped out, making sure to hit the lock-door button on his remote.

* * *

The first thing Jamie Martel was going to do when she got to the Sweet Spot was order a glass of wine. Not that she hadn't already tasted the Sweet Spot's brand of pinot. It might sound silly, but she was eager to see if her favorite wine tasted even better when she was standing on the sacred soil where the grapes were grown.

Tapping her foot, she checked her cell phone. Where was the guy who was supposed to pick her up?

She positioned herself smack-dab in the center of the Arrivals area and stood her ground despite the barely disguised annoyance of travelers detouring their rolling bags around her, her large checked bag, oversized tote, and guitar. No way could he miss her now.

The sliding glass doors swooshed open and closed as passengers and their loved ones came and went, doling out greetings, hugs, and backslaps. It seemed everybody had somebody except her. Soon all the familiar faces on her incoming flight had gone, leaving her standing there alone like a piece of unclaimed baggage.

She'd been counting the days until this trip. Now that she was finally this far, she couldn't wait to finish the last leg. She bit her lip as her eyes continued to scan the area. Maybe she'd been a little too impulsive, flying across the country all by herself to a place where she didn't know anyone. *Maybe I should have backed out of this trip when Kimmie did,* she thought for the umpteenth time.

Where was that driver?

She dug again for her cell. "Excuse me," she said when her tote bumped a full-bearded man with a sleeve tattoo. But before she could pull up the vineyard number, she heard the whooshing sound of the doors again, and striding toward her with the setting sun at his back came a broad-shouldered silhouette.

The man grabbed the fraying brim of a ball cap with the words TEXTRON AVIATION emblazoned across the crown and swept it off to reveal bottomless brown eyes and a head full of thickly layered, brown hair. "Miz Martel? Hank Friestatt. Sorry I'm late."

She had a vague impression of faded jeans and a denim shirt, a twisted red neckerchief in a loose U around his neck. But his eyes, filled with contradictions, were what held her captive. Something about them was injured, yet yearning. Vulnerable, but guarded. They drew her in while warning her: *Don't get too close.*

The warm strength in his hand surrounding hers was an unexpected comfort after having spent the last seven hours with only a teenage boy immersed in his video games and an overworked flight attendant for company.

"Just Jamie. I was starting to think you'd forgotten about me."

They stood motionless for a moment, while all around them the endless stream of people continued to ebb and flow.

Then Jamie heard that glass of pinot calling her name again.

"Would you mind giving me a hand with these bags?"

Though the famous teal-blue carpeting of the PDX did a good job of muffling the footfalls of the passengers, he must not have heard her.

"My bag?" She looked down pointedly at their lingering handclasp.

"Right." Swiftly, he divested her of not just one but both bags plus her guitar, leaving her empty-handed like some helpless, antebellum princess. "You play? Nice. I'm right outside. Let's go."

He led her to a dusty SUV with its blinkers flashing. With an economy of motion he tossed her gear in the back and slid in next to her, shifting into drive.

"Can't remember the last time we had a pickup on a Wednesday," he said, checking his rearview and pulling into traffic. "You joining a crew that's already up at the vineyard?"

"A friend of mine was supposed to be coming, too, but her plans changed."

He lifted a brow. "You came out here all by yourself?"

"For two whole weeks."

"Don't worry, there's lots of folks already on board, lots of things to do. We have meals family style. You'll meet people there. Hope you like wine."

"Do I! How else could I survive four hundred thirty-two precocious rappers-in-training?"

He glanced over at her, his interest mildly piqued.

"I teach music at an inner-city school for gifted kids."

At the mention of the city, he brightened. "Where'd you say you live?"

"Philadelphia."

"I went to school in Denver. Loved everything about that area. The nightlife. Coors Field. Loved every minute of it until—" He bit his tongue. "Going back for a visit soon, as a matter of fact. Can't wait."

"I've been living in Philly for a while now, but I grew up in Lancaster County and I'd do anything to go back there, even though some may not find it very exciting. There's something about belonging to a place . . ." A familiar melancholy arose in her, but she shrugged it off, looking out at the sights of Portland as they headed away from the airport. "I've been dying to get out here to wine country." Now that she was finally here, she refused to let the past intrude on the present.

"Tried any of our pinot noir? Or maybe you prefer white. Our Riesling's really coming along."

Talk of wine never failed to lift her spirits. "After music, Oregon pinot noir is my jam. Have you ever had a wine epiphany?" In her growing excitement, she shifted so that she was facing him, and tucked one foot under her bottom. "A moment when a certain wine rocks your world? Some people say it's like being baptized into the wine religion."

"Wine religion?" Hank laughed out loud. "Now I've heard everything."

Heat crawled up her neck. She'd have thought that Henry Friestatt VIII, of all people, would understand. "I was skeptical, too, at first. Wine was just a way to bond with friends over a meal."

"And then you had this epiphany?"

"As a matter of fact, I did." She turned her face to the window so he wouldn't see her cheeks in full bloom, remembering that chilly April evening with Kimmie and two other friends at a place called Entree in South Philly.

"Well?" Hank laughed. "You can't just leave me hanging."

"It was a 2015 Friestatt Sweet Spot pinot noir." She had been all set to go on at length about the choir of angels singing and the confetti fluttering down from the ceiling, but if all he was going to do was laugh at her . . .

"Good to know."

She'd just paid him a massive compliment. Was that all he had to say about it?

Whatever.

She sat back in her seat to the shush of tires on asphalt, thinking about the life she had left behind for a respite.

Just before school let out, the head of the music department had resigned unexpectedly and Jamie was offered the position, starting next fall. It was the career opportunity of a lifetime, making her the school's youngest-ever department head.

Jamie had accepted right then and there, before the committee had a chance to change their minds.

Her only misgiving was the look on the face of Aaron Beekman when he came up to her in the hallway the day after the announcement.

Aaron was a studious introvert with wire-rims, a thin, blond comb-over, and an earring. He was principal oboist in an orchestra on Philadelphia's Main Line. He was also Jamie's teacher-mentor.

Like all teachers, from Jamie's first day she was given a full program and expected to hit the ground running. Aside from the official checklist of mentor duties consisting of things like orientation, co-teaching, and goal setting, Aaron went out of his way to make Jamie feel respected. When she had a problem, he listened. When she met a small goal, he celebrated with her—and then challenged her to set a new one.

Most of all, he made her feel safe in coming to him when she made a mistake. That had made all the difference when she was still new and racked with nerves.

Aaron had been teaching for ten years. When he heard about the chairmanship opening, he confided that he was going to apply.

"You should apply, too," he said.

"Me?" replied Jamie. "They're not going to choose me. I've only been teaching for three years."

"But look what you've done in the short time you've been here . . . the festival you started for district band, chorus, and orchestra. What do you have to lose? Going through the interview process will be good practice for later, when you're really serious about advancement."

And so, like always, she had taken Aaron's advice.

When Jamie got the job, if he was hurt, he was far too professional—and generous—to ever let her see it.

"Congratulations," he'd said, taking both Jamie's hands in his. "I'm looking forward to seeing all the exciting things you're going to do for the department."

"Aaron, I—"

"I won't hear a word of it," he said, putting his

finger to her lips. "You got the job, fair and square. No hard feelings."

"You're a wonderful teacher, Aaron," she said. "I'm going to be so lucky to have you on my team."

One of the last things her superintendent had said to her was to make her last summer count. Starting next year, she'd be working admin hours; in other words, all year round.

That's when Jamie decided to come out West. She hadn't taken a real vacation since eleventh grade, the year Mom passed away. Dad had been squarely behind her decision. *Your mom would want you to,* he'd said. If not for that, Jamie would already be working on plans for next school year. But Dad said she deserved a break. Someplace far from the hustle and bustle.

Hank pointed out Portland's iconic Big Pink and the Wells Fargo Center right before they dipped under a bypass. On the other side, it was as if they'd crossed the border into another country.

"Ah. Look at this!" Jamie exclaimed. "Not a high-rise in sight. Those mountains look a lot like the blue hills where I'm from. Except for those spiky evergreens. They remind me of the way one of my students might draw a Christmas tree, pointy at the top with tiers that sweep outward, widening into the shape of a triangle."

She grinned at Hank, but he seemed strangely immune to the beauty of their surroundings. He kept his eyes on the road, leaning slightly forward as if that would help speed them to their destination.

"Soon as we get to the inn I'll hand you off to

my grandmother. She'll get you settled and tell you where to go."

She'd been dismissed—granted, in the nicest way possible, but still dismissed. But then, what was she to Hank Friestatt but one guest among countless others before and after her?

She opened her window, leaned back and sniffed. Unlike the dense humidity of a Mid-Atlantic June, the air here in Oregon was bone dry. The clean scents of sage and pine were already having a relaxing effect, despite her driver being in such an obvious rush to be finished with her.

Hank snuck a sideways glance at Jamie Martel. She was pale. Too pale, like she'd been stuck inside too long. Well, that wouldn't last. A little sun and exercise—to put the roses back in her cheeks, as Ellie liked to say—and by the time she was ready to go home again, she'd be almost pretty. Almost.

Then again, there wasn't a man alive who wouldn't appreciate that long right angle from her nicely rounded rear-end to her sneakers when she'd climbed into his truck.

With every grassy meadow, every swaying field of horsetail and dandelion they passed, her eyes had lit up anew. The way she gawked at the scenery reminded him of his first trip to New York. He'd gotten a neck ache from looking up at the skyscrapers.

As the inn loomed into view, Jamie sat up straighter.

Hank tried seeing the vineyard where he'd spent

most of his life through fresh eyes. The eyes of someone for whom green and brown corduroy rows of vines were simply pretty scenery, not yet another reminder of the magnitude of his responsibilities that had fallen out of the sky onto his shoulders.

Chapter Two

"There she is," Hank drawled as he slowed and turned left onto a side road. Tall pines on either side of the lane opened up to a clearing.

Jamie leaned toward the windshield to take it all in.

Across the road hung a weather-beaten sign on an iron-link chain. Burned into the wood was a heart shape with a bull's eye in its upper right corner, pierced with an arrow. WELCOME TO THE SWEET SPOT.

The ombré sky went from navy in the east to cornflower-blue where the sun had just dipped below the vineyards. Stars popped out before her eyes. And there was the rustic yet elegant inn, the stable, tucked within its paddock, and the little log cabins emanating out from them in a half circle. In the midst of it all, a still pond reflected the remnants of the day's clouds.

"Wow," she breathed. "It's even prettier than the pictures in the brochure."

Hank kept his eyes straight ahead. How could

he not be moved? If this place were hers, she'd never get tired of coming home to it.

Suddenly Hank veered right. Roaring down the middle of the lane came a black Escalade headed straight toward them.

Jamie's side of the truck dropped a foot when the tires descended into the roadside ditch concealed by knee-high weeds, narrowly avoiding getting sideswiped. Jamie's hand shot to the dash. "Jeez, buddy," she said, turning around to look at the vehicle disappearing into a cloud of dust. "Guess they didn't see the SLOW sign."

A moment later they crunched to a stop under the extended porch roof.

Before she had unbuckled her seat belt, Hank was already standing next to her, holding her door open.

Jamie stepped out, her legs stiff from sitting for so many hours.

Peering down the lane at the dust still settling behind the Escalade was a woman with a long white braid hanging over her shoulder and the same high cheekbones as Hank. In one ear she wore the latest-style Bluetooth headset.

"There's no land for sale around here," she muttered. "How many times do I have to tell them that?"

"Another Realtor?" asked Hank, depositing Jamie's bags on the ground at the woman's feet.

She shook her head. "Every week it's someone else. And every week, the offer goes up."

Tiny bugs hovered around the porch lights. A yellow Lab, tail wagging, sniffed at Jamie's ankles. She bent to pat his head.

"You're Jamie Martel." The woman swiped her electronic tablet. "I'm Ellie. Don't worry about your bags, I'll find someone."

"Where's Bailey?" asked Hank.

"Haven't seen her all day."

Hank picked the bags up again. "Which cabin?"

She peered at her tablet. "Looks like Chicory."

The woman lowered her readers to get a better look at Jamie.

"You hungry, Miz Martel?" Before Jamie could answer, Ellie shifted her attention back to Hank. "Why don't you two come in and have a bite? There's some leftover chicken."

Hank flashed Ellie a puzzled look, and then lowered the bags yet again.

"It's Jamie. And you don't have to do anything special for me." Her stomach rumbled. She'd been considering the dry, crumbling cereal bar somewhere in the bottom of her purse. Real food sounded fabulous.

"You been traveling all day. You need a decent meal in you. You can eat with Hank and me."

"If it wouldn't be too much trouble."

"Come on inside with me while Hank parks."

She followed Ellie up the porch steps, slowing her pace when the older woman groaned a little. "That's my knees complaining. They don't like these steps this time of day."

Easing the squeaky screen door closed, Jamie paused and got her bearings. In the cross breeze wafted the faint scent of pine. Recorded piano music played softly in the background.

"Make yourself at home. I'll see to supper," said Ellie, disappearing through a side door.

Jamie stepped deeper into the room. Her eye was drawn upward to an enormous moose head mounted above the river-stone fireplace that soared all the way up to the rough-hewn ceiling beams. Before the wood fire a young couple snuggled on a leather couch atop a well-worn Persian rug in muted hues of sapphire and ruby. Jamie eyed them wistfully. It'd been a long time since a man had looked at her like that.

She fingered the rough texture of an amethyst geode the size of a grapefruit, containing a hollow cavity lined with crystals, catching a glimpse of her reflection in the glass case of a grandfather clock.

No decorator had ever drenched a room with such a sense of cozy comfort . . . such solid reassurance . . . such contentment. The objects looked as though they'd been accumulated over years. Even decades.

On the west side of the enormous room was a long trestle table. She went over and stroked the polished wood.

The screen door squealed again and in strode Hank, letting it slam closed behind him. "C'mon back," he said with a wave of his arm.

Under the kitchen table the Lab looked up, then relaxed when he saw Hank and Jamie.

Jamie's gaze swept over ochre walls inset with stainless steel appliances. Harvest baskets heaped with cantaloupe and watermelons were arranged on the floor off to the side next to a couple cases of wine. Copper pots cluttered the commercial-size range. She breathed in the vanilla scent of freshly baked cookies.

Ellie's mittened hands carried a cast-iron skillet

to the table. "You can wash up over there," she said with a nod toward an apron sink.

Jamie felt Hank's eyes on her while she lathered her hands. But when she finished drying them and passed him the hand towel, he looked away.

"Help yourself now, there's plenty," prompted Ellie.

Greedily, she loaded up her plate.

"Wine?" asked Hank from where he stood directly across from her, inserting a corkscrew into the neck of a bottle with his family crest boldly emblazoned on the label, as casually as Jamie opened a carton of orange juice.

"You have to ask?"

Ellie looked up.

"She claims the 2015 gave her a wine epiphany."

The cork came out with a soft pop.

"I'll take that as a compliment," said Ellie with a nod to Jamie.

Hank poured the wine into three bell-shaped glasses, setting two down in front of Ellie and Jamie, then took his seat and raised his glass. "Cheers," he said without undue ceremony. He took a sip and then lowered his eyes to his plate and began to eat.

Slowly, Jamie raised her glass and peered through the translucent ruby liquid poured by none other than the owner of the Sweet Spot, in the family's private quarters, no less. She wanted to savor this moment, to remember it on a day years from now when this trip was a distant memory and a part of her doubted that it had ever happened.

It wasn't about prestige. Not for a minute. It was the all-encompassing sensations the wine awakened. She could practically smell the freshly turned earth the grapes had been grown in. Feel on her shoulders the warm sunlight that had nurtured the vines. Taste the faint hint of minerals from the ancient seabed beneath the soil, like the time when she was little and she'd licked a wet stone after a rainstorm.

While Hank focused on his food, she swirled and watched the legs run down the sides of the bowl of the glass. Finally, she sipped, letting the wine wash over the tip of her tongue where the sweet taste-bud receptors were, the sides, which perceived salty and sour, and finally the back, which picked up bitterness.

"Well?" Ellie had been studying her over her glasses.

A grin spread across her face. "Tastes like happiness in a glass."

Ellie grunted her approval, then picked up her fork.

"Your chicken is delicious, too," said Jamie.

"It's just like the wine. It's the love that goes into it. First you got to dredge it in cornmeal seasoned with paprika, then dip it in your egg batter, then dredge it again. Then you got to stand by the stove and watch the hot oil every minute so it doesn't burn."

"Kind of like when I used to babysit the neighbor kids. I didn't just plop them down in front of a video. I got down on the floor with them, gave them pony rides. Played board games. Read them stories. Guess that's when I realized I wanted to be a teacher."

"You cook?"

"My sister and I were each given our own little corner of the garden to learn how vegetables grow. Things like carrots and parsley. Sometimes, when I'm craving home cooking, I'll order one of those meal kits," she said sheepishly. "You know. The ones where the ingredients come premeasured and all you have to do is assemble them? But it never tastes anything like this. All that to say I end up eating out . . . a lot.

"Given the business you're in, I'm sure you know that Pennsylvania's one of the last remaining closed states. There are only so many liquor licenses to go around, and when one does come onto the market, the price is through the roof. As a result, Philadelphia's become known for its BYOBs. When a restaurant isn't saddled with the huge overhead that comes with a liquor license, they can focus more on the food—and charge less for it. The upshot of that is when you have to go out of your way to shop for your own wine, you can't help but eventually learn something."

She didn't disclose that she'd become so knowledgeable her friends had begun deferring to her to buy the wine whenever they went out.

A door to the outside swung open and a worried-looking man in Carhartts with a wisp of straw in his salt-and-pepper beard hurried in. When he saw them around the table he pulled up short, holding his rough, raw hands slightly out from his sides, as if they didn't know how to be idle. "Miss Ellie. Hank." He eyed Jamie curiously. "Sorry for interrupting. Thought you two ate earlier. When you're finished up here, can you stop over to the barn?"

But Hank was already out of his seat, headed toward the back door. "What's up, Bryce?"

"Gophers, that's what. Bright green holes between rows six and eight in Block Nine."

Hank pushed on the old-fashioned, spring-loaded screen door.

Bryce snatched a sugar cookie from the plate on the counter and followed him outside to the slamming of the door.

The men's voices trailed away.

"Did he just say *gophers*?" asked Jamie.

"That he did. Make themselves right at home in the vineyards this time of year. Drives Bryce up the wall. He used to wipe em out in one pass with Molex before my son—Hank's dad—started the long process of converting to organic about ten years back. Or, as Bryce calls it, voodoo viniculture. He knows better. Knows we're trying to get certified biodynamic. That means no chemicals. He's mostly good with it. But when it comes to those gophers, he's got a fixation.

"Hank is our vineyard manager. He oversees everything having to do with the grapes, from deciding what to plant to blending the wine along with our lead winemaker. I'm in charge of the housekeepers, the kitchen, and miscellaneous. That's over a dozen employees during high season, not counting the field-workers. The faces change. Some come back year after year. Others move on or go back to school. But that's only when everything's running smoothly, which, truth be told, it rarely is around here. Hank has been known to help serve in the dining room. And I know how to prune vines with the best of them."

Jamie scooped a second helping of rice onto her plate. "Do you do all the cooking?"

"Couldn't if I wanted to. We plate between ten and twenty breakfasts and lunches a day, in season. When it comes to dinner, the guests are on their own. A bit of a boon for the restaurants down in Newberry and even the surrounding towns, depending on how far people feel like driving. I plan the menus, and there are certain jobs I keep for myself—like the twice-monthly campouts, and such. And I always make one last sweep through the kitchen at night to be sure things are all set for the next day. To tell you the truth, we're a little shorthanded, what with Nelson's broken ankle and all. That sure put a spoke in the wheel. Might even be picking up a part-timer to help in the tasting room if we can find one this late in the season. The problem is, most of the usual suspects are hired out by now."

"Nelson?"

"One of our wine docents. That's his official title, but he's way more than that. He's been working here since Hank was still in that highchair."

Ellie nodded toward the antique wooden chair with a tray, sitting in a corner of the kitchen. A scene from a Mother Goose nursery rhyme had been painted on the seat back. By the looks of it, Hank had been far from the first child to sit in it.

"He helps with the horses, too, and I trust him with my banking and the mail."

When the meal was over, Jamie got up to help Ellie clear the table.

"I'll call someone to take you to your cabin. Won't have you walking back in the dark your first night here."

Ellie punched in some numbers and waited, to no avail. "I'm sorry about this. I have no idea why Bailey's not answering," she muttered. "I'll try again in a minute."

"Let's get these dishes started," replied Jamie as she carried her plate to the sink, cranked on the spigot and squirted some detergent into the rising water.

Ellie held up the wine bottle to the light. "Might as well finish this. There's just enough for each of us to have a sip. Little unusual, a woman your age coming here by herself," she added, replenishing their glasses. "You were booked with someone else at first, weren't you?"

"My friend Kimmie. We work together. She was really disappointed about canceling, but she was just awarded a summer fellowship she'd applied for on a whim. I told her she'd be crazy to turn it down. I was going to cancel, too, but I was dying to get out of the city."

"I've been racking my brain, but for the life of me I can't recall the last time we played host to a music teacher. You see the baby grand out in the great room?"

"Hard to miss it. Do you play?"

"Not since my arthritis started acting up. But the guy from Newberry still comes out and tunes it once a year. You're welcome to play anytime you want."

Jamie withdrew the serving bowl from the suds

and stared at the lush fruit and flower design. "This dish. My grandmother had this pattern."

"This is all that's left of my mother's very first set of dishes. She bought them at the old mercantile store in Newberry when she was a new bride." Ellie took it from her, turned it over and rinsed off the suds, and read the mark. "Johnson Brothers. Harvest Fruit pattern." She sighed. "Store's not there anymore. So many changes." She wiped it lovingly and reached to place it on a high shelf.

"Here. Let me," said Jamie.

"Maybe you'll get lucky and your grandmother will leave you hers one day."

"Too late," said Jamie before she thought the better of it. "When our farm was sold I was living in a dorm. My sister was a newlywed but her apartment was the size of a shoebox, and Dad was looking at a town house. None of us had room to keep all the crap that had been gathering dust for decades up in the attic."

Ellie flashed her a look.

"Not crap. I didn't mean it that way." Calling all those precious mementos crap in her mind made it somehow easier to deal with losing them. It had taken saying the words out loud to make her realize that.

But Ellie's expression held no judgment, only sympathy. "That's a shame. You ought to go check the list of this week's activities while you're waiting. Anything catches your eye, there's a sign-up sheet."

Behind her came the squeak of door springs.

"You're still here," said a deep voice.

Jamie whirled around to see Hank, and through the screen, the sky as black as ink.

"Would you please take this poor girl to her cabin?" Ellie scolded. "I imagine she's ready to drop. The whole day riding on planes, and then helping me with these pots."

Hank grabbed a cookie. "You ready?" he asked, biting off half.

Jamie opened her mouth to reply, but no words came out. Her eyes were glued to the lips of the Sweet Spot's owner, watching his tongue sweep a crumb neatly into his mouth.

After Hank showed Jamie where the light switches were and how the shower worked, he paused on her tiny porch.

"It's so peaceful here," she said beside him, as they looked out on the paddock and the vineyards beyond, her voice soft as velvet on the night air.

He jammed his hands into his pockets and listened. Only then did he hear the *kree-ek* of the tree frogs down by the pond.

"You good then?" he asked Jamie.

She glanced over her shoulder at the interior of the lamp-lit cabin, where her suitcase lay open on one of the beds.

"Looks like I've got everything I need."

He struck out for the inn. "Breakfast's at eight," he called over his shoulder.

But he didn't get far before he swung back around. "One last thing," he said, walking backward.

She peeked around the door. "Yes?"

"Oh." At the sight of her bare shoulder, he cast

his eyes to the dirt path out of a sense of propriety. "Sorry. What'd you sign up for tomorrow?"

"Riding, in the morning. I left the afternoon open. I want to take my time unpacking, wander around and get my bearings."

"You ride?"

"It's been a while."

"Then you'll meet people on the trail rides and round the campfire."

"Night then."

"Night."

Hank was halfway back to the inn when he realized the throbbing in his temples was gone.

He shook his head. What did he care what she was planning for tomorrow? Lord knew he had enough work for two men.

His trip to Denver couldn't get here soon enough. Delilah, a friend from college who still lived there, had invited him down for a visit.

Back in the kitchen, the dishwasher hummed in the background. Ellie set out a stack of gingham napkins for the breakfast crowd. "Get Jamie squared away?"

"Uh-huh." He hung up his hat for the last time that day.

"She seems like a sweet girl."

"I guess." He stopped halfway to the door between the kitchen and the great room. "Before I go up, tell me something. I get why you invited her to eat in the kitchen, seeing's how she didn't get any supper. But how come you acted like I hadn't already eaten, too?"

"Just a feeling I had. I didn't see the harm in getting better acquainted."

"What kind of feeling?"

As often as Grandma wished aloud about wanting him to find someone, she'd never singled out any particular individual. If this was her way of telling him that she'd picked Jamie—whom she'd only met that day—out of all the other women in the world, she'd sure picked an odd choice.

"Oh no you don't." Hank ran a hand through his hair, flattened down by his ball cap. There was no doubt in his mind.

"Why not? What's wrong with her?"

Because Jamie was as different from Hank as two people could be, that's why not. She had these romantic notions about winemaking and vineyards. What she didn't know was that growing grapes was in many ways the same as any other kind of farming—a tough way to make a living. If not for his parents dying unexpectedly, Hank wouldn't be here now. But fate had intervened, and now Ellie and he were all each other had left. She had raised him right alongside his parents. He could never do anything to hurt her.

"She's just not the one, that's all. End of story."

"When I was your age I was already married to your grandfather."

"That was then. This is now. People don't get married just to get married anymore."

"As far as supper goes, I thought you wouldn't mind eating again. You don't like my chicken?" She lifted a brow.

"You saw how much I ate." He bent and kissed her papery cheek. "G'night, Grandma."

On his way upstairs to his suite he pictured Jamie earlier, in his truck. Blonde or redhead? Her hair changed, depending on the light. At the airport, it'd glowed honey. But in the waning light in the truck coming home, it'd taken on a cinnamon hue.

Strawberry blond? Copper? While he brushed his teeth, stripped out of his clothes, and peeled back the covers, he kept hunting for the right word. For some reason beyond his grasp, it was important that he nail it down.

He lay down on his side and squeezed his eyes shut. Three years ago his world had shifted without warning. He'd left a life of unfettered freedom, skiing whenever the spirit moved him, on the brink of learning to fly. Now his every waking moment was dictated by a constant stream of income and expense statements, weather patterns and consumer buying trends. And even though he was raised to be a man who accepted his responsibility, he felt trapped. Thinking of it made his head start aching all over again. He flipped his pillow over to the cool side. What did he care what color her hair was? The coming months would bring a steady flow of visitors passing through his place, just like in every crush. They would drink his wine, ride his horses, and eat Ellie's old family recipes for a week or so, and then they'd fly away, most of them never to be seen again. Some of them were bound to be . . . what? What was it about Jamie Martel that had him losing precious sleep?

Chapter Three

After lunch, Jamie sat down on the grassy bank behind her cabin, pulled her sneakers and socks off, and wiggled her toes into the coolness of the creek.

Aaah, heaven. Slippery brown minnows swam around her ankles. She stretched her neck, and then lay back on the grass, closing her eyes to the sun's warmth until a strange, yet somehow familiar sound made her sit up and look toward the bend in the creek.

She'd heard that sound a million times on the farm, growing up. The rhythmic *shush* of a spade into damp earth and the sucking scrape as it was withdrawn.

She quickly put her shoes and socks back on, then rose and using the opposite creek bank as a guide, climbed up a gentle slope through tall grass, ducking beneath the branches of maple trees until she came upon a wheelbarrow along the edge of a cliff. She peered over and saw Hank and the yellow

Lab, Homer, standing in a few inches of water along the edge of the stream.

Homer looked up at the snap of a twig beneath Jamie's foot and Hank's eyes followed.

"Thought I heard the sound of shoveling," she called down to him. "What are you digging for?"

"Quartz."

Quartz? "Can I watch?"

"Suit yourself."

She started carefully down the bank. From the steep-sided wall of earth she saw that it was pock-marked with holes.

When she reached the bottom, Homer greeted her with a sniff and a wag of his tail.

"I saw the purple geode in the great room. Are you into rock collecting?"

"I remember the day I found that. I was with my dad, just a little north of here. That was a rare find. We use common quartz in our viniculture. Here." His wet, muddy hand held out a two-inch-long foggy ice cube with six equal sides. "Doesn't look like much, but it's a natural crystal. I'll admit the science is kind of squishy. But they say they have special powers."

She turned it over in her hand. "What do you do with them?"

"Grind them into a powder called silica. Then we pack the silica into cow horns and bury them in the vineyard. After a couple months, we dig the horns up, mix the silica with water, and broadcast it over the leaves."

Despite growing up on a farm, nothing had prepared her for that. She didn't know what to say.

He dumped the contents of his bucket into the

sieve. "My dad began experimenting with hyper-organic farming over a decade ago. He believed it helped with photosynthesis, healthier leaf growth, and protection from disease, among other things. All the better when you use crystals found on the same or contiguous property you intend to use it on."

His phone rang. He dried his hand on his pants and dug in the pocket of his overalls stained red with clay, while Jamie's eye flickered over Hank's equipment—a ten-gallon plastic bucket, a spade, and a digger bar.

"Hey, Tom. Thanks for calling me back. You looking for work by any chance? I already have a man laid up with a broken ankle, and now I'm short another hand all of a sudden."

Pause.

"What you heard is true. Bailey's gone AWOL. I need someone for the tasting room right away."

Pause.

"You can't. Well, all right. Thanks anyway, and good luck. Later . . ."

Hank shoved his phone back in his pants pocket. At the faint buzz of a small plane overhead, Hank looked up with his hands on his hips and longing in his eyes. Then he looked down with a sigh of resignation at his empty sieve. "Looks like that's all I'm going to get today." He straightened his cap and began gathering up his tools.

"Can I help you carry something?" Jamie asked, picking up his spade.

"If you want."

They climbed the creek bank, loaded the gear in the barrow and headed down the slope. "You say you're a farm girl?"

"Growing up we had twenty-five head of Holsteins and a handful of quarter horses. But I've been in Philly since college."

"What do you do when you're not teaching school?"

"Write songs. Sing in coffee shops and at church. I spent the last three summers working on my master's."

"You're a busy girl."

"If you want to do something badly enough, you find a way to fit it in. Now that my master's is finished, I'm looking forward to going to wineries and spending more time with my niece and nephew. My mom died when my sister and I were in high school, but my dad sees her family practically every week."

"Anybody else?" he asked off-handedly. "Anyone special?"

She kept her eyes on her sneakers as they strolled together. "Not anymore."

"Didn't mean to pry."

"It's okay." Tentatively, she added, "What's Textron Aviation?"

He looked up sharply.

"Your ball cap."

"Textron is the parent company of Beechcraft, my dad's old plane. Why?"

"The only time you don't have it on is indoors."

The cap had become a part of him. It was the one remaining vestige of what could have been. He couldn't bear to give it up. "I used to dream about being an airline pilot, but looks like that wasn't in the cards."

Hank had come up with an abridged version of

his life's defining event to date, paring it down to the bone. "I'd just started flight school when my parents' small plane went down on the way home from Seattle."

"I'm so sorry."

"I always knew I'd follow in the footsteps of my dad, and his dad before him. I just thought I had more time."

Jamie gazed out at the rolling acres of vines, the inn, the tasting room, and the outbuildings with a new appreciation. "It's a lot to take on."

"Didn't have much choice in the matter." He couldn't let Ellie shoulder it all herself.

When they got back to the stretch of creek behind Jamie's cabin, Homer bounded after something in the tall grass. Hank headed away from the creek toward the barns and sheep pen, Jamie still carrying his spade.

"Ellie seems like a wise lady."

"She's like a second mother to me."

"Is it just the two of you?"

"I have a cousin, Jack. He's got twin girls. And I got second and third cousins out the wazoo. Some of them are in the wine business, too." His various cousins had inherited Hank's uncles' shares belonging to their common ancestor.

But as the direct descendant of the original immigrant to Oregon, the main estate was his.

At the sheep pen, Hank got a slice of apple from a wood box hung on the wall. He handed the fruit to Jamie and nodded toward the animals.

"They like these."

Jamie took the slice and reached over the low

fence. Two ewes and their lambs strained forward, their damp, velvet noses tickling her palm.

"We use the sheep to keep down the weeds between the vines. Preserves the soil by eliminating the need for herbicides. Free fertilizer, too, if you get my drift."

Smelling the fruit, a couple more sheep tried to horn in on the action.

"Sorry, guys. All gone."

With an irrational desire to please her, Hank scraped the bottom of the box for the rest of the fruit and dumped it all in her hastily cupped palms.

She fumbled, and he surrounded her feminine hands with his rough, calloused ones, unnerved by the unexpected, sensual feel of skin on skin.

He turned abruptly. "Don't spoil 'em, now. I got work to do. I'm filling in for Bailey in the tasting room—that is, unless she decides to show up."

Abandoning Jamie with her hands full of apples, he strode back to the tasting room to make more calls for help.

But he'd already gone through a dozen old job applications, a list of former employees, and checked with his best vintner friends. Seasonal workers arranged for summer employment way back in March or April, and it was already late June.

He scooted his chair into his battered desk only to be interrupted by the image in his head of Jamie in a proper English riding habit astride a bay thoroughbred, cantering through gently rolling Pennsylvania countryside.

He stood up and looked out the window at the

paddock, thinking to distract himself with the view. But in place of his horses he saw her leaning against her teacher's desk before a class full of students, long legs extending from beneath her skirt, crossed at the knee.

He dropped back into his seat, adjusted the bill of his ball cap, and forced himself to try to think of one more person with a dependable reputation who might be able to help him out until Bailey showed up.

Her hair is reddish gold, he decided.

Either that, or goldish red.

Chapter Four

In the need to learn, as soon as possible, all of the varied aspects of the business that had suddenly fallen into his hands, Hank hadn't been back to Denver since college. He was still mourning his parents' passing when he'd had to start making crucial decisions affecting the business. Complicating matters was the fact that things were always in a state of flux. He soon realized the computer system was out of date, and he was faced with a bewildering number of choices with which to replace it. And no sooner had he memorized which grape varietals were planted in which vineyards, than consumer tastes began to change. Joy, his winemaker, was lobbying him to rip out some perfectly good chardonnay rootstock and replace it with pinot gris at a considerable expense of time and money. It wasn't that he didn't trust Joy, but his father had believed in the promise of that chardonnay. Hank didn't feel confident enough to second-guess his extensive experience. Besides, all Joy had to worry about was the wine. Staying within a budget and managing the vineyard crew wasn't her concern.

And then, one gray day last March when he thought the job of supervising the pruning and tying-up of two hundred fifty acres of vineyards would never end, out of the airport limo parked beneath the canopy of the inn at the Sweet Spot emerged a pair of brightly painted toes laced up in high-heeled sandals.

"Delilah?"

"Hank? Hank Friestatt? Is it really you?"

They hadn't spoken since graduation. Last Hank knew, Delilah had accepted a job as a flight attendant. He'd kept his ski lodge job and got his EMT certification. At twenty-two, he wanted to soar, not be tethered to one spot. He was all set to start aviation lessons when his dream of flying was whipped out from under him like a throw rug.

Once in a while, when Hank looked up and saw a jet contrail, he envied Delilah her independence, flying here and there. He never dreamed that one day she'd land at the Sweet Spot.

"What are you doing here?" he'd asked, looking her up and down.

Delilah had always been a head-turner. Now she had blossomed into full-blown womanhood.

"I could ask you the same question."

"I live here. This is my place."

"You own the Sweet Spot? I had no idea!"

To his surprise, something about hearing it on Delilah's lips awakened a latent pride in Hank. As if pride could be inherited, like brown hair or the enduring Friestatt sense of duty.

Over a glass of wine, she had explained the reason for her visit. "Some of my frequent flyers and first-class passengers are always asking for my advice on out-of-the-way destinations. I listened to what they wanted, started collecting business cards and reaching out to small resorts, making deals with the proprietors in return for commissions."

"You started your own travel agency," he said in frank admiration. As often as he felt trapped by his family business, it had given him an appreciation for what it took to become a successful entrepreneur.

"It's just a sideline," she said modestly. "I don't intend to stop flying. I came to the Sweet Spot to see if it would be a good fit."

Following a two-day tour, she'd seemed enthusiastic about partnering with him. When it came time for her to check out, Ellie gave her the standard industry discount.

"Thanks for the hospitality," Delilah told Hank as she said good-bye. "And if you're ever in Denver, you're always welcome in my guest room."

"Tell me," asked Ellie as she and Hank waved to the van receding down the lane. "How come I never heard of this Delilah before?"

"We went out a couple of times," replied Hank.

He'd only half noticed Ellie's raised brow. He was remembering the first time he'd spotted Delilah strolling across the campus of the University of Denver, laughing with the center of the basketball team at some private joke. With those long, tan legs and high heels, she was nothing like the girls back home. Delilah Arnold wouldn't be caught dead walking to first period bleary-eyed, wearing sweatpants and a messy ponytail. *Delilah.* Even her name sounded exotic.

He'd made it his mission to find out more about her. He'd spent weeks trying to figure out what her schedule was so that he could occasionally end up in the same place at the same time.

Then, one day at the cafeteria salad bar, Hank reached across Delilah for the salad tongs, his arm brushing against hers.

She scanned him from head to toe, her initial frown turning upside down. "I've seen you before. On the quad, the other day, coming out of Sturm."

He shook his head. "Tsk. I don't think so," he said, playing it cool. He turned to go, only to be stopped in his tracks by manicured fingers on his bicep.

She had the whitest smile he'd ever seen.

"It was in the morning. I was leaving Speech."

"Wait." He frowned and pointed to her legs, as if just remembering. "Black miniskirt?"

Her pursed lips and the tilt of her head said his pretense hadn't fooled her for a second.

Next thing he knew he was carrying her tray with its plateful of leafy greens back to the spot where she'd left her jacket when she'd gone up to get her food. "Speech, huh?"

"Yeah." She sighed, sliding into a chair. "Gotta get up early for Petrosky three times a week."

The following Friday, he was waiting for her outside of Sturm Hall.

She gave him a sly grin but didn't break stride, so he hurried to fall into step with her.

He drove to the local Dairy Queen, where they'd perched on a bench eating Buster Bars and talked.

"Hank?" Ellie brought him out of his reverie. "You say you two used to date?"

"Not really dating."

He'd spotted her a few times after that, usually on the arm of the basketball star. But he was carrying a full load, working nights and weekends at the slopes and hanging out afterward with a couple of search-and-rescue pilots he'd met après-ski. He couldn't get enough of their stories about their daring exploits.

"That's some coincidence, her picking the Sweet Spot out of all the other fancy resorts she could have picked. Ribbon Ridge is far from an Aspen or a Jackson Hole."

"Delilah's just getting her feet wet. Starting with smaller properties, hoping to move up to the big ones. She says there aren't many boutique inns on real, working vineyards. Plus, the horses. D says affluent vacationers are hungry for experiences instead of buying more things."

Ellie eyed him sideways. "Didn't I tell your grandfather, back when he sold the cattle? 'We need to keep the horses,' I said. Turned out I was right.

"If this Delilah can point more visitors our way, that's the bottom line."

The new partnership necessitated periodic phone calls to track its progress. During one of those calls, Delilah again invited Hank to Denver.

That time, he said yes.

And now, finally, he was on his way. He couldn't wait.

Chapter Five

Jamie was twelve years old again, riding her roan mare through the tall grass along the property line of the family farm. Her hips rolled with Dora's familiar gait, the saddle squeaking in time. Bees buzzed in the clover. The sun shone warm on her back. It was the start of a spring weekend, and the only thing pressing was her English paper due Monday, but that was easily brushed aside, given that she had all weekend to complete it.

Somewhere in the distance a rooster crowed. She turned over and slung her pillow over her head, longing to stay in that simpler time and place.

Er-er-er-er errrrrrr!

That was no dream.

She opened one eye. The bed across from hers was still neatly made. Kimmie should be lying in it.

She rose and went to the window, her bare feet slapping the floorboards. Something else was missing. No ambulances wailed their way into Methodist Hospital. No yelling came through the wall from the couple next door, who couldn't get through one morning without an argument. No rap music drifted up from cars passing in the street below.

She was a musician. How could she have become anesthetized to nature's silence?

From her porch she took in the sights of the vineyard waking up. Bikes with woven baskets attached to the handlebars leaned against a split-rail fence. In the paddock, steam rose from the mug of a workman making his way toward the barn. The swishing tail of an Arabian caught her eye. Nearer, a smattering of people moved toward the inn, the morning sun painting their long shadows across the ruts in the road.

Seven forty-five already. She'd gotten more sleep than she'd thought. It had been only a little past dark when she went to bed. Must be the quiet.

If she wanted to eat breakfast she'd better hurry. Out here, there'd be no dashing to a corner coffee shop for a to-go cup.

She showered, longing as she always did for a bath—with her increase in salary starting in September, maybe she could afford to move to an apartment with one of those soaker tubs—and pulled a clean pair of jeans and a blue top from her suitcase. Then she scurried toward the inn, the smell of bacon frying making her mouth water.

She thought of her first morning at the vineyard, just days ago. She had brightened when she saw Hank and a field hand coming down the steps as she was going up.

"I don't know what could have happened to Bailey," said the worker. "This is the first I've heard about it."

But either because he was intent on what the man was saying or because he simply didn't notice her, Hank didn't so much as acknowledge Jamie's existence.

She felt her smile fade then. He'd been polite to her when they were forced together, alone in his SUV and in his grandmother's kitchen. *But from here on out,* she thought, *I'm on my own.*

But inside the great room it had been just the opposite. Dozens of curious eyes looked up from their plates when Ellie had breezed through a swinging door bearing a basket of fragrant muffins in each hand, the ever-present Homer at her side, and announced, "Folks, make room for Jamie. She just came in last night."

This morning, Jamie took refuge next to a flaxen-haired child. She always felt at home around kids.

"We're going to ride the horsies today!"

"Well, what do you know? Me too," replied Jamie.

"Molly loves to ride," said her mother, seated on the other side of her. "I'm Dina. Don't mind the stares. You're a fresh face in the middle of the week. People are bound to be curious."

After breakfast they headed out to the paddock.

A character from off the lot at Paramount sized her up from under his cowboy hat. "I'm Bill," he said over the toothpick in his mouth, his voice the product of a thousand packs of Marlboros. "Ever ride before?"

She nodded, sizing up the quarter horses and ponies tacked up with Western-style saddles and bridles. "Where I'm from we mostly ride English, but I can adapt."

Bill glanced doubtfully at her sneakers. "We're down a man, so it's just me today. If you don't mind waiting I can tack up Dancer for you." He nodded toward the Arabian she'd seen earlier.

"I can help. I know how to saddle a horse."

He nodded toward the barn. "Through those doors, tack room's on the left. The pegs are labeled."

Jamie tacked up Dancer, mounted, and reined the horse out of the way while Bill helped the other riders with their reins and stirrups.

Finally, Bill sauntered over and checked Dancer's girth. "Don't let your guard down. He's got some personality to him."

Personality? Anyone who'd spent any amount of time around horses knew what that meant.

"So far, so good." Jamie patted Dancer's neck and his ears flickered.

Bill led the string of riders onto a well-worn path through the vineyard toward the tree-covered hills. A family of four rode directly behind him. Next were the newlyweds Jamie'd seen canoodling on the couch the night of her arrival. Then came Dina and her three daughters. Jamie picked up the tail.

The horses' heads bobbed along at a sleepy rhythm, long lashes half obscuring their eyes. Bill swatted at a fly buzzing in his ear.

Molly rotated at the waist to talk to Jamie, pulling the reins with her as she did. "My horsie's name is Kwystal."

"That's a pretty name."

Crystal responded as she'd been trained to do by turning herself sideways in the trail. She promptly began foraging on the dogwood branch right under her nose.

Jamie took hold of Crystal's bridle and straightened her out. Riding in tandem with Molly, she asked, "Can I show you a trick? The reins are only to steer with. If you need something to hold on to, grab onto Crystal's mane like this. It won't hurt her, no matter how hard you pull."

Daintily, Molly picked up a few strands of her pony's mane.

"Dig right in," Jamie demonstrated on Dancer.

The child wound her fingers in more tightly, her smiling face reflecting the security that came with the added connection with her mount.

"Thanks for helping her," said Dina. "Have you ridden a lot?"

Jamie shrugged. "It's been a while. But it's like riding a bike. You never forget."

On their way back, the sun was climbing to its apex. Some of the riders wondered aloud about lunch. Bill slouched even deeper into his saddle, tipped his hat down farther onto his forehead, and slipped into a half doze.

And then, without warning, Molly's pony reared up on her haunches with a startled whinny.

The roan behind her panicked and skittered sideways. Molly's sister landed on her back with a sickening thump and an unearthly moan.

"Lauri!" Dina slid off her mount without taking her foot out of the opposite stirrup, leaving her hanging awkwardly along her horse's flank. Inch by inch gravity tugged her toward the ground.

Dina's screaming terrorized Crystal even more.

The pony bolted off the path, zigzagging through the firs, Molly's fingers laced in her mane.

One touch of Jamie's heels was all the encouragement the Arabian needed. He bounded after Crystal.

"Whoa, horse!" Bill crackled impotently behind them, as he woke up to join in the chase.

"I'll get er!" he yelled to Jamie's back.

But Jamie was already several lengths ahead of him by the time she turned to see his legs flapping like goose wings against his mare's flanks.

Incredibly, Molly was still astride Crystal, as if horse and rider were sewn together, her little bottom bouncing off the saddle. It would have been laughable if it weren't so dangerous.

They were headed out of the firs and back to the vineyard. With fewer trees to swerve between, Molly was less likely to become unseated, even if her pony gathered momentum in the clearing.

Crystal emerged from the forest and just as Jamie had predicted, picked up speed. As Jamie's horse came astride Molly's in a wide row between vines, she leaned over and grabbed Crystal's bridle, reining both horses to a gradual halt.

Crystal snorted and huffed with the effort of her escapade.

"Whoa there!" Bill rasped, cantering up behind them. "I knew she'd run outta steam eventually," he said, breathing heavily.

Jamie was already off her mount. "Hey there, cowgirl! Way to hold on!" she praised Molly with a grin. "Some ride, huh?"

"That was scawy," Molly cried, shaking. The corners of her mouth dipped as a tear slipped down her cheeks and her face threatened to crumple.

"Yes, but you did just what I showed you, didn't you? You held on tight. And see? You're fine!" Jamie resisted the urge to scoop the frightened girl into her arms. If she got off now, fear might deter her from ever riding again. She untangled Crystal's reins, gave them to Molly and hopped back up on Dancer.

"Molly!" Dina called, rushing to meet them on foot. "Are you okay?"

"I'm a good wider!" Molly exclaimed, swiping bravely at a wet eye.

Dina looked at Jamie with pure gratitude. "Thank you so much," she gushed.

"You kidding? This one's a born cowgirl!"

By now the others had caught up. Bill motioned for Jamie to ride next to him.

"Looks like we got Dancer a little exercise after all today."

In contrast with breakfast time, at lunch people crowded around Jamie, regaling her with stories of what had happened earlier in the week, before her arrival, and trying to coax her into joining them in the rest of the week's activities.

"I thought this was supposed to be a relaxing vacation," she protested, laughing.

But she couldn't resist putting her name down for a variety of activities. This morning's ride had made her feel like she was back in her natural element. It felt good.

Chapter Six

From the airport, Delilah drove south an hour to Colorado Springs to take Hank on a surprise tour of the United States Air Force Academy. They spent a couple of hours touring the exhibits and the grounds.

Back in Denver, they drove through the UD campus so Hank could see the changes that had taken place over the last three years. Then it was on to Delilah's place, to shower and so that Hank could put on the sport coat Delilah had instructed him to bring for the charity dinner she was taking him to.

They checked in at a fancy hotel downtown and got their table assignment. Hank was given a bidding paddle and a table number in exchange for his credit card number on file. Then they entered a ballroom filled with Denver's glitterati, all of them seeming to talk at once.

Hank examined his paddle. "I've never been to one of these things," he said in voice loud enough to be heard above the din created by a couple of hundred people, all of who seemed to be talking at once.

"Don't worry," said Delilah, "I'll show you the ropes."

Across the ballroom, a man waved and Delilah waved back. "That's us," she said, taking Hank's hand and leading him into the crowd.

When they reached their table, the first thing Delilah did was save two seats by setting her program on one chair and her handbag on the other.

"Hank, I'd like you to meet Stewart Baker. Stew, Hank Friestatt, my friend from Oregon."

Stew took Hank's hand in his meaty one and shook it vigorously. "The Sweet Spot, right?"

"That's right."

"Delilah told me about you. I was just about to hit the bar. Get you anything?"

"I'll have a vodka tonic," said Delilah without hesitation.

"Beer," said Hank.

Stew gave him a knowing wink. "I getcha. Never order wine at these things." Before he turned to head toward the bar he patted Hank's arm familiarly, as if they'd known each other for years instead of less than a minute.

"Want to check out the silent auction items?" Delilah cocked her head toward the tables piled high with baskets wrapped in cellophane.

There were resort passes and sports memorabilia and every other kind of gift basket that could be imagined.

"How close is Eldora Mountain?" Hank asked Delilah as he contemplated a ski package.

"Just under an hour," said a male voice beside him.

Looking up to find a man in a tux peering down an aquiline nose, Hank was suddenly conscious of his sport coat, still slightly rumpled from his suitcase.

"Hank," said Delilah, "these are my friends the Willeses."

"You must be the wine guy," said the man. "Delilah's told us all about you."

Hank looked at Delilah in mild surprise. He hadn't realized he'd made such an impression on her. Was it because of their business venture, or—he hardly dared believe it—something more? Back when they were in school, she'd seemed so unattainable . . . so elusive.

Delilah leaned into Hank. "Suzy's my aesthetician and Paul's a stock broker."

"Anesthesiologist?" asked Hank.

"Minus about six years of schooling," said Suzy with a chuckle. "*Aesthetician.* I do facials."

"You lost me."

"You should try it sometime. It's amazing," said Paul.

Delilah laughed at Hank's ignorance. "Baby steps," she told her friends. "We're going to have to reintroduce Hank to civilization *slowwwly.*" Then she slipped her arm through Hank's and regarded her friends admiringly. "Suzy and Paul are building the most amazing house in the Washington Park neighborhood."

"It's got two public gardens and great shopping," Suzy added. "We're trying to talk Delilah into looking at a lot there."

Pulling Hank away, Delilah told Suzy, "We'll catch up later. I want to check out all the items up for bid before they summon us to our tables."

They arrived back at their table to find six of the eight chairs already occupied. Hank found himself seated between Delilah and Stew.

"So!" said Stew as Hank speared his salad. "The latest *Wine Spectator*'s giving last year's Friestatt pinot ninety-one points."

Hank nodded as he chewed.

"Must be tough in the wine business, always fighting to stay on top."

"I have complete trust in our winemaker. I prefer the vineyard management aspect of the business, myself."

"Nabbed her just out of UC Davis, right?"

As a matter of fact, he had—after spending a good deal of time vetting her.

Something about Stew put Hank on his guard. He couldn't tell if Stew truly cared about wine or if he'd only educated himself recently in anticipation of meeting him.

He turned to say something to Delilah, only to discover that she was nowhere to be seen.

"You know my winemaker?"

"I know she has a strong commitment to Riesling," Stew replied.

A strong commitment to Riesling? That sounded remarkably like a quote Hank had recently read about Joy in another wine journal.

And then it dawned on Hank that this seating arrangement was no coincidence. Delilah had intended to bring Stew and him together.

"Joy's responsible for our single-vineyard pinot."

"I just ordered a case of it." Stew looked at Hank expectantly.

Hank nodded out of courtesy. "Appreciate the business."

But he was grateful when the server materialized with his meal and Delilah reappeared and flounced down beside him.

Dinner was followed by a live auction. Program in hand, Delilah turned her chair to face the auctioneer. "This is the best part," she told Hank. "There are wines by the lot, trips, and so on up for bid."

The first item up was a trip to the Albuquerque balloon festival.

"Look over there," said Delilah, nodding toward the table where Suzy Willes whispered in her husband's ear. "Looks like the Willeses are thinking about going to New Mexico."

She was right. Paul raised his paddle in the first bid of the night.

All around them, other paddles went up in the air.

Hank was careful not to make any quick moves that might be misconstrued.

The bids mounted steadily. Finally it came down to the Willeses and one other bidder. After some more back-and-forth the gavel hit the podium. "Sold! For eight thousand five hundred dollars."

The Willeses kissed, to a roomful of applause.

Following the auction the lights went down and the band came out.

Delilah reached for his hand. "C'mon. Let's dance."

Mustering his enthusiasm, Hank followed her and dozens of others pouring onto the floor.

Halfway through the song a man bumped into Delilah. “Sorry,” he said, catching her by the elbow to steady her. He did a double take, followed by a scowl. “Delilah?”

Delilah’s eyes grew round, while the man maintained his awkward grip on her.

Hank closed the distance between them. He yelled to be heard over the music. “Everything okay?”

The man glared at Hank. “You with her?”

Delilah yanked her arm free. “Hank and I are friends. Just friends.”

Amidst the writhing bodies surrounding them, the man stuck out his hand. “Ryan Rowling. Delilah used to be my wife.”

Delilah has been married and divorced already? They’d only been out of school a few years.

Still, it was none of Hank’s concern.

“She didn’t tell you. Hah. I’m not surprised.”

Apparently, D’s ex thought she was downplaying the extent of her friendship with Hank.

“Piece of advice? Keep one hand on your wallet.” With that he dropped D’s elbow, grabbed the hand of his wide-eyed dance partner, and melted into the crowd.

Delilah exited the dance floor in the opposite direction, with Hank hurrying to keep up.

“It never should have happened,” she said over her shoulder. “It was a big mistake. He begged me, and I finally said yes. But it was never a good fit. Guess he’s still crying sour grapes.”

"Let's just go," said Hank. He'd accompanied Delilah to the benefit as a gesture of appreciation for letting him crash at her town house. But he wasn't disappointed to leave. Facials would never be his thing, and neither would paying three times the value of a trip, even if it was a tax write-off.

He found himself wondering what he had missed at the vineyard that day.

Chapter Seven

Sunday afternoon, Jamie finally made her eagerly anticipated trip to the tasting room, surprised to find a line to get in the door. Instead of waiting to be served, she headed straight to the front of the line, where she knew she would find the tasting menu. Flight of five wines, it said. Her eye skimmed over the bar. There they were, lined up, labels facing outward.

She stood back and took stock. Ellie was doing her level best to keep up. It didn't take a lot of time to serve the customers who bought a glass and carried it to a table or outside. But the ones who bought flights tended to hang at the bar and ask questions. That was the whole point of flights, to educate customers in a pleasant, relaxed atmosphere about the wine and the winery and provide a basis for comparison. Wine epiphany aside, there was bound to be one you liked better than the rest.

But one whole leg of the L-shaped counter was not being utilized. It seemed like such a waste of space.

On an impulse, Jamie went behind the bar, grabbed an apron hanging on a hook and slid it over her head.

Ellie poured with one hand and brushed back a strand of hair that had come out of her braid with the other. She lifted an inquiring brow.

"Put me in, Coach," said Jamie.

With Jamie behind the bar, a new line had already begun to form. An eager hand thrust a ten-dollar bill across the bar at her.

"You sure?"

"I'm yours as long as you need me. Just tell me what to do," she replied.

"The tasting fee is ten dollars. If you buy two or more bottles you get a refund. Don't serve anyone who can't stand up. That's it in a nutshell. That's all you need to know."

"Got it," said Jamie, slipping the ten into the cash drawer. Aping Ellie, she slid five glasses from the overhead rack and set up her first round.

Good thing she'd showed up when she did. The room was soon packed with people happily sipping and sharing their discoveries with their companions.

Jamie had always loved sharing her love of wine with close friends. Now that circle had expanded.

And she was no stranger to hard work. In her first year of teaching she had won the award for outstanding achievement by a rookie. Walking up to accept that plaque had meant the world to her.

All the extra hours, all the research, all the volunteering she'd done on the student assistant team had paid off.

True, she and her roommate barely made ends meet. But they were young and energetic and full of ideas. They barely noticed the sacrifice.

But next school year, everything would be different.

"Two flights," said a woman holding out a twenty.

Jamie took her money and reached up without looking, only to feel nothing where wineglasses should be.

There was a blast of warm moist air at her side. She turned to see a steaming bin of glasses straight from the dishwasher, which Ellie set on the counter.

"Perfect timing," Jamie said. "I needed you, and there you were."

"I'm the lucky one," replied Ellie with toothy grin. "Is there anything you can't do?"

Jamie lined up five more glasses.

Talk about change. Amid the fuss and bustle that went with the end of every school year—spring concerts, grades, the individual education plans required for all gifted students—Jamie hadn't had time to consider all the challenges her job change would entail. But the weeks that had gone by since school was finally out, plus three thousand miles, were lending perspective.

As department head she would be in charge of not just her usual four hundred, but all the students in the district. In theory, she would have even greater influence over them. She would have the power to implement her ideas. She'd been given a gift. A blessing. So why was she beginning to have an inkling that she'd be making less of a difference instead of more?

Change, even good change, is never easy, Jamie. That's what Dad had told her, to console her when he dropped the bomb about selling the farm.

She shrugged off her reservations and tried to look at the positives. Now there would be no more stocking bookshelves in the summer to pay for those odds and ends she'd got into the habit of buying to supplement her meager supply budget . . . a pack of clarinet reeds here, a new set of rhythm sticks there.

But that brought up a new worry. Who would supply those small but essential extras now? For one thing, buying things for the classroom with your own money was against the rules, although most of the teachers Jamie knew didn't abide by that particular rule. But not every teacher was willing to put her students' needs ahead of the occasional new top or concert ticket. And others simply weren't able to. For some, after the basic necessities were paid for, there was nothing left to give.

Well. Jamie had no control over her replacement's budget or what she did with it. She had bigger responsibilities now. And the powers-that-be believed in her ability to handle them. Who was she to argue?

She brushed off the list of concerns that was piling up. Since this truly was the very last summer she wouldn't have to work, she should make the most of it, not fritter it away worrying about things that she had no control over. And she couldn't think of a better way than to be standing right where she was, behind the counter of the tasting room of her favorite winery.

"Next?" she said with a smile to the women at the head of the line.

Chapter Eight

Late the next morning, Delilah worked on her laptop at her dining room table while Hank sat stiffly on her straight-backed white couch watching *Top Gun.* Back home he rarely got the chance to watch aviation movies.

When the credits started rolling he stretched his arms over his head and leaned back, only to snap his head forward with a sudden grimace and a hand to the pain in his neck. The sofa's back only came up to his shoulder blades, and wasn't designed with reclining in mind.

Delilah looked up. "Movie over?"

"Yup. Time to get a move on."

Before he had finished his sentence she was across the room, curled up next to him, glancing at the device on her wrist that did everything from tell time to graph the stock market. "Your flight's not for three hours. What's the hurry? Want another cup of coffee?"

"No, thanks."

"Something to eat? Otherwise you'll be stuck eating at the airport or worse, airplane food."

He patted his stomach. "I'm still stuffed from last night."

She tucked one leg under and turned to face him. "Did you have a good time this weekend?"

"Great. It would've been enough just to have a place to crash. Didn't expect you to drop everything and plan your whole weekend around me. The trip was worth it for the visit to campus alone."

"You liked the tour of the Academy I arranged for you?"

He scratched his head. He thought he'd made his appreciation clear, but maybe not. "Like I said when we were standing there in the chapel, looking up at that vaulted ceiling. If I'd known there was such a thing as the Air Force Academy when I was a kid, I might even have gone for it.

"Guess I'm just restless to get back. Not used to having spare time on my hands. Most days, there aren't enough hours to get everything done that needs doing. That's the way it is. How it's always been. Ellie and my parents were always constantly moving. Cooking food, cleaning up food. Planting, irrigating, and pruning the vines. Picking grapes, crushing grapes."

"Sounds intense."

"There's a few weeks' breather in the winter when the grapes rest on their lees. That's when we traveled. Usually Dad flew us in his own plane. The minute we got back, the racking—transferring wine from one barrel to another to get rid of the sediment before bottling it—began. Then, when spring came, the cycle started all over again."

"It was the opposite for me," said Delilah in a different tone, one that Hank didn't recognize. This new voice dripped with resentment. "My dad only worked when he felt like it. My mom supported the three of us on her wages from her factory job. Until Dad left for good. Then it was just the two of us."

"I'm sorry. I didn't know." Her polished image didn't so much as hint at a background steeped in poverty. "That must've been rough."

"I swore I was never going to be a single mother saddled with a kid in a dead-end job." She shuddered. "And mark my words"—she turned to face him head-on—"you won't find me schlepping a serving cart down the aisle of the plane into middle age, either. Why do you think I started the travel agency? Do you know what it's like taking orders from demanding, rich women with stacks of gold up to their elbows?"

"Er—"

"In fact, I started studying to get my real estate license.

"Sorry," she said, at the look Hank gave her. Her laugh sounded forced. "Didn't mean to . . ."

"Don't worry about it." He twined his fingers loosely as his eyes skimmed the stark white walls. Delilah had been ruthless in cutting anything that hinted of excess. The only objects that had survived the cut were a gourd-shaped, ice-blue bottle containing a single branch that sat on the credenza, a large, abstract line-drawing in a thin gold frame centered between two naked windows, and a porcelain bowl containing five oranges in the center of the dining table.

The total effect was reminiscent of the glossy, full-page ads from one of those home-goods stores that Ellie was always getting in the mail.

Apparently Ellie never patronized those stores. Back home, the inn was filled with the kind of comfortable clutter that sparked fond memories of shared experiences. Like the moose head that Dad shot on their hunting trip to Canada in the eighties, mounted above the fireplace. The picture of Hank next to his parents and their plane, the time they went to Alaska. And the geode he'd helped Dad dig out of the creek bank right there on their very own land.

He checked his watch. "Well . . ." He slapped his thighs. "Think I'll start getting my gear squared away."

He half rose, only to be halted by her touch on his forearm.

"Hank."

He looked down at red fingertips. *Is she flirting with me?*

"Wait."

He lowered himself back to the couch uneasily, racking his memory of their conversations leading to this visit for some subtle cue he'd missed.

The sofa cushion shifted as she changed position, facing him where he sat looking straight ahead, arms propped on his knees.

"You sacrificed a lot, growing up the way you did."

"I'm really sorry about the way you were raised," he replied, springing to his parents' defense, "but you might be transferring your bad experience onto mine. I actually had it pretty good. Loving family. Three squares a day." He neither wanted nor deserved anyone's pity.

"Still. You just got finished telling me how hard you had to work, even on the weekends and holidays. Think of all there is to do here in Denver. The shopping, the skiing, the snowboarding—don't even get me started on the restaurant scene. And that's just for starters. There's so much more I've found since I've been living here. So much more I'd be happy to show you, if you wanted."

Her enthusiasm was contagious. "I'll be the first to admit—Denver's a veritable Disneyland for grown-ups."

She threw up her hands in excitement. "I know, right? Why do you think I've passed up transfers? I loved this city from the get-go. Of course, anything's better than the hick town where I grew up. Denver has everything anybody could ever want. Concerts, theater . . ."

"Just what are you getting at?"

"Do you ever think of what you would you do if the sky was the limit? Anything. You know. Like—take a cruise around the world?"

"The one time I went on a cruise I was bored to death."

She laughed. "Duly noted. A cruise is out. I know—how about a home in Hawaii? One overlooking the ocean with a lanai?"

"Rock fever."

She sighed, exasperated. "Haven't you ever thought about doing something more with your life?"

He opened his palms where they hung between his knees. "What are you getting at? The Sweet Spot isn't just a job, Delilah. It's what I was born to do."

"Says who—your parents? I'm sorry, Hank, but they're gone. And I have to believe that if it were between carrying on some old, outdated idea of a 'legacy' and being happy, they'd choose the second for you in a heartbeat. This is your future we're talking about. Your whole life!"

Of course, there had been times when he had thought of giving up, just walking away. But he'd never uttered that thought aloud. Hearing Delilah say it made his heart race. With excitement or guilt, he didn't know. He didn't want to examine it too closely.

"No. Not really." It was too much to fathom. Abandoning the vineyards would be going against everything he'd ever been told that he should want.

"Are you sure?" She gave him a provocative look. "You used to want to be a pilot."

"Yeah, and some kids want to be firemen or race-car drivers. Sooner or later, we all have to grow up." He stood then, her hand sliding off his forearm, pulled out his phone and checked the time yet again. "Now it really is time to get going."

With that he jogged up the stairs to the guest room, aware of Delilah watching his every step.

The summer solstice was almost here. The night he and his dad always used to bury the cow horns in the vineyard. Whether the tradition had any real scientific benefit or was done to appease the harvest gods or whatever, now it was Hank's job, with Ellie's help, of course. He would do it in deference to his dad.

He quickly finished packing his bag, suddenly anxious to get home.

Chapter Nine

Hank caught up with Bill when he was feeding the horses not long after daybreak, then returned to the inn to find his grandmother watching the sun come up through the window above the sink.

"Scrambled eggs on the stove. Didn't hear you come in last night. How was your trip?"

"It was good to see the campus again."

Ellie cradled the mug she carried over to the table and sat down across from him.

"It's a shame you had to leave Denver before you were ready."

Hank looked up from his eggs. They didn't often talk about what had happened. It hurt too bad.

"It is what it is," he said, taking a bite of toast.

"Sometimes I regret making you come back here, saddling you with all this."

"You didn't make me come back. I came because I wanted to."

That wasn't quite true. But he wouldn't have his grandmother shouldering any guilt on account of him. "All that rain we got in May's going to give us a high grape yield," he said, changing the subject. "You know what that means."

"More thinning," she replied gravely.

"Hear from Bailey over the weekend?"

"Not a word."

"I was afraid of that. On top of everything else, I can't be tied up with personnel problems. Been racking my brain trying to think of someone I could hire to take her place. Can't be guessing if people are going to show up for work or not."

"I'm sure something or someone will turn up sooner or later. More milk?"

"Mm." He nodded between mouthfuls.

She poured him some from a gallon jug. "Did you hear about Jamie Martel on the trail Saturday? Bill had her up on Dancer when Crystal got spooked and tore off with that young child. Lucky she was there. Bill's getting old. He was probably asleep at the wheel."

Grandma, calling Bill old? Hank hid his amusement behind a gulp of milk. What she said was true, though. "Bill told me just now when I was out at the barn."

"I took the trouble to peek in the dining room at lunch to check on her. Not only was she not eating alone, she was the most popular one in the room. There's something about that girl."

Hank kept his eyes on his plate and tried to keep his voice even. "She said she could ride a little, but you never know. Sometimes people say that and then you find out they don't even know what side to mount up on. Sounds like she's the real deal."

"That's nothing. You should have seen her at the tasting room yesterday. We were swamped—"

Hank looked up from his plate. "I was afraid of that."

"Jamie saw how busy I was, and instead of adding to it, she put on an apron and helped me pour."

He went back to his eggs. "That so?"

"Kept up with me all day. Then she refused to take the cash I handed her after we closed out."

Hank imagined the apron with the Sweet Spot logo tied around Jamie's slim waist.

"You can't let her do that. She's a guest. We'll give her a partial refund on her trip."

"You read my mind."

Ellie fingered her napkin. "Too bad Jamie doesn't come from around here. She'd be a real asset."

Hank's knife clattered to his plate. "Jamie Martel is a paying guest. From the other side of the country."

"She grew up on a farm."

He got up for more coffee. "A *dairy* farm."

"She kept her own vegetable garden. You know what they say. 'You can take a girl out of the country . . . '"

"Vineyard work is out," he said, sitting down again, taking a careful sip from his mug. "Suckering and shoot-thinning are skilled labor."

"Not the vineyard. But she could help out with the stables and the tasting room."

"She already has a job. She's a teacher. Remember?"

"Last I knew, teachers didn't work in the summertime."

"Grandma. Do you hear yourself? The woman is here for two weeks. She's not looking for a job. She's got a round-trip plane ticket and, probably, big plans for the rest of the summer."

He grabbed a fourth slice of toast from the plate and reached for the butter dish.

"Might be worth us paying the fee for changing her ticket."

"Seriously?" he asked around his mouthful of toast.

"You don't want to wait too long. I know she just got here, but the sooner you ask her, the more wiggle room she'll have to change her plans."

Hank wiped his mouth, laid his napkin by his plate, and scraped his chair back. "I don't even know why we're having this conversation."

Ellie threw her hands in the air then. "You're probably right. You do whatever you feel's best." She pushed back from the table, too, and replaced the milk in the fridge. "I was only thinking out loud. Like you said, though. It would never work. I'm just an old woman. What do I know? You're the one with the fancy business degree."

But Hank knew Ellie. She'd planted the seed. And she wouldn't be satisfied until it sprouted.

"What about tonight? You got the quartz ground to where you want it?"

"Horns have been steeping since last night. Pit's dug. You picked out the wine?"

"Over there, in the bag." She pointed to what looked like a heap of burlap fabric beneath the coat hooks by the back door.

"Maybe Bailey'll show up yet," he grumbled as he slapped on his cap and headed out the back door.

The stars were coming out as Hank made his way back to the house, covered in a fine layer of dirt and smelling like wood smoke from burning a pile of pruning debris.

"How do the grapes look?" asked Ellie. She was rocking in her chair on the back porch with Homer at her feet. From there she had a panoramic view of the fire along the bank of the pond and beyond that, the vineyards.

"The plants are budding out like gangbusters, thanks to the rainy spring. I walked through several blocks, removing suckers and buds from the trunks. Easier to do it now than later."

"It keeps you in touch with what's going on out there, too. Are you seeing many bees?"

He nodded. "A few."

"I saw a good number when I was weeding my herbs. And my peonies have buds on them."

He wiped his brow with his sleeve. "Think I'll go in and call Bailey one more time before it gets too late."

"I see Bill," said Ellie, squinting toward the guests lined up on log benches, finishing the tail end of a song. "Who's that other guitar player?"

"Must be a guest. You know how it is. When they read about the sing-alongs on the website, lots of guests bring their instruments with them," replied Hank without looking, one hand already on the doorknob.

"Looks like a woman."

At that moment a creamy soprano voice swirled into the clear evening air, and he glanced over his shoulder toward the campfire.

"Who hasn't searched for a life of her own?
To find a new place, a new setting, a new home?
Who knows what it's like to chase a dream?
To find the woman she was meant to be?"

"I believe that's Jamie," said Ellie.

Following the first line, Hank's hand had fallen from the doorknob. His feet carried him of their own accord to the edge of the porch.

The firelight brought out the gold highlights in Jamie's hair. He watched her lips, full and ripe, as she mouthed the words to her song.

Even the kids had stopped elbowing one another.

"Wow, she's good." Some nights, when the temperature near the ground dropped before the air above it, sound waves refracted upward, so that anyone on the porch could hear every word that was said at the campfire. That was Brynn, talking to her friend sitting next to her on the log. The two teens lived nearby and helped Ellie bus breakfast tables during the summer. Brynn often returned to the Sweet Spot later in the summer evenings, toting her guitar, though Hank had yet to hear her play.

The song ended to a smattering of applause and whoops. Jamie smiled and began tuning up for her next number.

"Thought you said you were going in," said Ellie.

"Huh?" He'd forgotten all about calling Bailey, and Ellie sitting behind him. "Oh."

In the failing light he thought he saw the faintest hint of a smile cross Ellie's face.

He headed back to the door. "See you at midnight."

Around ten, Jamie thanked her audience and stood up to find her guitar case, when the two teens who had been paying rapt attention came up to her.

"Can I see your guitar?" one of them asked shyly.

"Sure."

The girl handled it with respectful admiration. "Wow."

"I see you've got your own. How long have you been playing?"

"Not long."

"Yes, she has," her friend chimed in. "She's been playing ever since I've known her. She's just embarrassed to play in front of people."

"Have you had any lessons?" asked Jamie kindly.

"Some." She looked at the ground. "My teacher moved away, though."

"That's too bad. Have you checked online? You might find some lessons there."

"I've seen some. But it's not the same as real life. You don't get any feedback on what you're doing wrong."

Despite the late hour, Jamie sat back down and patted the empty space next to her. "Have a seat. Let's see what you can do."

"Me?" She shrank back.

"Yes, you."

"See?" said the girl's friend. "This is what always happens. She carries that dumb guitar around everywhere she goes, but whenever someone asks her to play it, she won't do it because she's too chicken."

"I can't help it! I just don't like to play in front of people."

"All she does is play in her room," said the other.

"Look around," said Jamie. "It's only us now. Everyone else is gone."

"But you're this supergood musician."

"How do you think I got that way? By playing. The more you play in front of people, the easier it becomes."

Reluctantly, the girl sat down and brought her guitar onto her lap. She started out haltingly, but once she got going, Jamie saw what she'd kept hidden.

"You have potential. What's your name?"

She grinned and looked into her shoulder. "Brynn."

"Me and Brynn work for Miss Ellie, bussing tables," said her companion. Sometimes we come back here to the campfires in the evenings."

"Tell you what, Brynn. I also teach music. Here's your homework assignment. Sometime in the coming week I want you to play that song you played for me, for someone else, just to start getting comfortable with it. Okay?"

"Okay," she said, so softly Jamie could barely hear her.

Despite Hank deliberately slowing his pace, Ellie was huffing and puffing by the time they got to the center of Block Five.

The moon was so bright he could easily see her chest rising and falling.

"I don't know how much longer I can do this," she said.

"I told you, you don't have to come. Or, we could take the golf cart."

"It's a job for two people. As for the cart, no sense waking the guests."

"Why? Afraid they'd think we're crazy?"

"If we're crazy, so is every other vintner in the Willamette Valley. And half of them in Europe."

She was right, of course. There wasn't a vintner Hank knew who hadn't adopted hyper-organic methods these days.

"Joe Bear likens it to the Three Sisters crop rotation, practiced for eons by his people," she continued.

Joe Bear managed a motorcycle dealership down in McMinnville. He wore a do-rag and a black leather vest, was a ceremonial leader, and as unlikely as it seemed, Ellie's closest friend.

"They plant corn, beans, and squash together, but at different times. The corn stalk supports the bean vine; the beans, being a legume, improve the soil; and the squash leaves provide shade to the other plants. Eating all three in the same meal provides a complete, meat-free protein." She sighed. "There is so much I want to teach you yet."

"I wish Bryce would buy in a hundred percent," said Hank. "He doesn't think raptors and peppering to control rodents works."

"He's coming along," said Ellie. "Last full moon he helped me burn morning glory runners and spread the ash around their burrows."

"If it weren't for Dad promising Bryce a job for life, I'd have given him his walking papers by now."

"Think long and hard before you do that," Ellie said. "You'd be going against your father's word."

At times like these, as hard as Hank tried, he still felt like an apprentice.

Delilah's voice came back to him from just yesterday. *There must be a million things you'd love to do, things you'd be really good at.*

Maybe Delilah was right. What might his life look like now, if he hadn't spent the past however many months busting his butt to keep the vineyards running, squinting over profit and loss statements, and staying up late to enact some neo-pagan agricultural ritual? He could be piloting a 747 or be part of a search-and-rescue crew.

He wondered if there would ever come a time when he felt like he owned the Sweet Spot, instead of it owning him.

He knelt in the moonlight between two rows of vines, by the pit he had dug earlier, and reached out his hand.

Without speaking, Ellie handed him the first of two dozen long, curved horns packed with ground quartz.

He inserted it into the ground, point up.

They repeated the process, their shadows moving with them eerily across the ground, until the pit was filled.

"Last one," said Ellie. "Ready for the wine?"

He nodded and she withdrew two bottles from the burlap sack. Carefully, Hank laid them on their sides among the horns.

"When I think of how many thousands of years people have been doing this, going all the way back to ancient times. It's more than just a sacrificial rite. When it comes to storing wine, the finest climate-controlled cellar can't compete with the earth. Still, dark, and a constant temperature. I'd be all for fermenting all our wine underground if it was practical."

He stood up and brushed his hands together. "See you at the equinox," he told the wine.

"God willing," added Ellie.

He shot her a look. He might not feel fully invested in the Sweet Spot, but the thought of drinking the wine from these symbolic bottles without Ellie was too much to bear. "Don't talk like that."

Ellie tossed in a handful of dirt. Quickly and efficiently, Hank finished the job with his shovel.

After the pit was filled in, he scattered a handful of clover seeds across the soil. Clover improved the soil, kept down the weeds, and provided pollen for the bees and grazing for the sheep.

"There," he said, lifting the handles of the wheelbarrow as he turned to go. "Sleep tight."

Chapter Ten

"There's sloppy joe in the pan on the stove, and I made more sugar cookies," said Ellie the following day at noon when Hank came in for lunch. "And you can quit wondering about Bailey."

"She back?" he said hopefully over his shoulder.

"Not back. Gone. I made some inquiries. She bought an old Airstream and headed south. Probably crossing the border into Mexico as we speak."

Hank dried his hands and tried to absorb the news. "Where'd you hear that?"

"Seth Thompson. Who else?"

If there was such thing as a town gossip, Newberry's head postal clerk was it. Hank shook his head.

"Seth heard it from Denise at the pharmacy, who heard it from her brother-in-law."

"Bailey always talked about dropping out and taking off to see the country." But then, everybody daydreamed. Most of the time, their dreams didn't come true.

"I never thought she was one to ride the river with. She had a spotty employee history before she came here, remember? Anyway, Nelson's wife called."

"Oh, boy," said Hank, spooning sloppy joe onto a bun. Poor Nelson was probably going stir-crazy. Everybody knew his wife drove him nuts.

"How's he doing?"

"Not good. Leg's infected. She had him at the doctor Friday and they got him on antibiotics to try to clear it up. But we shouldn't expect him back directly."

"Par for the course, lately."

"I know you were hoping to have him back sooner than later."

"Nelson's got to take care of himself," Hank said, setting his plate down. "I'll post a help wanted ad tomorrow."

"You think any more about asking Jamie if she wants to help out?"

Hank winced. "Not that again."

"What's it hurt to ask? All she can do is say no."

"Mark my words, that's exactly what she will say."

"You never know till you try. We can scrape by another weekend. But what about next week? Could be days before you get any kind of response to your ad. Jamie can hit the ground running."

"Fine. If you think it'll work."

Ellie grinned from ear to ear. "I'll go put a bug in her ear right now." She got up and went out to the dining room.

Fifteen minutes later, Jamie stepped gingerly through the swinging door. She looked from Hank, still seated at the table, to Ellie, wiping the range. "You wanted to talk to me?"

"Sit down, why don't you," said Ellie, pouring from the bottle she and Hank were drinking from. "Here you are. A nice glass of Riesling."

Jamie pulled out one of the four chairs, followed by Ellie.

Hank cleared his throat. Might as well get this over with. "Grandma says you were a big help while I was gone. Want you to know I appreciate it."

"You're welcome."

"What are your plans for the rest of the summer?"

"I have a summer job at a bookstore that starts the day after I get back. And some intense planning to do for next school year. Oh, and I also have to find a new apartment."

"Sounds like you're pretty tied up." He raised an eyebrow at Ellie as if to say *I told you.*

But he should have known Ellie wouldn't give up easily. "You've heard we're shorthanded," she said.

"Nelson, and Bailey." Jamie nodded, still looking perplexed.

"We just got news that Nelson will most likely be out the full six weeks that the doctor ordered," said Ellie. "That takes us right up to August."

It had to be dawning on her by now, why they'd called her back here.

"You're interested in wine, you know your way around a horse, and you pitch in without being asked. Most important of all, you're well-liked." Jamie's hand rested on the table. Now Ellie placed her hand atop it. "I know it's asking a lot, and we're probably way out of line for asking. But what would you think of staying on for a while? The pay's no great shakes, but we'd be willing to at least match what the bookstore pays. You're exactly what we need around here. Someone who can float back and forth from the winery to the stables."

She blinked. "I'm not sure . . ."

Hank saw his chance. "We understand if it's a no."

Jamie rose, paced slowly to the sink, and then turned around to face them. "I'm sorry, but I'm going to have to decline."

Hank waited for the inevitable relief to wash over him. So then why did his heart fall into his stomach with the weight of a ten-pound hammer?

For a long moment, no one spoke.

"I can't," Jamie repeated for emphasis, her mouth twisting with regret.

Hank knew that look on Ellie's face. She was racking her brain for a go-around.

"I have to get back to Philadelphia," said Jamie. "Like I said, I have a summer job. And I have to get ready for the fall. It's going to be a lot of work. A ton of preparation."

"You really love the city, don't you?" asked Ellie.

A new tactic, as Hank had both hoped and feared.

"I really do," she said with emphasis.

"What is it that means so much to you?"

"Well . . . my students, first and foremost. Do you know how hard it is to get those kids to show up for rehearsals, when basic daily attendance is way below that in the suburbs?"

Ellie grinned. "Sounds like you're one of those lucky people who's truly found her calling. But what is it about Philadelphia in particular that makes you so anxious to go back?"

In anticipation of what she would say, Hank bit into a sugar cookie, recalling the wealth of things Denver had on offer. Four major sports teams. Its advanced flight-training center geared specifically for airline pilots. Three hundred days of sunshine a year.

Jamie paced the kitchen tiles. "Well, there's the energy, and there's the diversity. The art museum's world-class. And then there's the Italian Market and the Magic Gardens mosaic gallery—" She stopped, facing Hank. "There's something you should understand. Moving away from my home was the hardest thing I ever did. I'm really proud of the way I adapted. If not for those BYOBs, I never would have gotten into learning about wine like I did. Even got a big promotion. But I have missed our farm. That's one of the reasons I came *here.*"

"Promotion?" asked Hank.

"I'm going to be department head next year."

"How come you didn't mention that earlier?"

She shrugged. "There was no reason to." Besides, she didn't like to toot her own horn.

"I have no doubt you'll be a wonderful leader to your fellow teachers," said Ellie. "But what about the children? Won't you miss them?"

"Absolutely! But I couldn't very well turn down a chairmanship, could I?"

"Of course not."

"Well," said Hank. "Guess that's that." He rose and went for his cap on its hook by the door. "I'll get that ad posted tonight instead of tomorrow. I'm sure we'll get a couple of hits before long."

"Wait." Jamie held up her hand.

Hank stopped in place, his hand already on the back door.

Jamie looked from Hank to Ellie and back.

She was so open, so lacking in artifice, anyone could see that she was second-guessing herself.

"Maybe you'd like to take a couple days to think on it," said Ellie, rising with considerably more effort than it had taken Hank.

Jamie had seen it, too.

"I got my evening chores to do. You can let us know for sure Sunday evening. In the meantime, thank you for hearing us out. Enjoy the rest of your stay. And if there's anything you need, be sure and let us know." She opened the linens drawer to get tomorrow morning's napkins.

Hank gave Ellie a desperate look. *Now who's giving up?*

"I guess it wouldn't hurt to sleep on it," said Jamie.

That evening, Hank was surprised to receive a call from Delilah.

"Do you remember my friend Stew?"

"Stew," he said, racking his brain.

"He liked you. He said when you're in town for your convention next week, the four of us should go out to dinner. You, me, Stew, and his wife, May."

"Oh, yeah. The guy we sat with at the gala." Hank recalled Stew's comments, meant to impress him. In his experience, the people who were truly knowledgeable about wine didn't need to flaunt it. "I don't remember his wife, though."

"She wasn't there. Anyway, I got us a reservation at Bennett's."

"Before you asked me?" He wished he had never mentioned the upcoming convention to Delilah.

"You can't wait till the last minute."

"I'll have to look at the schedule."

"You'd rather eat hotel food at the convention center than at one of the best steak houses in Denver? Please? As a favor to me? You can sneak away for a couple of hours."

She had gone out of her way for him the last time.

"Sure." Then he could rest easy that he'd paid her back.

"Great! I'll pick you up at seven in front of your hotel."

Chapter Eleven

"I don't believe I've ever had a group that eats as much as this one," said Ellie, scurrying to fill yet another napkin-lined basket with yet more biscuits.

There was a soft knock on the kitchen door.

"I'll get it." Hank got up from his bacon and eggs to find Jamie on the other side of the door.

He stood there looking at her while behind him, Ellie said, "Thank goodness it's only Jamie. I was afraid it was someone who'd drawn the short straw to come back and tell me they were out of jelly again."

He had no choice but to let her in. Wordlessly, he stepped aside.

"Help yourself to some toast and bacon," Ellie told her. "Hank got the last of the eggs, but you're welcome to scramble some more if you want. Might as well take this out to the table. Good thing I made extra."

Ellie disappeared behind the swinging door, leaving him alone with *her.*

He was acutely aware of her every move.

She got some toast and coffee and turned to the table. Ellie's half-eaten bowl of oatmeal still sat at her usual place. A basketful of freshly folded laundry sat on a third chair. That left only the place right across from him.

In the loaded silence, Jamie scooted her chair in, poured some half-and-half from the carton into her coffee, and took a sip.

Why was he suddenly so tongue-tied this morning? One thing was for sure: He didn't think he could take a whole summer of seeing her around every corner, studying that unique hair of hers, feeling uncomfortable in his own place.

Ellie breezed back in, took her seat, and picked up her spoon. "There! Now. Have you thought any more about staying on?"

"I have," said Jamie.

"And?"

Hank's breath stalled in his throat.

"I'll do it."

"Wonderful!" said Ellie.

Jamie laughed nervously. "It'll be kind of like getting paid for a vacation that lasts the whole summer."

"What about finding a new apartment for next fall?" he said.

"I'll research some places online. My sister won't mind inspecting a couple of places for me if I don't feel like I can make a decision any other way. How long will you need me?"

"September would be ideal," said Ellie.

"Only until we find someone else," said Hank, his words getting tangled up with Ellie's.

Confused, Jamie looked from grandson to grandmother. "I have to be back the third week of August."

Ellie shrugged bony shoulders. "Beggars can't be choosers."

"What about your job at the bookstore?" asked Hank.

"The store's in Rittenhouse Square . . . it's a busy area, surrounded by colleges," she added when she realized they probably weren't familiar. "University of the Arts, the Art Institute. They probably have a pile of résumés this high"—she set her hand atop an imaginary stack—"to choose from."

Must be nice, thought Hank.

"Family?" asked Ellie.

"I haven't lived at home since college. I go back for holidays and a few weeks in the summer. But there are no expectations. I do have a question for you, though. Can I still take part in the guest events? That is, if there's room and I'm not scheduled to work? For example, I'm signed up for rock climbing."

"As long as the activity isn't filled. And you'll have flexible time off," said Ellie. "If there's something you really want to do while you're in Oregon, let us know. Matter of fact, there's a big wine festival coming up that you might like. Maybe you can get Hank to take you to it."

"Sounds great," she said, taking a delicate bite of toast.

Behind Jamie's back Hank gave Ellie a scathing

look. He'd been planning to meet up with his group of friends who weren't part of the wine industry, after the fest. They were his escape. His release valve.

"Well then," said Ellie, "it's settled. The cabin you're in now is already reserved for the remainder of the season, but there's an empty suite upstairs. I'll get it spruced up and then you can move right in. No sense waiting."

Now his grandmother had gone too far. The Sunflower Suite was sacred. It had belonged to his parents. No one else had ever slept there.

And . . . it was located right across the hall from his.

He got up, rinsed his plate, and put it in the dishwasher.

"Where do you need her most, Henry?" asked Ellie.

Hank glanced over at Jamie's willing eyes, full of innocence, and was hit by a vision of her bronze hair fanned out across his white pillowcase. Immediately he turned away.

Now, thanks to Ellie, Jamie Martel was going to be around for the rest of the summer, dammit. And not just in one spot where he could easily skirt her, but popping up in all the same places he went throughout his working day . . . the tasting room, the stables, and now even sleeping right across the hall.

"Tasting room, tomorrow from two to five," he managed to spit out.

A server came into the kitchen carrying a tray full of sugars and creamers and the other extras that went with the breakfast meal.

Ellie clapped her hands down on the table and used them as leverage to get up. "Time for me to start thinking about lunch. Jamie, welcome aboard. I'm looking forward to hearing more of your playing in the evenings."

The campfire. She'd be a presence there, too. He'd forgotten about that. "Maybe you can get Bill to update his song repertoire to something after 1960."

Ellie extended her hand.

But instead of simply taking it, Jamie threw her arms around her. "I come from a family of huggers. Hope you don't mind."

"I never turn down a hug," said Ellie into Jamie's shoulder.

Before Hank knew it, Jamie was standing in front of him with her arms wide open. With no alternative, his arms went around her ribcage. He felt her breasts mashed against his chest, smelled the heady blend of vanilla and the voluptuous peonies Ellie cherished above all other flowers in her garden because their blooms were so fleeting, while his hands hovered uncertainly above her back.

In her excitement, Jamie didn't seem to notice his reticence. She pulled back quickly and said, "If you don't need me right now, I have to make some phone calls to the East Coast."

With that she disappeared out the back door, already holding her phone to her ear, leaving Hank still wondering what had just happened.

"I had a good feeling," Ellie said after Jamie left.

Hank hid his conflicted emotions behind his

eyes as he clapped on his ball cap. "You heard her. She's a city girl."

"Is she?" replied Ellie. Busy clearing away the rest of the breakfast dishes, she didn't seem to notice his disorientation. "Sometimes in life, you have to look beyond the obvious to find the answers."

Hank left without knowing what else to say. How was a man supposed to step into his role as a leader when his grandma was always interfering?

The upstairs hallway led to two doors right across from each other.

"That suite belongs to Hank," said Ellie to Jamie. "This one's yours." She opened the door and stepped aside for Jamie to enter first.

Jamie stepped into a sunshine-yellow room anchored by a bed made up with plump feather pillows. Through the flowered curtains she could see miles of vineyards extending all the way to the distant hills.

"There's a little sitting area here for you to read and play your guitar."

"It's perfect."

Jamie followed her into the spacious bathroom furnished with fluffy white towels.

"There's a bathtub! I've been stuck taking showers since college. A tub is one of the things I'm looking for in my new apartment."

"I hope you'll feel at home. This room's kind of special. It belonged to my son and his wife."

"Hank told me what happened. I'm so sorry for your loss."

"There comes a time when you have to move on. Can't think of anyone I'd rather have stay here than you."

Her hand flew to her breast. "I'm honored, Miss Ellie. Truly, I am."

Her eye was drawn to a row of framed photographs on the dresser next to a tiny vase packed with violets. She was immediately touched, picturing Ellie toddling out to the meadow to search the ground for the low-growing wildflowers, then making her creaky knees endure repeated bends until she had enough to make a bunch.

Jamie picked up a silver frame. "Who's the young couple with the old pickup truck?"

"That's me and my husband. Henry Friestatt the sixth. Sounds pretty fancy, doesn't it? You'd never match the name with the man. He was as down-to-earth as it gets. That was our very first grape harvest."

Jamie's eyes lit up. "That's the same heart-shaped sign I saw over the lane to the inn."

"The very same." A fond look came over Ellie's face as she took the photo from Jamie. "My husband carved it to look just like the one his grandfather carved, and his before that." She set the picture lovingly back in its place. "This has been a sweet spot for generations."

"This little boy missing his front teeth—is that . . . ?"

Tenderly, Ellie took the frame from her. "That's my grandson, all right, in front of my son's plane. Hank was the center of his parents' world. Not to say that he was spoiled. His daddy taught him by example. One time in sixth grade he got kicked off the school bus for a week, for swearing. His father not only made him walk the five miles to school, he walked with him. And it was wintertime, to boot. They had to leave the house before it was light.

"And then we lost them." She sighed heavily and put the photo back on the shelf.

"It must have been a terrible time."

Ellie smoothed the afghan hanging across the back of an upholstered chair. "I don't know what I would have done without Hank. He gave up his dream of flying to come back and take over the vineyards. He's come a long way these past three years. But, time marches on. I just can't help but worry about the next big change . . . when he's left to handle everything himself."

Jamie laid her hand on the woman's freckled arm. "Hopefully you'll be around for a long, long time. But even if, God forbid, you aren't, Hank will be fine. You said yourself how he was raised, with all that love."

"I just hope and pray that he'll be able to keep ahold of the vineyards for the next generation. Aren't many places as special as this."

"No. There aren't," murmured Jamie, thinking of a certain farm three thousand miles to the east.

If there were this many wineaux here in July, Hank wondered what was in store for August through October, the Willamette Valley's peak harvest season.

No sooner had he poured for one group and started explaining what was in their glasses and the care and skill with which it was made, when the next thirsty gang came in.

As he poured yet another sample, he educated his potential buyers. "Grapes grown in the Willamette Valley benefit from a wide variety of diverse soil origins—"

And then, from the corner of his eye, Hank looked up and saw Jamie enter.

"Be right with you," he called to her.

"Take your time," she said with an easy smile. "I'm in no hurry." She slid into a seat at the end of the bar.

He went back to his customers. "Where were we?" Somehow he'd lost his train of thought. "Right. I was explaining about soil types . . ."

After he rang up his sale, he only had time to pour Jamie a sample when the next group arrived.

Every time he had a moment, Hank glanced at Jamie to find her calmly sipping her wine, watching him work, listening intently to what he said.

When her glass was empty, he refilled it before being asked, in between selling.

When at last he got a breather, he headed toward the end of the bar, where he found a young couple listening to her with rapt expressions.

"The special magic of Sweet Spot pinot noir comes from communicating a sense of the place. When you fly over Ribbon Ridge, the white fog lying in the surrounding valleys make it look like some ancient island-hill from another time. Ribbon Ridge soil is very fine. It doesn't contain many nutrients. Now, that may sound like a bad thing, but a too-rich soil means more foliage and less fruit . . ."

His heart swelled. Jamie wasn't just reciting facts. She was painting a picture. Her off-the-cuff description was ten times better than the script his paid docents were required to memorize and regurgitate.

". . . fresh, smooth, and jammy. The sneaky tannins creep up on you and grab you when you aren't looking. And aging in both old and newer oak gives it complexity and depth."

"How do you know so much about this place?" asked the woman.

Jamie looked over the woman's shoulder at Hank. "I like learning about wine. Guess you could call it a hobby. But I'm not the owner. Here's the guy you want."

After Hank served them, he suggested they take their glasses outside and check out the view.

When he and Jamie were finally alone, he leaned on the bar. "When have you ever flown over Ribbon Ridge?"

She shrugged. "I haven't. But I've seen pictures."

He rose to his full height and straightened the brim of his ball cap. "I think we need to fix that."

Her smile transformed her features and her eyes shone.

It wasn't like Hank to be impulsive. The last time he'd flown over his land had been in his dad's Beechcraft. But once he made a promise, he always kept it.

Chapter Twelve

"Circle round," said Hank, holding a clipboard. "Let's see who's brave enough to tackle Raven's Rock. Jamie, I see you made it." One by one he checked the others off his list. Taylor and Amanda, the newlyweds, and Cole, a fit Californian in his forties.

"This is Lewis." Hank indicated a sinewy young man with tangled blond dreadlocks. He stepped up to help Lewis finish squeezing the last of some bulky equipment into the back of the topless Jeep Wrangler. "Lewis and I go way back. He's what they call a rock hound. Knows every good climb from here to Hood River."

"What are those?" Jamie asked, pointing to what looked like bundled-up crib mattresses.

"Crash pads. We're going to lay one on the ground beneath each of you when you climb."

Lewis drove off in the Jeep along a dirt road toward the rock formations. The rest of them mounted their horses and followed.

"Bring Dancer over here," Hank indicated with a toss of his head.

She fell in next to Hank's big chestnut gelding.

"How're you two getting along?" Hank sat his horse easily, one hand resting on his thigh, the other adeptly controlling the reins.

"I let him know who's boss," she said, stroking the gray's neck.

"Ready to show me your skills?"

Jamie blushed. "Skills?"

"Riding skills I heard so much about. Want to race?"

Her eyes flew to the horizon line, scoping the distance. "I'm not very familiar with the terrain."

"Just stay on this road till you get to that stand of firs." Hank indicated the spot with his chin.

As if understanding Hank's words, Dancer lifted his head a fraction.

"In that case . . ." At the lightest touch of her heel, Dancer sprang forward.

"Hey!" came Hank's yell from behind her. "I didn't say *go*!"

"Ride it like you stole it!" hollered Lewis from the Jeep when Jamie thundered past him.

Dancer's hooves thrummed against the hard-packed earth, gaining momentum with every stride. Jamie thrilled to the feeling of flying down the valley toward the distant trees. The rush of speed and the wind whipping her hair made her giddy. She heard pounding behind her and from the corner of her eye saw Hank's quarter horse gaining on her. For a second they rode neck and neck. Then Jamie asked Dancer for more speed and he willingly, thrillingly obliged.

"I won," she said, laughing as Hank's horse trotted up to her.

"Closest thing there is to flying," Hank said. The rumors were true. Jamie Martel could ride. "What did you say you rode in Pennsylvania?"

"Arabians, just like Dancer. But they're gone now." She felt her smile fade. "A couple died of old age, the rest we had to sell with the sale of the farm."

"Shame. Tell me more about your work. You've got a great singing voice, but then, I bet you get told that all the time."

"Singing's fun, but teaching's what pays the bills."

"Do you like it?"

That brought her smile back. "I love the kids. Unlike the regular classroom teachers who have a set number of students, I teach the whole school. They cycle through a class at a time, once a week. Music is a bright spot in their week. They're always happy to come."

With her as their teacher? *I'll bet.*

"Everybody loves to sing. You should hear them at the holiday concerts, after they've been practicing for months! They make me so proud."

With some effort, he tore his gaze off the easy roll of Jamie's hips with the rhythm of her horse's gait.

"How long have you been teaching?"

"Three years. In my part of the city, teaching, even at a gifted school like mine, can be . . . complicated. Most families, if they can afford it, send their kids to private or parochial schools. It's only the poorest who go to public. Lots of them are being raised by a grandmother, or an aunt, or in foster homes. A few are even homeless from time to time. Sometimes they get so clingy I have to pry them off, which goes against all my instincts. But we're not supposed to hug." She winced. "Lawsuits, you know. There's one I still lose sleep over. Jasmine, a second-grader. One Monday morning she kept falling asleep at her desk. Her mom had gone off with her boyfriend for the weekend, leaving Jasmine to watch her three-year-old brother and new baby sister. When I asked her if she'd been afraid, she said, *No, my mom gave me a big knife in case anyone tried to hurt us.*"

When Hank found his voice again, he asked, "What happened to her?"

Jamie shrugged. "The next school year, she was gone. Moved to who-knows-where."

"What keeps you going?"

She smiled again. "Like I said. I care about the kids."

Hank gazed out at the rugged horizon without seeing it. Jamie's job back East made his problems running the vineyard seem trivial in comparison.

But now the other riders were catching up with them.

Hank turned in his saddle. "Okay, everyone. See that rock formation?" He pointed through the trees to what looked like an unimpressive rock formation off in the distance, where the Jeep now sat waiting.

"I know what you're thinking. That little outcropping hardly seems worth climbing when you compare it to Mt. Hood in the distance. Trust me, once we get up close, you'll change your minds."

As the riders drew nearer, the rocks seemed to grow, until they had to tilt their heads back to see the top.

Hank paired them off. You could barely drive a wedge between the newlyweds, so that was that. Lewis had already claimed Cole. That left Jamie with him.

Lewis placed a crash pad at intervals along the base of the rocks for each pair of climbers, and demonstrated some basic techniques.

Hank offered to let Jamie climb first, while he spotted.

At first glance upward, the crag looked vertical in places, but Hank pointed out chalky spots, previously established handholds she could grab on to.

Jamie lifted her trembling leg up to the first foothold. She scouted out a niche for her other foot, and she was now up off the ground, her flesh pressed against the unyielding stone.

She clung to that first jug for a full minute, searching for her center of gravity, before she found a sloper within her reach.

"Feel for it," Hank instructed. "Sometimes what looks like the obvious solution won't be. You have to stretch. Use new muscles you're not used to using."

Gingerly, she slid her palm across the sun-warmed stone, seeking any small protrusion she could grasp onto. Finding one, she placed her feet on the jugs where her hands had originally been, halted, concentrating, and looked above her again for new handholds. Climbing was hard work. Already she was winded. The muscles in her hips and thighs were beginning to ache with the strain of fighting against gravity, keeping her body plastered onto the rock. She tried again to focus, but her arms were shaking with the effort needed just to hold her body weight against the rock.

As Jamie tacked doggedly left and right on her ascent, Hank remained grounded beneath her, arms out, thumbs tucked in to prevent snapping them in case she fell and he had to catch her.

"Spotters," called Lewis. "Don't take your eyes off your climber's back. It's the best indicator of when they're in danger of falling."

There had never been an easier job. Jamie's engaged lats stretched taut the fabric of her thin cotton knit T-shirt. For a solid half hour, Hank's eyes were fixated on her anatomy, permanently imprinting it on the back of his retinas. There was her wingspan extending from her spine, across her shoulder blades, over the rounded small hills of her shoulders, to her contracted biceps. And the hourglass of her waist, exaggerated by her spread-eagle pose on the rock. He could see the tight half spheres of her glutes through the featherlight fabric of her pants.

Everything on Jamie's body hurt, even her hair. But she was determined not to give up. She pushed on, buoyed a little more with every inch closer to the top.

It was a lot like horseback riding, she realized. You had to let your body become one with the rock. To find that combination of effort and effortlessness.

Gradually she slipped into an alternate state of consciousness. She stopped listening to the others—stopped thinking at all—and let her instincts take over.

Toward the top of the wall, she found more handholds, or maybe she'd just learned to recognize them better. She'd forgotten the people far below, who were gazing skyward, pulling for her.

And then she was scrabbling across the top of the rock on her knees.

She stood up, panting, planted her hands on her hips, and looked out on acres upon acres of vineyards.

It was hard, she thought, *but it was worth it.* She wiped her brow and grinned.

Far below she heard Lewis say, "Dude! She freakin' flashed it!" and high-fived Hank.

She looked down to see everyone else at the bottom, looking up. Even from here she could see Hank's grin.

"Your first try, and you made it!" hollered Hank. "Take a minute and catch your breath."

Why was he worried about her breath? She was finished.

And then she looked down again and realized: She'd only thought about climbing up. Now, she had to get down.

Her smile evaporated. Streaks of perspiration trickled down the nape of her neck between her shoulder blades. Locks of hair stuck to her chest. She reached back and fixed her ponytail.

Then she turned to see the view behind her and saw the sheer drop-off. She gasped, froze, and stepped backward, her foot bending in half over the edge of the rock. She teetered and spread her arms for balance.

"Lower your center of gravity," yelled Lewis, cupping his mouth.

"He means sit down," Hank translated.

She sank to her haunches. "How do I get down?" she yelled back, trying not to cry.

"Trust me," said Hank. "I've got your back."

Her eyes met his steady ones, but fear paralyzed her. She couldn't believe she had never thought past climbing up.

But then, wasn't climbing all she'd ever done? After all, what was college, but a climb? What was learning her craft but getting to the point where her music moved listeners? What else was becoming a competent teacher?

What other choice had she had? Did she have, now?

"Jamie. Just listen to what I tell you. I'm going to talk you down."

She took a deep breath. She could hardly stay up there forever.

And then she turned around to face the rock and tentatively, oh so tentatively, lowered her foot, feeling for a foothold. With nothing else to cling to but the rock and his instructions, Hank's voice became her world. She felt oddly disassociated from her body, as if coming out of a dream. Try too hard to capture it, and it evaporates. She only knew that he was the way, the only way, to the ground and security.

Hank rubbed sweaty palms against his pants as he talked Jamie down from the rock. It was one of those rare Oregon summer days when the air felt like a sauna. He could see the heat radiating off the rocks.

He had spotted a hundred new climbers over the years. And yet he'd never been so anxious about one. He had the insane urge to take Jamie into his arms as soon she was again within reach . . . to hold her tight and never let go.

She was a quarter of the way down now. Her initial adrenaline rush would have long since faded, leaving her weak.

"Halfway home," he called. It was a miracle how steady his voice sounded, given how rattled he was inside.

She stumbled, and beside him, Amanda gasped and her hands flew to her mouth.

"Fifteen feet. Hang in. You're almost there." Hank moved in closer. The coast was far from clear. He could see her triceps tremble with the effort of trying to stay plastered to the rock.

Six feet to go.

Then Jamie's foot slid, and she fell backward off the rocks into Hank's outstretched arms.

The crash pad did its job of cushioning the brunt of their fall. But momentum kept Jamie going, rolling them over a couple of times onto the hard ground. They came to a halt with Jamie straddling him on her hands and knees, his hands planted on her damp ribcage.

With every breath she took he felt the exhilarating rise and fall of her chest beneath his hands. Time stopped. Eye to eye, their world closed in tight, the only sound their breath rushing in and of their lungs, the only smell, that of triumph over defeat.

Lewis was already dragging the crash pad over. "Here," he said. "Roll onto this."

Gingerly, Hank rolled Jamie over onto her back, scanning her body for blood or swelling. "Does it hurt anywhere?"

Dazed, Jamie came slowly to a sitting position and examined the bloody nicks on her hands. The tips of her fingernails were torn ragged, and her palms were still white from the chalk.

She blinked. "I don't think so."

He exhaled a breath he didn't know he'd been holding.

She smiled and attempted to stand on wobbly legs. Hank rose with her, steadying her with a hand on her elbow, reluctant to let go.

She swayed a little bit. "Whoa."

"Dude, that was sick," drawled Lewis in admiration.

Amanda, who, along with the other first-time climbers had failed to reach the summit, rushed over and asked if she was okay.

Jamie smiled gamely despite her scrapes and what would no doubt be bruises tomorrow. "That kicked my butt. It was hard physically. But it was a lot harder, mentally."

The rest of the climbers followed Lewis to the Jeep, but Hank held Jamie back a few steps.

"Sure you're all right?"

"Honest, I'm fine. Lord knows, I didn't have any nails to begin with, from playing instruments." She chuckled, showing him the tops of her brush-burned hands with their long, tapered fingers.

They caught up with the others preparing to picnic on the ground. While they ate, Cole wanted to rehash his own climb with Hank.

Lewis took advantage of Hank's distraction to sidle up next to Jamie.

Hank could barely keep his attention on Cole over straining to hear what Lewis was up to.

"Dude, for a girl, that was damn good. Not that I'm sexist or anything," he hastened to add. "But guys have a lot more upper body strength." He flexed his carved bicep as if to prove it. "It's rare as hell to solve the problem on the first time out."

Jamie wouldn't be the first Sweet Spot guest Lewis put the moves on. Rock or woman, what drove Lewis was the conquest. Once he'd triumphed over them he promptly lost interest and moved on in search of the next adventure.

Hank got up, tossed his sandwich into the woods for a squirrel or a raccoon to feast on, and disappeared behind the Jeep.

How Jamie chose to handle Lewis was none of his business. But he didn't have to sit there and watch.

Chapter Thirteen

Ellie insisted that Jamie eat her meals in the kitchen. She claimed it was because Jamie was an employee and didn't have a place of her own to go home to at the end of the day. But Hank suspected it was more because Ellie had taken an instant liking to her.

"Mr. Rawlings can't have gluten and Mrs. Farabelli is allergic to eggs." Ellie sighed, skimming over the special requests of the current crop of guests.

"It must be hard keeping up with so many different dietary needs," said Jamie, on her way to the fridge carrying her mug of coffee.

"All in a day's work," said Ellie. "Did you bring boots with you?"

Jamie stopped pouring milk into her coffee and followed Ellie's eyes downward to her feet. "I had a good pair of riding boots in high school, but they're long gone. I meant to buy a new pair before I came out here, but time got away from me."

"You need boots," said Ellie matter-of-factly, returning her attention to her laptop. "Why don't you take her to Walker's tomorrow when you go to the wine fest, Hank? She'll like the festival. And while you're there you can show her where the market and the post office are, in case I ever need her to dash into town for something."

The first time Ellie brought up taking Jamie to the wine fest, he'd chafed at the idea. Now it didn't seem so bad. After all, his resident friends weren't going anywhere, but Jamie would only be here for a while.

"That work for you?" he asked her.

"A heel to put in the stirrups would be better than these. And yes, I'd love to go to the wine fest."

The next afternoon, Hank was in the great room waiting for Jamie when a woman descended the stairs wearing a flouncy white skirt and an off-the-shoulder blouse embroidered in bright colors. Flame-colored hair fell forward over her shoulders. Her skin was newly bronzed, cheeks rosy from riding and giving tours through the vineyards.

"Jamie?"

Her smile faded. She spun in a circle, making her skirt swing. "Is this okay to wear to a wine fest?"

"Er, yeah. It'll do."

On their way to town, Hank pointed out some of the local landmarks. Friends Church with the white spire. His old elementary school with the flag out front.

The early summer rains had been beneficial for flowers. As they neared the residential neighborhoods, gardens spilled out onto sidewalks, and front yards boasted roses as big as saucers.

He parked in a spot along Main Street from where they could walk to Walker's Wild Western Wear.

The entire store was stacked from floor to ceiling with boxes of boots of every kind.

"This is overwhelming," Jamie said, fingering the boxes as she wandered down an aisle, Hank trailing behind her.

"I got every pair of boots I've ever owned at this place," he said.

"Do you think they have any English style? Something I'll get some use out of when I go back home?"

"You're not in Pennsylvania anymore. Why not go with something different? A souvenir to remember your vacation by. Like these Noconas. Or over here, these Luccheses."

"I don't know one of these brands from the next."

"What size are you?"

He pulled a box from the middle of a stack and with his foot, dragged a couple of benches to face each other. "Have a seat."

Jamie sat down and reached to unfasten the buckles on her strappy sandals, but Hank stilled her hands with his.

"Let me."

He slid his left hand down the back of her calf and caught her ankle, laying it across his blue-jeaned thigh.

Jamie watched as Hank's thick fingers carefully unfastened the tiny, delicate buckles, allowing them to fall open one by one. He cupped her heel, slipped off her sandal, and eased the first, sturdy boot onto her foot.

"Stand up," he ordered in a voice that sounded different. Softer, yet somehow gruffer.

When she did as he said, his eyes slid lazily from her toes upward, past her knees, over her shoulders, bared by her peasant top, and on up to meet her eyes. "How's that feel?"

She wiggled her foot and winced. "Tight."

"Let's try the next size up."

She sat down and raised her knee to pull off the boot.

But Hank was already there, positioning her leg straight out between his, firmly pulling the boot off.

They repeated the routine twice more without success.

"Maybe it's the style." He looked around, grabbing another box that caught his eye.

He opened it up, peeled back the white tissue paper, and dangled a snakeskin number. "How about this one?"

"I like it."

She slipped in on. "It feels good, too."

"Here, try its partner." He peeled off her other sandal as deliberately as he had the first.

Jamie turned this way and that in the full-length mirror Hank found for her, twisting her hips to make her skirt swirl around her legs.

She grinned. "I'm starting to feel like a real Oregonian."

"Want to wear them out?"

She shrugged. "Might as well."

He put her sandals into the boot box, stuck it under his arm, and headed to the checkout.

Jamie followed him to the register and reached into her bag.

"I got it," said Hank, slipping a couple of large denomination bills out of his wallet onto the counter.

"Oh, no you don't. Did you see how much they are?"

"I said, I got it. It was Ellie's idea. The Sweet Spot will pick up the tab."

"Thank you," she said as they went out onto the sidewalk. "When Ellie asked you to buy me boots, I didn't think she meant it literally."

"Business expense," he replied in a tone that said the subject was closed.

The wine fest was set up in the town square. At booth after booth Hank was greeted with warm handclasps and smiles. In turn, he made sure to introduce Jamie.

She marveled at the way he seemed to take it all in stride. For her, the chance to ask questions and touch the hands of the people who actually grew the grapes and blended her favorite wines was beyond thrilling.

They whiled away the afternoon wandering from booth to booth, sampling wines in tiny plastic cups, not getting the sales talk that Jamie was used to hearing at wine festivals, but chatting easily in the way of old friends.

"You must know everyone in Ribbon Ridge," said Jamie.

"Not only do I know them, my parents knew their parents, my grandparents knew their grandparents, and so on. But we don't see much of each other during the grape season. We're always in the vineyards or the cellar. Winter's our only slow time. That's the social season, and when we do a little traveling to spread the word about our wines."

"What's it like here in the winter? Do you get a lot of snow?"

"You might think so, given that we're on about the same latitude as you in Pennsylvania, but we have a maritime climate. Cool, misty winters and mild summers. That's one of the reasons why grapes love it so much here."

"Where do you go when you travel?"

"Mostly just up and down the coast."

"What about all the other big cities? It seems like there'd be a lot of opportunity there."

"I used to think that, too," he said, returning the wave of a wine writer in town for the festival. "I've been to Chicago, New York, Miami. And I'll go again. Actually, I'm leaving again tomorrow for a conference in Denver."

"Weren't you just there?"

"That was a rare exception. Friend from college invited me out. But on any given night in a major metropolitan area, a wine tasting—even a big one featuring vintners from places like New Zealand and South Africa—is just one option among many. Now, places like Des Moines and Harrisburg . . . those people really appreciate it when a vintner comes to town. They come out for us in droves."

* * *

As dusk fell, they were ambling back toward the field that served as a parking lot when they heard live music coming from a band playing in a gazebo strung with white lights, behind the Turning Point Tavern. More lights were suspended from tree to tree, marking out the perimeter of a leaf-canopied dance floor on the grass, where people danced to the infectious tune.

Hank was about to suggest they head back when Jamie began to sing along.

"They're good," she said. "Want to listen for a while?"

He looked down at her eager eyes and caught a bit of her enthusiasm. How was it that she made things he took for granted seem new again?

Tentatively, he led her toward the dance floor.

The ballad ended and the band launched into a swing dance.

Hank wasn't expecting it when Jamie reached for his hand and twirled around to face him.

What choice did he have? He pressed Jamie's right palm to his left. His hand went to rest lightly on her waist.

"You're so lucky to live here in this beautiful place where you have so many friends."

She was light on her feet, a delight to dance with. He swung her around and pulled her into him in time with the music.

The song ended with them both laughing, and with barely a pause, a slower one began.

Hank hesitated. "We ought to get going."

"Just one more?" she pleaded breathlessly. "I haven't danced in ages. Aren't you having fun?"

"A lot more fun than a benefit dinner."

"Pardon?"

"Nothing," he said, drawing her lush body against his and holding her close, breathing her in, her perfume mingling with the tang of trampled grass from all the feet that had passed by that day on the way to the wine fest.

Holding her hand aloft, he eased her fingers apart, intertwining them with his.

She returned the pressure, sending a thrill through him, and together they swayed to the music. Hank closed his eyes to block out everything but the feel of the curve of her lower back against his hand.

Her breasts pressed against his chest. Behind her back, he rubbed a lock of spun gold between his thumb and finger.

They danced to the next number, and the next, until Hank lost count. When the last song ended and the band said their farewells, he pulled slowly back and opened his eyes to find Jamie staring softly up at him, her lips parted. His gaze traveled down her swan neck to the sensitive cord of her shoulder, bared by her peasant top.

He swallowed, forcing his hands to fall from her waist to skim lightly over her hips on their way back to his sides.

Only then did their glances sweep around the floor to find that they were the only ones still there.

Jamie smiled up at him, her eyes sparkling with expectation.

Just what did she expect? Despite this one, perfect day, the reality was that she didn't belong here. Soon she would vanish into thin air and his days would drag on as if she had never existed, pouring wine in the tasting room, keeping a close eye on the vines for signs of trouble. It was going to be hard enough trying to forget her hair and her boots and this evening's dances, he realized. If he let it go further . . .

The sooner they removed themselves from temptation, the better.

Without a word, Hank took her hand and led her away, heedless of his long, brisk strides that forced her to skip a step now and then to keep up.

When they reached the SUV, he held her door, then slammed it shut almost before she was all in, then booked it around to the driver's side, revved the engine, and vented his frustration on the gas pedal, spinning a tire on his way out of the grassy lot.

Clenching the steering wheel, he homed in on the road, focusing all of his pent-up energy on staying in his lane.

The vehicle was warm from sitting closed up in the sun all afternoon. Hank needed air. He stabbed at the window control with his thumb, impatient for the glass panes on both sides of the cab to descend faster, their smooth downward course in irritating contrast to his erratically pounding heart.

But when the cool air finally rushed over him, instead of bringing relief, it brought the heady scent of the summer blossoms lining the sidewalks and the scent of Jamie's perfume where it had rubbed off on his shirt.

As they sped through the soft night toward the inn as if he could run away from his feelings, he was acutely aware of her sitting beside him. He could see how the wind lifted her hair . . . the easy grace with which she smoothed it down again . . . the movement of her head turning his way, and then, her lack of comprehension when he refused to meet her eyes, and she turned away.

Jamie stared out at forest-green shapes rushing past, not knowing what to say, how to act.

This day had turned out to be memorable. Hank had noticed it, too. She was sure of it. Hadn't he been the one to start it—whatever *it* was—with his outright flirting at the boot store?

She'd seen his face when she was talking to his vintner friends. He'd been almost—dare she even think it?—*proud* to be strolling the wine fest with her.

And the barely restrained longing in the way he held her in his arms when they danced . . . well, even if she couldn't put it into words, a woman *knew* when a man was attracted to her.

But ever since the dancing ended, it was almost like he was afraid of her.

Had she done something to offend him?

Or maybe she was wrong, after all, about him being attracted. From the way he sat over there as if they were complete strangers, staring at the road with the concentration of a NASCAR driver, maybe she'd been hallucinating.

After all, it wasn't his idea to take her to town today. Ellie had foisted her onto him with her boot mandate.

She chanced another sideways glance at him,

now that her eyes had adjusted to the dark. One arm rested on the window ledge, the other straight-armed the wheel. She could even make out a hint of a frown, and that he chewed the inside of his cheek, deep in thought.

She sighed softly, swooned a little bit inside, and bit back a telling smile. Today wasn't the first time she'd noticed the way his hair waved around his ear . . . his well-proportioned body . . . his hands, carefully-groomed, yet rugged from his seeming inability to walk down a row of vines without ripping off every stray sucker that caught his eye.

Romance was the very last thing Jamie had come to wine country for. Never in the wildest stretches of her imagination had she dreamed of coming across a sexy, sulky hero.

And now she was stuck here until the middle of August. What was she supposed to do? Quit, like Bailey, and leave Miss Ellie, and Hank—even if he resented her presence—in the lurch?

It seemed to Hank like forever until they finally pulled up to his space in the back of the inn.

"Thanks again for the boots," said Jamie, climbing out of the SUV.

Hank nodded curtly. "You go ahead in," he said, his voice cracking, which only irritated him more. "I got some things to do before bed."

He lingered by his truck, eyes glued to the sway of Jamie's hips as she walked away. As soon as she disappeared through the front door he threw his cap on the ground, jammed his hands on his hips and paced the length of the truck and back. He looked to the sky for answers, but the stars weren't talking.

How could it be that the subtle nods of approval that he'd received from the growers and vintners with regard to her had made him want to puff out his chest with pride? That the thrill of dancing with her, pretending for a few precious moments that they were more than just employer and employee, had inflamed him to the point of wanting to run out and conquer the world, something even his beloved Ellie hadn't been able to spur in him in three years of trying?

He cursed and kicked up a rooster tail of dust.

Finally, he walked around to the back door and entered the dimly lit kitchen, where he found Ellie folding laundry.

"Did you have a good time in town?"

"Great." He ran himself a tall glass of well water and gulped it down, wiping his mouth with the back of his hand.

"Jamie like the wine fest?"

"What's not to like?" he grumbled.

"Pull in yer horns, Son. I'm just trying to be sociable."

He shook his head. "Sorry. Got a lot on my mind."

"Jamie said she was going up to take a bath. I'm headed up too, soon as I finish this laundry."

"See you in the morning," he said as he trailed out toward the great room and up the stairs to his suite.

"What time's your flight?" she called after him.

"I have to be out of here by nine."

He braced himself for Ellie's usual hand wringing over his trip. Ever since she'd lost her son and daughter-in-law, the mere thought of him flying made Ellie anxious. But mercifully, all she said was good night.

He had just switched off his light, fallen onto the mattress, and squeezed his eyes shut tight against the turbulence of the day when he heard water running across the hall.

His eyes flew open to nothingness. He lay flat on his back, listening. A fence post away, Jamie Martel was stepping out of that white cotton skirt. He pictured her sleek hips and legs with the skirt in a pool around her feet.

The sound of water running through the pipes stopped. Now in his mind's eye he saw her step over the rim of the bathtub and lower herself into the deep bubbles . . . washing away the dust and the damp excitement of the day that they'd shared, and he wondered if the memory of dancing in each other's arms beneath the twinkling white lights was etched as deeply in her mind as it was in his. For he knew beyond a shadow of a doubt that, even decades from now, when he was old and grizzled, there would still be nights when he would lie awake and marvel over the woman who came to work for him one summer. The one who got away.

Chapter Fourteen

Denver

Hank and Delilah ducked into a dimly lit, masculine space with leather banquettes, blood-red carpeting, and a vaulted ceiling. Hank shook the water off the umbrella he'd been holding over Delilah and handed it and their wraps to a waiting staffer.

"Tell me again," he said in a low voice, straightening the tie that threatened to choke him as the host showed them to their table. "Why are we having dinner here?"

"Bennett's is known for their aged Kobe beef and their cellar."

"I meant, why the Bakers? I only met him once."

"I told you before. He and his wife are clients of mine as well as being wine lovers. They've entertained me at their home. He has a built-in cellar. When I told him you were coming to town again, he asked if they could buy us dinner. Smells great, doesn't it?"

The tantalizing aroma of sizzling beef and promise of cold beverages lifted his spirits. The soft buzz of civilized conversation filled the air.

He shrugged off his misgivings. Delilah had been a generous hostess yet again, picking him up at the airport and letting him crash in her place, neither of which he had asked for.

A few cocktails did their intended job. The conversation was light, centering on the weather, travel, and cars. As they finished their salads, Hank listened quietly while Delilah, Stew, and Stew's wife, May, argued the relative merits of her Lexus versus their BMW.

"How bout you, Friestatt, what do you drive?" Stew asked Hank, in an obvious effort to include him.

"My dad's old 2003 Outback," he replied, tipping his glass of the pinot Stew had graciously insisted he choose for the table.

"Champagne-colored, so it doesn't show the dust," chimed in Delilah. "Hank's very practical that way."

"All-wheel drive?" Stew asked.

Hank sliced off a bite of his Delmonico and nodded. "Any vehicle of mine has to earn its keep."

"When I travel I always rent an Escalade. Clients like the legroom, and the suspension automatically adjusts to bad roads."

Once the small talk was out of the way, Stew began asking Hank's opinion on current affairs in Oregon, such as taxes and local politics, while

Delilah engaged May by asking about where she'd found the dress she was wearing.

Finally Stew worked his way around to wine. "How is this year's grape crop looking?"

"We had above average rainfall in the spring. We're looking for a high yield."

"Last I read, your share of the greater Friestatt Vineyards was two hundred forty acres. That still the case?"

There was an unwritten rule. Never ask a man how many acres he owned. A man's acreage was nobody's business but his own. If Stew had asked that question of the right guy at the Turning Point Tavern a sufficient number of beers into the night, he'd have been likely to learn that lesson the hard way. But instead they were here, in this ritzy Denver restaurant, and there were ladies at the table, so Hank settled for cracking his neck, still stiff from his flight and from working outside in the damp.

"Which journal'd you read that in?"

"I subscribe to several of them."

"Delilah says you travel a lot," said Hank, steering the conversation in a different direction.

"Mostly for work. Though lately, May and I have been to some places we would never have discovered if not for our friend Delilah, here."

Next to him, Delilah sat back. Hank glanced at her just in time to see her and Stew exchange what looked like a meaningful glance.

"Worked in the real estate division of Snacks Galore for ten years," Stew continued. "A regular paycheck. Safe, but I learned a lot."

"And now?"

"I'm making deals on my own."

Hank raised his glass. "Congratulations on your new venture."

Stew drank, then cleared his throat and with an obvious glance around the room he lowered his voice a notch and said, "You're well aware that there's been a flood of new investment in the Willamette Valley. Fifty years ago there were only a handful of wineries there. Now seems there's a new one every month. Land prices are skyrocketing because they can't make enough pinot to meet demand. You got investors from all over. California, even as far away as France and Australia. Yamhill County's the best of the best, and also the most expensive."

Hank's eyes flew to where Delilah kept May occupied with idle chatter. And he'd thought she was just being a gracious hostess to a fellow alum and she'd arranged this dinner for his entertainment.

"But in spite of the outward success, I know how hard it is to manage vineyards the size of yours. Day to day, year in and year out, it's no different from traditional farming. It operates on rolling debt. Every bad year weather-wise puts you farther and farther in the hole. Nowadays you're lucky if you have one kid who wants to stay on the family farm. Even if he does, chances are he'll have to sell off part of the land to buy out his siblings, or at least to pay inheritance taxes. That means more farmland available to be converted to vineyards.

"I have a client who has a proposition I think you'll want to hear. Your land is exactly what he is looking for. It has the elevation, the gentle slope protected from the weather by the mountain, and the southeast aspect. Everything you could ask for in a vineyard."

"That was you."

Stew drew a blank.

"Last Tuesday night in June. Dusk. The black Escalade."

Stew frowned. "I didn't see you there."

"No. You talked to my grandmother. I was pulling in as you were leaving. I had to swerve into the ditch to avoid getting sideswiped."

"The Subaru."

Stew apparently failed to register that an apology was in order.

Hank took a long swallow from his glass. He and Ellie routinely watched the small planes flying above their southeast-facing slopes, which maximized the afternoon sun needed to grow and ripen grapes. An hour later a Realtor would come driving up, wanting to talk about selling. You could set your watch by it.

"I take it you didn't get very far into your spiel before she told you to take a hike."

Stew swirled his wine while he measured his next words. "Your grandma Eleanor's a pistol."

"Ellie doesn't pull any punches." Hank visualized her cutting Stew off at the knees and smiled to himself.

"I was counting on you to be more . . . how should I say it? Open-minded."

"That land has been in the family for a century and a half."

"There's a bunch of new investors out there," said Stew, mopping up the pool of A.1. Sauce on his plate with half of a dinner roll, working it sideways into his mouth. "It's a rising tide."

"The Willamette Valley is more than a brand," said Hank. "It's my home. We have a vibrant culture. Ever wash down coho salmon fresh from the Clackamas River with a 2009 almost-dry Riesling, the kind that's only made in small batches?"

"I understand your sentimental attachment. But outside investment's not a bad thing. It's beneficial for the entire industry. We get your passion. We do. We're in it for the long haul, too, just like you."

Hank fingered the base of his wineglass. "We small guys can't compete with giants like your client."

"This interest by out-of-state investors is only going to grow," said Stew as he sawed at his steak. "It's not *if* you'll sell. It's when, and to whom."

Hank spread his arms. "As Ellie told you, we have no interest in selling."

Stew sized up Hank with beady eyes, a shiny film of grease clinging to his fleshy lips as he chewed.

"Have you thought about what this means, Hank?" Delilah interjected, her eyes round. "You wouldn't be tied down anymore. You could take up your flying lessons again."

"I get it," said Stew. "Change makes people nervous."

For some strange reason, the glow in Jamie Martel's eyes at her first sight of his property came back to Hank.

"You're sitting on a gold mine," Stew pressed. "Aren't you interested in hearing the details of the offer?"

Delilah's eyes glittered. "Why not hear him out? What do you have to lose?"

Whose side are you on? Hank wondered.

Stew scribbled something on the back of his card and slid it across the table to Hank. "This is our price per acre for all two hundred fifty."

Despite lots of fishing expeditions and drive-by Realtor inquiries, never had a conversation about selling gone this far. Hank wondered how Stew had inveigled Delilah into getting him an audience.

Delilah leaned over to read the number, then eyed Hank with a catlike grin.

Hank's pulse began to race in spite of himself. It wasn't the money. Money had never been in short supply, thanks to the hard work of his parents and grandparents. Consequently, it didn't hold any special magic. And he didn't care about fast cars or the latest toys.

Freedom was what excited him.

Rather than spending his summers babying grapes, he could go skiing in Argentina. Instead of having his autumns tied up with the crush, he could fly his own plane over the fall foliage. Hunt and fish in Alaska. Revisit all the places he'd gone to with his family, back before he had so many responsibilities.

He took a gulp of wine.

"Fewer than two hundred fifty, the price starts dropping in direct relationship," said Stew. "You don't have to answer now. Think it over. You've got forty-eight hours."

"That's not much time."

"That's the way it works."

It only took Hank a second to grasp the reasoning behind what at first seemed to be an unreasonable request. "You don't want to give me time to go look for a buyer willing to pay more, and then pit the two of you against each other."

Stew's grin couldn't disguise his admiration for Hank's powers of deduction. "Right on one count. We want to avoid a bidding war. But we have another property on our radar, too. If you're not willing, we want to offer immediately on that one before it's gone."

The server brought their check, and Stew handed her his credit card between two fingers.

"I'll need to hear from you early next week," he said in parting.

Back in wine country

Jamie was laying down fresh straw bedding in Dancer's stall.

"What are you doing mucking out?" asked Bill from where he worked across the aisle. "I can handle this."

"I like mucking out. It reminds me of when I was growing up."

"Suit yourself."

For a minute they worked to the soft music coming from the ancient barn radio.

"Lewis's got some beef brisket in the oven over at his place. Puts beer in it. There's plenty if you want to join us."

She rested her hands on her pitchfork. She had never been around Bill and Bryce and Lewis outside of the Sweet Spot.

"I don't know . . ."

"Can't have a fire tonight, thanks to this rain. What else are you going to do all night? Sit inside by your lonesome? It's not far. I'll bring you back after a while."

Lewis's kitchen was small, but it was dry and toasty warm from the oven having been on all day, and the men were in good spirits.

"I'll say grace." Bill folded his sun-speckled hands atop the table.

Jamie sneaked a peek at the tops of the heads bowed around the table: Lewis's tangled blond dreads. Bryce's buzz cut. And Bill's surprisingly naked pate, usually disguised beneath his ever-present felt hat.

"Lord, bless these gifts we are about to receive," said Bill in his bass voice.

The men's big, work-hardened hands made the cutlery seem like children's toys as they ate.

After dinner, while Lewis was preparing a pot of coffee, Bill pulled out a deck of cards and began shuffling.

"Five-card stud. You in?" he asked Jamie with a twinkle in his eye.

"Oh, no, I couldn't," she said, shaking her head.

"What's the matter? You never played poker before? Come on, we'll show you how."

She glanced at the dark, rain-streaked window and shivered.

Lewis set a steaming cup of coffee down in front of her.

A couple of hours later, Jamie laughed as she scooped up her winnings, heedless to Lewis's loud accusations that she was a ringer, and Bryce's usual grousing.

And when it was time for Bill to take her home, the same men who'd just given her a rough time jockeyed for position in the narrow doorway, fairly tripping over each other to bid her a good night.

Chapter Fifteen

"That was fun," said Delilah in her car on their way back to the convention center. "The steak was delicious. I won't have to eat for a week."

Hank grunted a response, looking straight ahead from his seat on the passenger side as he jammed the male part of his seat belt into its female receptor.

"Tell me how you met Stew, again?"

"Same place I meet most of my clients, on a flight a year or so ago. Stew likes nice things. Fine wine. Upscale accommodations. Since I started my company, he's stayed at two or three of my resorts. A while back I was having dinner with another flight attendant at the Springs, and Stew was at the bar talking about Oregon. He asked us to join him for an after-dinner drink. I happened to mention the Sweet Spot, and that I had gone to school with the owner.

"Did you know before tonight at dinner that Stew wanted to talk to me about selling my vineyards?"

"He said he had a business proposition for you," she said, pulling her car away from the curb. "He made it sound like something you could benefit from. I thought I was doing you a favor. You've seen how Stew is. A little overbearing, though he means well. I guess I got a little caught up in it. Honestly, Hank, was it that bad?"

Hank raised a brow.

"I've been to the Sweet Spot," said Delilah. "I've seen what it takes to keep a place like that going. You're on your feet from sunup to sundown. And that's just the lodging aspect of the place. Everyone knows how dangerous farming can be. Climbing around on that tractor, cutting vines with those big old shears, or whatever they're called. What if something happened to you?"

Hank frowned at the column of cars sitting in front of them. "Is traffic always this bad here this time of night?"

"I thought you and Stew had something in common."

"It sounds like you're encouraging me to sell."

"I'm not encouraging you to do anything. But you have to admit, selling would make your life a whole lot easier."

"I'm not the type to live my life putzing around without a purpose."

"Without the vineyards to tie you down, you could get your pilot's license."

"I told you before. That was a pipe dream." He turned away from her and gazed out the opposite window. "The Sweet Spot has been in my family for generations. It's always been understood that I'd keep it in the family. Can you imagine what losing the only home she's ever had would do to Ellie? The woman is seventy-one years old. The Sweet Spot is sacred ground to her. Without it, what would she do? Where would she go?"

"She's getting up in years, Hank. She can't expect to keep going like she has been, forever."

"Try telling her that."

"Give it some thought. How can that hurt? Maybe you can come up with a good alternative for your grandmother. A nice house, all on one level, in a gated community. Someplace warm, like Palm Springs. Who wouldn't love that?"

"You don't know my grandmother."

Twelve hours after Stew had laid out his offer, Hank watched the lights of Denver recede as his plane ascended.

Despite what he'd said, he couldn't help but think about it. What if Delilah had a point? Running the business was a relentless job. Not long ago he'd attended the funeral of a hard-driving vintner friend of his father's who'd been found in his vineyard with his sprayer still strapped to his back.

Selling would free him to do anything he pleased. Take those flying lessons, even buy his own plane, just like Dad. He cherished his dad's old aeronautical charts that noted the locations of key waypoints, as well as the routes connecting them. Nowadays airliners were equipped with autopilot. You could get up from your seat in the cockpit of a 737 to use the head and stop to flirt with the pretty crew chief on your way back, while the plane virtually flew itself.

But small craft were still hand-flown. Only then did it occur to Hank that just maybe, the old way suited him better.

He peered down at the Rocky Mountains. Just a few weeks ago Jamie had seen a similar view on her cross-country flight. He imagined how her face must have lit up at the majestic view of white-capped peaks and deep blue ravines. She was drawn to natural beauty, difficult kids, and good music. He bet she didn't give a fig about black tie affairs or cultivating friends in high places.

After he landed he took a van to the long-term parking lot where he'd left his truck and drove the hour and a half to the inn, still thinking about all the possibilities open to him.

It was nearing midnight when he climbed the stairs to the floor where Ellie, and now Jamie, slept.

In the quiet hallway outside his and Jamie's rooms, he paused.

Bags still filling his hands, his gaze fell to Jamie's door. Behind it was the bed his parents had shared. Memories of joyous mornings crawling in between them, getting his hair roughed up and being tickled breathless, went through his head. For a short, sweet time, that bed was the center of his universe. A place where he belonged, where nothing bad could ever happen.

Now that bed had a new occupant.

Hank set down his bags in the hallway and slowly turned to gaze at the knob of the door leading to the Sunflower Suite. None of those old, upstairs doors had locks on them. In one step he was standing in front of it. The glass knob felt cool in his hot palm, the oval shape a perfect fit.

His heart pounded in his throat.

And then what? What would he say when Jamie woke up and saw him standing over her like some crazed psychopath?

Before he ended up sending his newest employee tearing off for the airport at first morning light, he let go of the knob, carried his bags inside his own room, and barricaded himself behind his door.

Chapter Sixteen

The canes, so green and springy in May and June, were growing firm and brown, right on schedule.

Hank pulled his July vineyard journal from the row of identically bound books above his desk, each representing a year in the vineyard. Starting with volume one, created that spring when his grandfather grafted vines from Burgundy onto American rootstock to increase their vigor and resist disease, every handwritten, wine-stained volume was a practical resource for comparing annual weather patterns, the best days to perform seasonal chores, from planting to picking, and how different grape varieties performed in Ribbon Ridge's marine sediment soil.

In July of volume five, Grandpa's big, loopy lettering ended without explanation on the day he died, continuing without a break the very next day in Hank's dad's tighter, more precise script.

Hank wondered if his grandfather and father

could ever have imagined getting a multimillion-dollar offer on their ground. If only they were here now. He could use their advice.

The past three annual journals were written in Hank's similarly careful hand.

Thin crop. Monitor gophers. Let flock loose in Block Three for weed control, Hank scribbled.

The inn was booked solid in anticipation of the annual campout. Thank God for Jamie. The only people who'd replied to his help-wanted ad were ones no one else would hire. If it weren't for her, he didn't know how he would get through this summer.

His phone rang. Barry, one of the workers, came up on the screen.

"Hank? The Newberry All-Stars made it to the World Series. You know what that means."

"Something tells me it means I'm going to be shorthanded for the campout."

"Sorry to leave you high and dry, but looks like I'll be headed to Portland that day."

"You go and support Maddie."

"She's fourteen. This is her last year of eligibility. Next thing you know she'll be wantin' to go riding in cars with boys."

"No, you can't miss the championship. Tell Maddie I said good luck."

Hank tapped his pen against his teeth and thought. Lewis and Drew could probably handle the campout. Lewis knew these hills like the back of his hand. But Drew was young and Hank didn't know him that well. And he outright refused to send Jamie out alone with that womanizer Lewis, or with Bill. Jamie didn't know the procedures or the territory, and if something happened to Bill, she would be hard-pressed to take care of both him and the guests. But if Hank and Jamie went out, Bill could cover the tasting room.

He scratched his chin and thought. He didn't like it. Anything could happen on an overnight trip.

He'd been giving Jamie mixed signals. She had to be confused. Maybe even annoyed. Even worse, hurt. And no wonder. What with him growing more attached to Jamie than an employer ought to be, this mysterious new urgency Ellie had about teaching him the ropes, and now the offer on the land, his head was spinning.

But he liked the alternatives even less.

The next morning before breakfast, he called the affected staff members into the tasting room before it opened.

When they were all there, lounging around at tables and talking, Hank cleared his throat.

"As you probably heard, Maddie got into the softball finals, so Barry'll be in Portland during the campout. Means I had to do a little shuffling. Bill, can you cover the tasting room?"

Chewing on his toothpick, Bill nodded.

"Bryce, you stay here and cover the campfire for the folks who aren't going on the campout."

Hank paused to look at his notes. As if it were an afterthought, he added, "Jamie, you and I will do the campout."

Heads whipped toward her.

"That's it." Hank rose from his perch at the bar.

Everyone but Jamie headed off to his respective job.

"Are you good with that?"

"Anything I can do to help out. Just consider me one of the boys." Smiling saucily, she tossed her jeans jacket over one shoulder and went out to tack up for the trail ride.

"Temptress." *Did I just say that out loud?*

Jamie whirled back around. "What did you say?" Her eyes danced. She swatted at him with her jacket.

He arched his spine, missing getting swatted by a hair.

She took off after him then, swinging as he swerved and ducked.

Laughing, they circled the room, once and then twice, weaving in and out of high-top tables and chairs. But Hank knew where all the nooks and crannies were. He ducked behind a door, then popped out behind her and pinned her arms to her sides.

She struggled briefly, then, knowing she was beat, stopped, her breasts rising and falling rapidly above his arms.

Her ponytail tickled his nostrils but he couldn't scratch it without letting go of her body, warm and firm pressed up against his. He wrinkled his nose, narrowed his eyes, and peered down at where her neck disappeared into the edge of her T-shirt. He had an overpowering urge to bend and kiss that spot. To taste her soft skin with his tongue.

Instead, he took the high road and freed her with a playful shove.

Jamie picked up her jacket, yanked down the hem of her shirt, and gave him a defiant parting glare. But try as she might, she couldn't contain her smile.

Evidently, despite his erratic behavior, Jamie Martel wasn't one to carry a grudge.

"Truce?" he asked.

She pretended to think about it. "Truce," she said finally, flouncing out of the tasting room without a backward glance, to go help with the trail ride.

Hank stayed behind, watching the bounce of her ponytail with each step. A few more weeks and she'd be gone and life would go on as before.

In the meantime, he and Jamie were going camping together.

Chapter Seventeen

The day of the campout dawned warm and mild, with just enough clouds to break up the monotonous expanse of sapphire.

Jamie was in the kitchen helping Ellie prepare the food for the excursion, thankful that the tension that had lingered between Hank and her after the wine fest had vanished just in time for them to spend the better part of two days and a night together.

"We got this campout routine down. I fry enough chicken to feed everyone at the vineyard, including the workers. Then I make a couple buckets of potato salad and simmer a cauldron of baked beans. Half of the meal gets packed up for the people who're going out to the Peak, the other half stays."

The buzzer on the range went off, and Ellie grabbed her hot pads to withdraw battered metal sheets of puffy sourdough biscuits from the oven.

"How's that look?" Jamie called to her. Ellie

peered into the oversized bowl of potato salad Jamie was composing according to Ellie's recipe.

"Looks dandy. Would you go in the pantry and see if you can find some more catsup, and then give those beans a good stir while I start this chicken?"

"How many people will there be on the campout this year?" Jamie asked, standing at the stove where the beans bubbled.

"The campout's always our most popular event. There's only three sleeping tents. Those who want to go have to let us know when they make their trip reservations, months in advance. As usual, today's trip is full."

"Where do the packers sleep?" What she really wanted to know was, *Where will Hank and I sleep?*

"If it's raining, in the food tent. It has a wood floor and a picnic table that can double as a cot for your sleeping bag. If it's fine, they sleep on the ground, next to the campfire. Looks like it's going to be nice out tonight. You'll find it's pretty rustic up there, but there's a latrine and a shed where we keep equipment, horse feed, and fishing gear. The main supplies that need to be transported are fresh food and drinking water.

"Everyone takes his own sleeping bag and water in his saddle bags. You and Hank will ride your own horses, plus lead horses packed with the food and ice. You leave room for your guitar?"

"Do you think I should?"

"Absolutely."

On an impulse, Jamie gathered her dishtowel to her heart. "Ellie, thank you for everything you've done for me this summer."

"Pooh. I should be thanking you. From the minute you walked through that door, I felt like you were part of this place."

Hank led the packhorses up to the back door of the kitchen and showed Jamie how to load them up with the food.

"C'mon up," he called to Jamie when they were mounted and had gathered the rest of the crew. "Flora and Chico like to ride together."

Lewis saw them riding out and gave a wolf whistle. "Hey, Hank. While you're up there on the Peak, don't let her tell you she doesn't know how to play poker."

Jamie smiled and waved back.

"What was that about?" asked Hank, doing his best not to look too interested.

"The guys invited me to sit in on their Saturday night poker game."

Hank had heard about those poker games for years, but never once had he been invited to play. And they'd asked Jamie after she'd barely started working here. Obviously, they saw her as one of them.

While he was miserable dining on Kobe beef in one of Denver's finest restaurants, she and his men were having the time of their lives, playing cards at Lewis's humble ranch house.

"Took 'em for twelve dollars and sixty cents," Jamie added proudly.

He led Jamie and the others along a rough trail through sun and shade until they came to a meadow. "Red columbine," he said, pointing to where flame-like, orange-red flowers emerged through the rocks. "And see that little purple flower over there? That's Oregon iris."

The riders didn't do much talking. The green ones were focused on keeping control of their mounts, and the more experienced ones, like Jamie, were seizing the day, taking in the countryside.

Farther along, Hank reined in Blitzer and turned in his saddle to face the riders behind him. Putting a finger to his lips, he pointed to where a herd of deer grazed not far away.

The shadows lengthened and the slope gradually became steeper. The setting sun cast a bronze glow on everything in its path.

Hank reined in again in a tract of Douglas fir stripped of their needles and motioned for the others to gather around.

"Those trees look as if they've been burned," said Jamie.

"That's what I wanted to show you. There was a controlled burn here late last fall," Hank explained. "It's a practice continued from the Native Americans to prevent a small fire, say from a lightning strike, from turning into a large one. Plus, periodic fires are healthy for the forest. It prevents overcrowding of trees and promotes new growth of flowers and plants, improving habitat."

On they climbed, the scrubland gradually being replaced with evergreens.

"Won't be long now," said Hank.

One last curve and they emerged from the woods to see a patchwork quilt of brown, green, and blue spread out beneath them.

"What do you think?" asked Hank.

Jamie stared out at the vista, speechless.

Hank squinted again at the bright orange horizon. An osprey rode a thermal current in the foreground of Mt. Hood, while a flock of Canada geese descended noisily into a thicket of cattails to spend the night. How many times had he been out here since Dad died without really seeing this? He had allowed the campout to turn into just another chore.

He slid off Blitzer and led him to a small pool. "There's a spring over here," he called to the others. "The horses got us up here. They get their drink before we do."

While Jamie helped the riders feed and stake their animals for the night, Hank unlocked the remote kitchen shed, retrieved a few bottles of wine, and submerged them up to their necks in the spring to chill.

The campers found their tents and unpacked their saddlebags, while Hank lit the camp stove so Jamie could warm up the baked beans.

"It's the same food as down at the inn, but for some reason it tastes better up here," said Jamie.

After supper Hank showed Jamie where to lock away the leftovers to keep wild animals from getting them during the night.

While Hank built a fire, the others gathered round. Jamie brought out her guitar, and they talked and sang until the flames burned down to embers.

"Listen," said Hank. "Hear that?"

"What is it?" asked a wide-eyed woman from Chicago, dressed head to toe in expensive new outdoor gear.

"A Great Horned Owl. They've been living in that stand of firs for generations, ever since I started coming up here as a boy."

A while later, a howl went up, answered by an identical one farther away.

"Coyotes calling to each other. Don't worry, they won't bother us."

"Are you sure?" asked the woman, hugging her knees to her chest.

"Jamie and I will keep the fire going through the night. We'll lay out our sleeping bags right here, next to it."

"Speaking of sleep, you might want to get some. I'll be rattling your tent flaps at sunup."

One after another, the campers yawned, stretched, and retreated to their tents.

Hank showed Jamie how to lay out a plastic tarp to protect her sleeping bag from moisture, then he laid his own tarp at a respectful distance from hers.

But instead of lying down, Jamie went back to her camp stool. With no explanation, Hank disappeared in the vicinity of the spring and returned holding another bottle of wine. He dried it off with the tail of his shirt, pulled the cork, and poured some into the collapsible cup she held out.

For a while they sat in silence.

Hank wondered if Jamie, too, was thinking that this was the first time they'd been alone together since the night of the dance. Though with the others just a stone's throw away in the tents, they weren't technically alone.

Then Jamie tipped her head back and gazed up at the glittering night sky. "I don't think you can get any farther from Philadelphia than this," she murmured. "The stars look so close I can almost touch them."

Hank tipped his head back, too. "Getting here's a hassle. All that prep, then the hour-long ride. But then there's . . . *this.*"

"I have to give you and Ellie and the guys credit. Between all the daily chores, the sometimes finicky guests to take care of, and then the glitches that seem to crop up just when you're least expecting them, you work awfully hard to keep things running smoothly."

"I give Ellie all the credit. But then, she's been doing it for years."

"How long has the Sweet Spot been in your family?"

"The Friestatts came out here from Missouri at the start of the Civil War. Missouri was supposed to be a neutral state. But with stars on both the Union and Confederate flags and some members of the same families taking different sides, there were skirmishes everywhere. A woman named Arabella O'Hearn had a teenage son who was chomping at the bit to run off and join the fighting. She had already lost husband number one in the Mexican-American War. She was scared to death of losing her son, too. She came up with this plan to head west. But she knew it would be hard to travel two thousand miles on her own. There was a widower at her church, Henry Friestatt, who also had a teenage son. So, she proposed to him."

"As in, marriage?" Jamie's fingers flew to her breast.

Hank noticed yet again how long and expressive they were, like angel's hands in paintings of Biblical times.

"How romantic."

"Not sure romance had anything to do with it. Once they finally found their new home on the West Coast, far from any wars, where they could start fresh—"

Her eyes lit up. "The Sweet Spot."

He shrugged. "They did end up having more kids. Lots of them."

"So it *is* a love story."

"In those days, they needed as many hands as they could get to run the farm. The Friestatts started out planting hazelnuts. They lived frugally, plowing all the profits into buying more ground, till eventually they accumulated enough acreage to add beef cattle to their operation. Of course, all that came to a screeching halt when it was discovered that the Willamette Valley is one of the best places in the world to grow pinot noir. Grandpa was one of the first to see it coming. About twenty years ago he tore out all the nut trees, sold the cattle, and planted wine grapes."

"It's nice that you kept the horses."

"That was Ellie's doing. Can't get rid of those as long as she's around. Not that she rides much anymore.

"A decade later, Dad started getting into biodynamic viniculture. We've gradually been building up the soil using natural methods and finding ways to use fewer pesticides and herbicides. Now not a week goes by when some rep from one of the big beverage conglomerates or snack-food companies doesn't fly into the private airstrip down on Dopp Road."

"And now, it's all come down to you. Do you realize how lucky you are, Hank Friestatt?" she asked emphatically. "There are millions of people who'd give anything to be in your shoes. Though, it must have been overwhelming, at first."

"Sometimes it still is."

"But you did it. Some people would have been too scared. Or would have refused to try."

"That was never a consideration," he said quietly. "Ellie needed me."

"But she didn't insist that you come back, did she?"

"She would never do that."

"The fact that you came through for her shows what kind of guy you are. Someone to be trusted. To be depended on."

If she only knew.

Hank got up and put another log on the fire. "It's not that I'm not grateful. But with privilege comes obligation. It takes a lot to keep the plates spinning."

"Still. There's got to be more good than bad. The advantages outweigh the disadvantages."

"Do they?" He shot her a look. *Should I tell Jamie about the offer?* He'd been carrying it inside until he was ready to burst.

Jamie wrinkled her forehead. "What do you mean?"

He leaned forward in his camp chair, made a teepee with his fingers, and stared into the flickering flames. There, atop the Peak, it was just them sitting around the campfire under the stars. There was no Bryce bringing him yet another problem with the gophers, no grandmother whose mere presence served as a reminder of his legacy. "The wine boom has jacked up the value of our land exponentially. And there are people out there who're more than willing to pay for it."

"You've had an actual offer?"

Hank laughed drily. "You could say that."

She waited for him to explain.

"I have a chance to fold, Jamie. Throw in all my cards and start over. You remember that black Escalade that almost ran us off the road the night you arrived?"

"Ellie said something about a Realtor."

"His name is Stewart Baker. We had dinner when I was at the wine conference."

"But, what would happen to the vineyard? What about you? Where would you go? How would you make a living?"

Jamie was a music teacher from back East, not an expert in the specialized field of wine country real estate site selection. She had no way of knowing that in the past five years alone, the price of Willamette Valley land had quadrupled. It was an embarrassment of riches.

"Any damn thing I wanted."

"Exactly what is it that you want?"

He looked up to see a blinking light of an airliner on its way toward the vast Pacific and from there, the exotic Far East. "Fly. I always wanted to fly."

If only he could trade places with that pilot with a snap of his fingers, soaring west until he caught up with the sun.

"I was all set to start flight school when—*it* happened."

"There must be flight schools around here. What's stopping you?"

Hank took off his Textron cap and turned it over in his hands. "Ellie's been anxious to teach me as much of the business while she still can. Plus, since the accident she hates it when I fly, even as a passenger. I could never fly commercially and manage an operation the size of the Sweet Spot at the same time. I can barely keep up as it is."

"I don't understand how you could give all of this up."

Hank stifled a snort. How could he have expected her to understand? To her the Sweet Spot was just a temporary post before she went back to her real life.

"That's just it, Jamie—I *can*. The company Stew represents is looking to expand. They're offering me an obscene amount of money."

She leapt to her feet. Behind her hung the half moon. "You've just finished telling me how precious this land is to you. How your ancestors drove cross-country in a prairie schooner for it, and it's been carefully cultivated for generations since then. Now it's your turn, and you're considering selling out to some"—she cast about for the right word—"some modern-day prospectors?"

"Careful." Hank nodded toward the tents where the others lay sleeping. "I don't want just anyone to know about this. It could start a rumor that would hurt business.

"Those advantages you're talking about come at a heavy cost. Some might think of me as a big landowner, but that's within a very small viticultural zone. In most ways, I'm like any small farmer: I do it all. The crop and the winemaking are only the tip of the iceberg. There's maintaining the buildings and equipment, keeping up with legislation . . . Sure, I have an accountant. But who do you think keeps the records that she needs to do her job? You've seen what it's like. Most days I'm up before dawn and don't get to bed till after midnight. And then there's the weather. Droughts, flooding, the whole gamut. The whims of the market—fads, competition, and so on. Is it any wonder Ellie has high blood pressure?"

"But you have complete autonomy. Granted, it's hard for you now, starting out. But you'll get a handle on it. You'll figure out how to strike a balance . . . where you need to ask for help and what jobs you want to keep for yourself because you enjoy them, the same way Ellie does the campouts and readies the kitchen at night for the following day."

She thought for a moment. "Speaking of Ellie, what did she say?"

He didn't say anything.

"Hank. What was Ellie's response when you told her you're considering the offer?"

He was beginning to regret sharing.

Suddenly he wished Jamie had never come to Oregon. She forced him to talk about things he'd rather keep buried. He ran a hand through his hair. What was it about her that brought his carefully stored feelings to the surface?

She sighed. "You haven't told her."

"She's on blood pressure medication. The doctor—"

"She is? Why didn't anyone tell me?"

Hank gave her a blank look.

"Sorry," she mumbled. "I'm just an employee. It's none of my business."

"Jamie—"

"Well, it's true, isn't it?"

"Ellie would never allow someone she didn't think pretty highly of to stay in my parents' old room."

Blue eyes met his. "What about you?"

"What do you mean?" he asked, hedging.

"What do you think of me?"

It would be easy to tell a white lie and say he'd been a fan from the start. But something told him she wouldn't hold his honesty against him. "I admit, when Ellie first brought up hiring you, I wasn't sure I wanted to."

"You didn't think I was up to the job?"

"Far from it. Maybe I saw too much of my ideal self in you. The Hank Friestatt everyone wants me to be."

"Which is?"

"You know. Someone who passively accepts his fate without questioning it."

"You think I'm passive?" She huffed in indignation. "You don't know me at all."

"No. Not that." He squirmed. "I'm making a mess of this. It's that—what I'm supposed to want, you seem to want without trying."

"And that is?"

"To squelch your desires and spend your life in the same place your parents and grandparents did, doing all the same things."

Jamie picked up her guitar and began to sing softly, so as not to wake the others.

"I met a brown-eyed boy that summer
Between the meadows and the vines
Never intending to be lovers
Then came the taste of sweet red wine.

"Now in the moonshine in my wineglass
I swear I see his face
And though it wasn't meant to be
Still in my mind I see
That summer time, that summer place."

"That's your song?" asked Hank.

"That's how it works sometimes," replied Jamie. "The lyrics spring up fully formed from out of nowhere, like a dandelion puff on a breeze. I have to hurry to catch them before they blow right past."

"You *wrote* that."

She shrugged and laid her guitar down carefully at her side. "That's what musicians do."

Hank hesitated. "What inspired you?"

"You mean, who did I write it for?"

He held his breath.

"It's about somebody I used to know. His name was Ben."

Ben? Who the hell was Ben?

She clenched her hands between her knees until her knuckles were white, and drew a deep breath. "Ben and I went to the same high school. He followed me to college. Oh, he didn't admit it was because of me at first. But once he finally did, we were exclusive from then on. He was my rock when my dad sold our farm. We were talking about getting married. It was understood, even if we hadn't made it official. And then a new guy transferred to our school. A football player, looking to step up to a bigger league. He was as charming as he was talented. Overnight he became the hottest guy on campus. And of all the girls he could have had, guess who he wanted?

"I was flattered. I broke up with my rock for him. You can guess what happened next."

Hank studied the intricate topstitching on his boots. "I take it it wasn't good."

"Appearances can be deceiving. Oh, well. Lesson learned. I survived." She pasted on a smile. "I'm here, aren't I?" She laughed without bitterness. "It's kind of surreal. If anyone had told me senior year that in three years I'd be pouring wine in Oregon, I'd have said they were crazy. Back then I thought my future was all sewn up. I was going to marry Ben and settle down in the farmhouse. Dear old Mrs. Anderson, my elementary music teacher, all but came right out and said that when she retired, her job was mine if I wanted it. Ben was going to work the farm."

And there would be children. At least one boy and one girl, maybe more. Jamie would watch their faces light up when she showed them where trout lurked on hot summer days in the shaded areas of the stream that flowed through their farm, and the autumn miracle of pulling big orange carrots out where months earlier their fingers had pressed tiny seeds into the damp earth.

"Ben married another girl from our community. After that, I couldn't have gone back to Lancaster County even if there'd been a home for me to go to. I couldn't bear to see my childhood best friend living the life that was supposed to be mine. I gave away Mrs. Anderson's job. Dad had moved into a town house. That's why I went to Philadelphia. I had nowhere else to go. A year or so later, my sister called to tell me that Ben's wife had given birth to a baby boy."

Hank cleared his throat.

She looked at him steadily. "I still have my teaching. Or did." She averted her eyes. "This coming school year's going to be different."

"Are you having second thoughts about your promotion?"

"It's starting to hit me how much I'm going to miss the classroom, that's all."

She began to strum again.

"If I could turn back time
Take you there with me
Maybe then you'd see
Into my past.

"If you'd just take my hand
Walk a mile with me
Baby then you'd see
The best things are those that last."

Hoo? Hoo? Hoo cooks for you?

Jamie looked up from her guitar toward the fir grove where the owl lived, and couldn't help but smile.

Hank sang along in a rusty voice that was a little off-key.

> *"I thought that we'd be more than friends*
> *But time, it marches on.*
> *You were there for a while*
> *When I needed a smile*
> *But you stole my heart in the—"*

Hoo cooks for you? called the owl.

With growing confidence, Hank placed his hand over his heart, threw back his head and belted it out with Jamie, accompanied by the owl in the background.

> *"If I could turn back time*
> *Take you there with me*
> *Maybe then you'd see*
> *Into my past . . ."*

Aaah-ooooo . . . The coyotes chimed in, too.

> *"You were there for a while*
> *When I needed a smile*
> *Now I'm yours—"*

Ar ar ar a-oooooh!

> *"Till the end of the line."*

One sleep-tousled head after another popped out of the tent flaps to witness the spectacle of Jamie playing and Hank acting the fool, with the owl and coyotes providing backup.

The song ended with Jamie's head thrown back in gales of laughter and Hank clutching his sides.

Finally, Jamie returned her instrument to its case, leaving only the sound of crickets over by the spring.

The campers retreated into their tents, but not before exchanging secret looks of amusement.

The fire had burned down to a bed of red coals.

Jamie carried her guitar over to the picnic table.

It was high time to get some shut-eye, but sleep was the furthest thing from Hank's mind. His body was vibrating with energy. Without thinking, he strode purposefully over to where Jamie stood in the shadows, and with a touch on her shoulder he turned her from where she had just covered her guitar case with a tarp to keep out the dew, and slid his hand down her arm to entwine his fingers in hers.

She looked up in mild surprise, but didn't pull away. He took her other hand, slipped his fingers through hers and let it drop, and for a moment they stood there face-to-face, the lines and mounds etched on their palms that some might say were a portent of their future melding together.

He swallowed thickly. Blame it on the music. For the first time in a long time, Hank felt free . . . as free as the red tail hawks that hung on the hot, ascending air above the ridges on summer afternoons. All the burdens and expectations that had been weighing so heavily on him were left behind on the valley floor.

He reached up and brushed a lock of hair away from her face. The moonlight shone down on her too-long nose, her soft eyes. He dropped his forehead to hers and for a moment listened to the sound of their breathing. Then he took Jamie's head in his hands, and gently pressed his lips to hers.

Their first kiss started out soft and chaste, almost reverent.

But it whetted his appetite for more. With the slightest nudge of his tongue, her lips opened, warm and slick.

Her willing response sent him soaring even higher, as though they'd been hurtling toward each other on a collision course and they'd finally made impact.

Jamie threw her arms around his neck and pressed her body against his and suddenly he was awash in a tsunami of sensation. He slid his hand into the hair tumbling down the back of her head. Skeins of long hair entangled his fingers like tentacles. He wound himself into them tighter, a willing captive.

The kiss grew and deepened until it was a living thing, evolving . . . expanding . . . eclipsing all else. They explored each other with heated desperation.

Suddenly they heard a smattering of soft pops far in the distance. They broke the kiss to look out across the sky at starbursts of color from the fairgrounds south of town. When their eyes met again, they smiled in wonderment. It felt like a sign.

Hank put his hands on Jamie's hips and turned her around so that they could watch the fireworks together. The length of her back felt warm up against his torso. He peered over her shoulder at the sight of her breasts rising and falling.

He slid his hands up her ribcage and cupped her breasts, squeezing them together and lifting until the shallow line of cleavage deepened into a seemingly bottomless crevasse between two high mounds.

Twin strokes of his thumbs revealed the hard nubbins of her nipples.

Her head fell back onto his shoulder on a sigh.

He slid his hand into her jeans along her soft belly and found the crisp edge of her panties.

"Hank," she breathed, her hand atop his, stilling it.

He sucked in a ragged breath. "Is it because we work together? Because I don't care about that."

"We don't just work together. I work *for* you. There's a difference."

The words *then quit* were on the tip of his tongue. He bit them back just in time.

"This summer is going to fly," she said.

"I know."

The fireworks had ended, but she still felt so warm, so lithe in his hands.

"Before I know it, it'll be time for me to go back to Philly and start my new position."

She had only been there a matter of weeks, and already he could barely remember what it had been like before she'd arrived.

"I can't risk doing anything that would put that in jeopardy. It's all that I have. I don't have choices. My home is gone. There's nothing left to go back to."

Reluctantly, Hank slid his hand out of her pants and slowly turned her around to face him again.

Her arms went around him in a restrained hug that was more friendly than passionate.

They clung together, reluctant to part, until finally their breathing returned to normal.

Then they went back to the fire circle and crawled into their respective sleeping bags, still acutely aware of each other.

It took some experimentation to get comfortable on the hard ground.

"Jamie . . ." murmured Hank when they'd been still for a few minutes.

Her head, resting on his shirt that she'd rolled up and fashioned into a pillow, turned toward him.

He wanted to tell her that he wished things were different. He wanted to curl up next to her in her sleeping bag. He wanted to utter sweet nothings to her all night long.

"Good night."

"Night." Jamie looked away and folded her hands across her chest.

Hank stared at her profile until her breathing relaxed into sleep.

But a seed of hope, so tiny he hardly dared acknowledge it, had been planted.

If experience had taught him anything, it was that things don't always work out as planned.

Chapter Eighteen

Jamie awoke to a metallic clanking and the shuffle of boots. She opened her eyes to see Hank squatting in front of the fire, setting up a tripod on which to cook breakfast.

She rubbed her eyes and sat up.

"Morning," she said, her voice cracking.

He twisted around at the waist. "Well, if it isn't Sleeping Beauty." He grinned. "I was starting to think you were going to sleep the day away."

She looked around to find much of their equipment already packed up and waiting to be loaded onto the packhorses.

"What time is it?" she asked, bending her knees and planting her feet and leaning forward to rise. "Whoa," she said, landing on her butt with a dull thud. She'd forgotten she was zipped into a sleeping bag.

"Careful, there."

She automatically fished for her phone, only to

remember there was no service up there on the peak.

He tipped his head to the sky. "I'd say around six thirty."

"Uggggh." She groaned, falling back onto the padded flannel, still warm with sleep.

"I'd like to get everyone fed and be off the trail before the rain hits."

"Rain?" The sunshine sparkled in the dewy foliage surrounding the campsite. "It looks like it's going to be a beautiful day to me."

"See those clouds that look like an outstretched horse's tail at about forty thousand feet?"

She held a hand over her eyes and squinted in the direction where he pointed with his chin, trying to adjust to the light. All she saw were some feathery wisps.

"It'll be raining by suppertime. Wait and see."

They spent the next hour working in tandem, feeding the guests, putting the campsite back in order, and helping riders back onto their horses. It was as if last night had never happened, and yet it was all Jamie could think about.

Only after they were headed downhill with the others out in front, where Hank could keep a watchful eye on them, did he fall back to where Dancer picked his way delicately along the trail.

At first, the only sound was the squeaking of their saddles as they rocked gently back and forth in pleasant rhythm with their horses.

"You okay?" Hank asked.

Those two words held a world of meaning.

"I'm fine." She smiled and brushed back her

windblown hair. It gave her a warm feeling inside to know he cared.

"Hope I didn't talk your ear off last night."

"Did you?"

"You know I did. At least, it seemed like it."

"It was fun imagining your however-many-greats-grandmother coming out here in a covered wagon wearing a long dress and a sunbonnet."

"A lot more fun than actually doing it. Those old wagons were so bumpy that most of them preferred to ride or walk alongside. Add to that, no doctors if you got hurt or sick. Only about twenty percent of the people who started out on the Oregon Trail actually made it all the way to Oregon."

She reached over and squeezed his bicep playfully. "You come from hardy stock."

Her lighthearted touch had a profound effect on him. His eyes burned into hers like black beacons, starting a peculiar melting feeling low in her belly.

"What about you?" asked Hank when he found the ability to speak again. "I told you all I know about my ancestors. What about yours?"

"My family came from Scotland, back in the eighteenth century. Do you know anything about Scottish history?"

"Nada."

"It's not like I've been to Scotland or anything. But we had this big photo album with lots of pictures when I was growing up. My sister and I used to sit with my dad, and he'd page through it with us.

"Back in the day, clans would rent a small piece of the chief's land to grow their own grain on. The clans were basically a military society. Your rent took care of the chief, and in exchange, the chief took care of you in times of war.

"Well, after the English won a certain battle, the clan chiefs were stripped of their power. The Scots were forbidden to speak their native Gaelic, wear their tartans, and so on. It was the end of the clan system. The chiefs had to figure out a new way to survive. At the same time, the price of wool was skyrocketing. They came up with the idea to put sheep on all the farmland to take advantage of that. You had to have a lot of sheep, and therefore a lot of land, to make a profit.

"But—as you know," she said, thinking of the sheep that kept down the weeds in the vineyards, "raising sheep doesn't require many people. So the farmers were 'encouraged' "—she drew air quotes—"to leave the Highlands. Dad told us about how the roof of his family's cottage was set on fire to hasten their departure."

"Is that when they came to America?"

"Not yet. They were given a tiny plot of ground high on Scotland's windy west coast. But the rent was so expensive that their crops didn't cover it. Both the mother and the father had to farm seaweed. Not only that, the coastline was so treacherous that the mother routinely tethered her two small boys and the milk cow when she went to work, to keep them from blowing away. Of course, the kids put up a terrible fuss. And so one day she left them untied, and—"

"No way."

Jamie nodded. "The littlest one was blown right off the cliff. They started dreaming about America, saving every penny they could. They knew they'd never be able to save enough to emigrate themselves, but they worked until they had enough to send their only surviving son.

"His mother sewed all their savings into the lining of his coat, put him on a ship, and sent him across the ocean, knowing she would never see him again."

They rode for a while, thinking without speaking until a single ringtone sounded from the vicinity of one of Hank's saddlebags.

"Pull up," he said to Jamie.

She reined in and waited for him to pull out his phone.

"We have service again," he said, looking at the screen. He punched in a number and waited.

Dancer shifted his weight and flicked his tail at a fly on his rump.

"Stew? Hank Friestatt. I'm calling to tell you that I've made a decision. I'm not going to sell."

A smile overspread Jamie's face.

Then something over Jamie's shoulder caught his eye.

Jamie followed his gaze to one of the guests backtracking toward them.

"Something's come up," Hank said into the phone. "Got to run."

"What is it?" Hank asked the guest, shoving his phone back into his saddlebag.

"My wife's horse refuses to move. It's like she hurt her foot or something. She's holding it with her knee bent and when she kicks her, she just limps forward one step and then stops."

"Probably a stone lodged in her shoe," said Jamie.

"Welcome back to reality," Hank grinned, gave Blitzer a nudge and trotted up to the others to take care of business.

The lame mare had a small cut and a dark spot, a bruise, on her near hind sole. She would be fine, but she needed care and rest before she could be ridden again. Hank boosted his stranded guest onto the back of Blitzer and told Jamie to go ahead with the others while he walked the injured horse back.

Jamie returned to the Sweet Spot much happier than when she'd left. Bill came out to the paddock to meet them. After Jamie explained Hank's absence, she rode to the back door of the inn, where she dismounted and carried the first armload of supplies into the kitchen, to the smell of chili cooking on the stove.

Ellie sat at the table, partially obscured by her open laptop and a jumble of half-unpacked groceries. Heads of lettuce appeared to have rolled out of a biodegradable grocery bag lying on its side. It struck Jamie as odd that Ellie would let the produce sit out unrefrigerated like that, long enough for the edges of the lettuce to start to curl.

"We're back! Whew, what a trip. Where do you want me to put this cast-iron pot? I rinsed it out as well as I could, but shouldn't it be reseasoned before it's put away?"

Ellie sat intensely immersed in her computer screen without response.

"Miss Ellie?"

From the stove came the *ting-ting-ting* of a metal lid against its pot. "Ellie. The chili!" Couldn't she see? "It's boiling over." Red stuff filled the well surrounding the burner and oozed down the front of the gas range.

Jamie leaped across the room, straddling the puddle at her feet. With a quick flick of her wrist she turned off the flame, then moved the heavy pot to a cold burner and turned toward the sink for paper towels to mop up the mess, swallowing the growing panic in the pit of her stomach when Ellie still didn't react.

"Ellie? Miss Ellie!"

Chapter Nineteen

"Hate to think of what would've happened if that young lady hadn't walked into the kitchen when she did," said Ellie's doctor.

If the stroke hadn't killed Ellie, the near–kitchen fire would have.

"How long do you figure she'll be hospitalized?"

"Plan on at least a couple of days until we've done a complete assessment. Couldn't even venture a guess at this point." The doctor clapped Hank's shoulder. "My advice to you is to go on home and get some sleep. You look like you could use it."

Hank looked down at his dirty jeans and wrinkled shirt he'd ridden and slept in. He rubbed his stubbly chin. The clock on the wall of the ER waiting room said eleven thirty. It had been forty-some odd hours since he'd had a shower and a shave.

He nudged Jamie, slumped over on the vinyl couch.

"How's Ellie?" she asked, sitting up straighter.

"They're keeping her as comfortable as they can. C'mon. I'll take you home."

Home. Ellie was the ship's rudder. It wouldn't be the same without her there in the kitchen first thing in the morning and last thing at night, on the front porch greeting guests, and watching over the campfire out back.

In the car, he bought Jamie up to speed.

"Doc said she hadn't been sitting there long. But she still can't talk or move her hands."

"It's only been a few hours. Give her some time, let the doctors figure it out."

He gave the upper arc of the steering wheel a sharp rap with the heel of his hand. "That forty-five-minute drive to get to the trauma center couldn't have helped. When someone's having a stroke or a heart attack or falls off a rock, time matters." Then he whipped off his ball cap, tossed it into the back, and massaged his jaw.

"Ellie wouldn't live anywhere else." Jamie laid a hand on his arm. "Everything seems worse when you're tired. You'll feel better after you get some rest."

"Won't get much rest tonight. There's green harvesting to be done, and we have a dozen guests arriving in"—he glanced at the dashboard clock—"a matter of hours. Who's going to take care of the inn? Supervise the meals? Handle reservations?"

"Green harvesting?"

"When there's too much rain, the grapes grow too vigorously. Every single bunch has to be cut in half."

"But that's like throwing away half the grapes."

Hank nodded. "That's why you don't look back on the ground behind you as you work. Breaks your heart while you're doing it. But culling pays off in a stronger yield, later."

"I'm here. I'll man the inn."

"Look," said Jamie a short time later when she and Hank walked in the kitchen door. "Some anonymous good Samaritan cleaned the kitchen."

There was a note stuck on the fridge. "It says they hope Ellie will be okay," said Jamie. "It's signed by all the men."

By the next morning, everyone for miles around had heard about Ellie's stroke. When Ellie's teenagers came to serve breakfast, they brought along some unexpected help.

Brynn took one of them by the hand and inched toward Jamie.

"Theresa Morgan," said the woman. "Brynn's mom. I know about you helping Brynn with her guitar playing. It's too bad we have to meet under these circumstances. But I'd been hoping someday I'd get a chance to meet you in person to thank you for all you've done for her."

"Of course," said Jamie, wiping her hands on her apron. "I'm happy to give Brynn some pointers."

"Joan," she said with a nod to the other teen's mom, "and I work in the high school cafeteria during the school year. We thought you could use an extra hand in the kitchen."

"Can we?" Jamie faked a swoon. "Hank, did you hear that?"

"I did. Much appreciated."

"And they're professionals."

"Hardly. That's what neighbors are for," said Theresa. "Now. Time's a-wasting. Put us to work."

A car horn beeped. Hank and Jamie went outside to see an older model pickup bouncing down the drive.

"What the . . ." said Hank, hands on hips. "It's Nelson."

The truck pulled under the porch overhang. Nelson was still wearing his black therapy boot. He handed Hank his crutches while he limped out.

"Bored to tears, lying on that crusty ol' couch all day. If I have to watch one more of Lorraine's soap operas, I'll put a bullet in my head. Gimme something to do."

"I'm happy to be rid of him for a few hours." Nelson's wife leaned over to talk to Hank from her seat behind the wheel. "How's your grandmother doing?"

"We're waiting to hear the results of her tests."

"She's in my prayers. Call me when you need me to come pick up the old coot."

Nelson and Jamie sized one another up.

"I just realized," said Hank, "you two haven't yet met. Nelson, meet—"

"I know who she is." Nelson cut off Hank's words, pulling Jamie roughly into a body hard as a tree trunk. "Not a person within twenty miles of the Sweet Spot that hasn't heard about Jamie Martel."

Soon afterward when the new crop of guests arrived, Jamie took Ellie's place on the front porch. As Hank unloaded baggage from the van, he kept an eye on Jamie checking off the names and greeting guests as if nothing were amiss.

After she'd directed them to their cabins, Hank came up behind her. "If I didn't know better, I'd think you'd been checking in guests here for years," he said in a voice for her ears only.

She glowed inside. "I learned from the best."

"I need to see how the green harvest is going. You be okay here?"

"I'll supervise Theresa and Joan and field the inevitable newbie questions."

Hank adjusted his ball cap and set out for the vineyards.

By midafternoon, the guests were finally settling in, making dinner plans on their own. Joan and Theresa had gone home. Jamie looked out the kitchen window. Hank was still out there, somewhere in the vineyards. The hoodies of the field workers were spots of color among the vines. Here and there, they sat on the tailgates of their pickup trucks, eating food from the lunch pails sitting open next to them.

It wasn't Hank's custom to take a break in the hottest part of the day. He was used to eating at six. By then, when it was cooler, his men would be back at work.

Jamie looked at the clock. Then she looked around at the sparkling kitchen.

When Hank came in from the fields he'd be ravenous.

Cooking wasn't Jamie's forte.

She poked around in the fridge, looking for

possibilities. The first thing that caught her eye was a package of chicken parts. Fried chicken was Ellie's specialty. No doubt that's what she'd been planning to make.

She got it out, laid it on the counter and stared at it, trying to remember what Ellie had said the night Jamie had arrived at the Sweet Spot. She'd dredged it in something. Flour? Jamie had a vague memory of her mother coating meat with flour before browning it. There was some spice, too. She sat down and put her head in her hands and tried to remember, wishing she'd paid closer attention.

She gave up trying to duplicate Ellie's recipe and fell back on the old-fashioned way of finding a recipe: the internet.

The look on Hank's exhausted face when he finally came in through the back door and saw Jamie standing at the range made it all worth it.

He hung up his ball cap and came over to where she turned the chicken in a pan of hot oil.

"What's this?"

"What's it look like?"

"Looks just like Ellie's chicken." He peeked under the foil-covered pans resting on the back of the stove. "Mashed potatoes? Buttered carrots? Thought you said you couldn't cook?"

She smiled modestly, rolled her eyes skyward, and shrugged a shoulder. Why confess how nervous she'd been earlier? Her virgin attempt at making a dinner from scratch was actually turning out pretty good, if she said so herself.

He rubbed his stomach. "This is great. I'm so hungry I could eat the north end of a southbound bear."

"Well, you got here just in time. It should be just . . . about"—she poked a thigh with a fork—"*done.*"

She flicked off the burner and carried the dishes to the table, set just the way Ellie did it.

"How'd Nelson do today?" Jamie asked Hank as they unfolded their napkins and laid them on their laps.

"Still not a hundred percent. But at least he knows the ropes."

She spooned some potatoes onto her plate and passed the bowl to Hank. "Any news about Ellie?"

"Specialist says there's definite damage in the part of her brain that controls speech. She can't use her right side and has minimal control of her left. They think she understands what's said to her, but she can't respond. She's on blood thinners. Going to transfer her to the rehab wing tomorrow."

"Sounds like she's getting good care."

"She starts physical therapy tomorrow. We'll have to wait and see."

Their filled plates looked just like the picture on the web.

Hank cut off a sizeable chunk of chicken and forked it into his mouth while Jamie watched eagerly for his reaction.

Hank bit down. Then froze and looked up at Jamie with full cheeks.

Seeing her anxious look, he worked his jaw again, then swallowed what remained of the semi-chewed bite, whole.

"What's wrong?" asked Jamie, full of concern.

Hank drank half his glass of water. "Nothing," he assured her.

He set to work on his carrots, keeping his eyes studiously on his plate.

"What's wrong with the chicken?"

Hank shook his head vigorously. "Just getting my vegetables in before I get too full."

She cut off a tiny piece and deposited it onto her tongue. A second later she leapt out of her chair and ran to the trash can. "Blah!"

Hank looked up innocently from where he shoveled potatoes into his mouth but made no comment.

"This is terrible!" exclaimed Jamie.

"You don't like it?" asked Hank.

"It's terrible, and you know it."

"It's okay," he said, bravely trying it again.

"You don't have to pretend to like it," said Jamie. "You won't hurt my feelings."

"Who's pretending? It's good," he said, washing it down, getting up for more water.

She cocked a hand on her hip as she stood there, wondering what to do. "You're a poor liar."

"Not lying."

She sighed. Feeling suddenly unworthy of Ellie's apron, she took it off and returned to her seat. "I'm glad I made the vegetables. At least we won't starve," she said, subdued, her hands on the table to scoot her chair in.

Hank reached across the table and laid his hand on hers. "It's the thought that counts," he said.

She looked up at him with eyes full of tears.

Before she knew it Hank was around the table, his arm around her, lifting her out of her chair.

She melted into his arms and swallowed the hard lump in her throat, trying as hard as she could not to cry while he stroked her hair.

For long moments they stood together without speaking, taking comfort in the simple goodness of each other's embrace.

Finally, Hank pulled back and looked down at her with a look of tender concern that touched her so, she couldn't bear to worry him anymore over a silly chicken. Somehow she managed a feeble smile and angled back toward her chair.

"Go ahead. Finish what's edible while it's still warm."

He did as he was told.

"This is the peak of the tourist season," he said when they were through. "And we still have the crush to get through. The inn has to keep on going, even without Ellie. I've got to come up with a plan."

"Tell me what I can do."

He considered for a moment. "Let's get these dishes out of the way and get on Ellie's computer and I'll show you how the reservations work. She has the menus already planned for the whole summer, and they're on there, too."

Side by side, they cleared away dinner. Jamie recalled Ellie telling her that Hank wasn't averse to waiting tables. Now she was seeing that for herself.

"Here." Hank rolled a wheeled chair out from the built-in kitchen desk. "Have a seat and I'll show you how Ellie does the day-to-day accounting."

Jamie sat down and he pushed her in, then squeezed a dining chair in next to her for himself.

They worked until the sun went down and the only light was that of the screen. At one point Hank rose to open a window and fetch them glasses of water. He set hers down next to her and, standing behind her, rested his hands on the back of her chair, staring at the information over her shoulder, trying to ignore Jamie's vanilla and floral scent wafting upward.

Jamie asked him a question and he leaned over her, splaying his left hand on the table to see the fine print on the screen.

The cursor hesitated over a column. Without thinking, he put his hand over hers to guide the mouse to where he thought it should be.

"You want this one."

"No, I was right before, see?" she said, frustration in her voice.

Sleep deprivation, thought Hank. They'd been up since before dawn. *And maybe, malnourishment.*

"You're looking at the subtotals column. Scroll over. The grand total goes here."

He sensed her start to fight him but immediately seeing the futility in that, changed tack. She slipped her hand out from under his and swiveled around, slapping Hank's chest in mock anger. "I knew that. I was only seeing if you did."

He caught her wrist and held it.

She raised her other hand to strike him and he grabbed that wrist, too.

"Now what?" he said, arching a brow.

The faint sound of contented guests singing out

in the yard seemed as though it came from another world.

"Looks like Miss Martel's not used to being the student, is she?" he teased softly.

Her grin melted as her pupils dilated into jet-black disks.

Tilting her head becomingly, she pursed her lips and raised her chin in cocky defiance.

"Actually, I loved going to school. In fact, I consider myself a perpetual student."

"I bet there's lots I could teach you," he growled.

Her mouth parted in surprise.

Seconds passed, the air crackling with anticipation.

Jamie licked her lips and swallowed.

It took everything Hank had in him to drop her wrists and spin her back around to the computer screen.

Chapter Twenty

Hank woke up one morning after his first full night's sleep since before the campout, feeling clearheaded and focused.

From now on, things were going to be different, starting with his grandmother. When she came home from the hospital, she wasn't going to lift a finger unless she wanted to.

He was pouring himself a coffee when Jamie breezed into the kitchen. "What's the latest on Miss Ellie?" she asked, setting down her guitar case.

"She's alert but still hasn't spoken. You going someplace?"

"Is it okay if I go into her room and get a few of her things, like her hairbrush and maybe a robe? I thought I'd pay her a quick visit this morning. And I also want to stop at the market and get some dinner things that are a little less . . . complicated."

"I don't want you feeling obligated to cook me

supper every night. Do I look like I'm wasting away?"

"I don't mind."

"I'm sure Ellie would appreciate having some of her things from home. I've been there twice this week, but it never occurred to me."

"Maybe it's a woman thing. We like to be surrounded by our favorite personal belongings. Surprised the nurses didn't mention it. No matter, I'll do it. Now that you've put Joan and Theresa on the payroll, I don't have to be here while the guests are eating breakfast. I can do the errands while I'm in town, too, if you want."

Hank thought for a moment. "I could go with you. But why don't we spread out our visits? Give her more time with friendly faces that way. I talk to the docs every day, and the nurses hold the phone up to her ear for me. Tell you what. You go now; I'll get some work done here. Tell her I'll see her tomorrow. Oh, and would you mind making a bank deposit?"

From behind a cupboard door, she said, "Do you know where Ellie keeps the vases?"

"Sorry."

"Not a problem. A glass will do. I'll bet a bouquet of her gerbera daisies will cheer her up. Be right back."

She dashed out the screen door, leaving Hank standing holding his coffee cup in the wake of her delicate scent. He sipped as he watched Jamie snip red and yellow blossoms from Ellie's cutting garden. She had put on that white skirt, the only item of clothing she had with her that wasn't jeans, for her visit to town. He couldn't see that skirt without it dredging up memories of their dance after the wine fest.

And she was good for his grandmother. His heart swelled with appreciation. As bad as this week was, without Jamie it would have been exponentially worse.

"Good morning, Miss Ellie! Look what I brought you—"

The man at Ellie's bedside holding her hand looked up. He had bushy eyebrows and a head of thick, black hair that sprouted from his scalp like a bed of nails.

"—gerbera daisies . . ." Jamie's words faded away.

Ingrained creases curved downward from the corners of his mouth, suggesting a perpetual frown. On the whole, he looked like he'd survived being electrocuted but wasn't too happy about it.

"Sorry. I'll come back later." She turned to go, considering filing a report of an intruder at the nurse's station.

"You're Jamie."

She stopped in her tracks. Slowly, she turned back around. "How do you know?"

"Ellie told me about you."

If that were true—and it must be—then this man couldn't be as fearsome as she'd thought. She screwed up the courage to venture a step farther into the room.

"You've been a blessing to her."

Now he was talking about blessings. *Who is this guy?*

She shook her head. "I didn't do anything special."

"When Ellie needed you, you were there."

"I'm the one who needed *her.*" Come to think of it, needed everything about the Sweet Spot, from the idyllic setting, to the steady work, to Ellie. And Hank.

"You're not from around here."

"No. But I'd like to be." *How is he getting me to say these things that a minute ago, I didn't even realize I felt?*

Fear morphed into fascination with the scars and wrinkles, indistinguishable from one another, that snaked across the man's face. She stepped closer. "What's your name?"

"I'm Joe Bear. Friend of Ellie's. How's Hank doing?"

"How come the blinds are drawn?" Jamie asked, adjusting the blinds to admit more light into the room. "It's a beautiful day outside."

"I hear he's got an offer to sell the vineyards and the winery."

How does he know that? Jamie just looked at him.

"It's happening all over the valley. Especially in Yamhill County. The market is buying up every drop of pinot noir as fast as it's made."

She ran water into the glass she'd brought from home and began arranging the flowers where they would easily be seen from Ellie's bed.

"I see what Ellie meant by you being there for her."

While Joe Bear stood back and watched with his arms folded, Jamie gently washed Ellie's face and hands. Then she unbraided her hair, brushed it, and rebraided it. The whole time, she kept up a running monolog of amusing anecdotes of the past week.

"Would you mind stepping out for a minute while I change her gown?"

When he left, she followed him into the hall. "Ellie wasn't supposed to find out about the offer."

"She knows."

Jamie and Joe Bear shared a long look, communicating without words.

"Well, once she's better she'll be glad to know that he turned it down. Though I don't know why Hank would even consider selling. Why can't he see that his inheritance is worth more than any amount of money?"

Joe Bear thought for a minute. "Often it takes losing something for a man to realize what it was that he had."

Jamie sighed. "Come back in a minute? I still want to dress her in the gown I brought her from home."

"I'll go now. She's in good hands." His mouth turned up at the edges.

They clasped hands. Then he left without saying good-bye.

Jamie went back into the hospital room. "There," she said to Ellie. "Feel better? Well, you look better, I can tell you that. That hospital gown did nothing for your complexion."

She looked into Ellie's vacant blue eyes for a sign that she understood, but they only stared straight ahead without moving.

Then she pulled up a chair and tuned her guitar.

At the sound of her singing, a nurse popped in from the hallway. "I put this pen and pad of sticky notes on the blanket within easy reach," she said. "Maybe Miss Ellie can show you her writing progress."

At that, Ellie's eyes shifted Jamie's way.

"She looked at me!" exclaimed Jamie. She sprang to her feet and set her guitar aside.

The nurse helped Ellie wrap her fingers around the pen to scribble what was allegedly a wobbly version of her name.

Jamie followed the nurse into the hall on her way out. "How much does she understand?"

The nurse hesitated. "Are you family? Sorry. Have to ask."

"No. I'm living at the Sweet Spot this summer, as an employee. But Ellie and I have developed a special bond in a short amount of time. I care about what happens to her."

The nurse made a sympathetic face and a decision. "We think she's in there. There's nothing wrong with her hearing. You can probably assume she gets most, if not all, of what we're saying. That's why it's important to communicate with her, not talk over her as if she weren't there. Keep talking about home and she'll be motivated to get there sooner."

Chapter Twenty-one

Jamie left the hospital with the most optimism she'd had since Ellie had gotten sick. Flying down the country road in the topless Jeep, the sun shone warm on her shoulders and the breeze whipped her hair. The ripening vineyards rippled out from both sides of the road to hills dotted with pines.

Back in Newberry, the sweet bungalows with their distinctive windows, the colonials with their colorful front doors, and the ornate Victorians came into view. She got the bank deposit out of the way, then headed down Main Street on foot. When she spotted a new romance novel in the window of the bookstore, she went in and splurged on it to curl up with in her sitting room. She would miss that cozy nook when she went back East.

When she came to Walker's Wild Western Wear, she slowed down and peered in the window. The clerk who had sold her her Noconas spotted her and waved to her through the glass.

It struck her that if she ever came back to Newberry, it would probably look much the same, no matter how much time had gone by. The town had a sense of permanence about it. This was a forever kind of place.

Last stop, the grocery store. Along with some prepackaged dinner fixings, she picked up the perishables that couldn't wait until the next delivery truck came, and a new bottle of shampoo. Hard to believe she'd already gone through both the travel-size bottles she'd packed in her suitcase when she thought she was only going on a two-week vacation, plus another full-size bottle. And, of course, more bubble bath.

Juggling her bags on the way to the car, she paid no attention to the tavern sign hanging over the sidewalk, though she had to walk right under it.

On the other side of town, just visible through the trees, was the tall flagpole that marked the school that served the town and its surrounds.

NEWBERRY ELEMENTARY SCHOOL—HAVE A SAFE SUMMER said the sign sitting perpendicular to the road in the center of a neatly trimmed patch of lawn.

Beneath the school's name was a line of text that hadn't been there on her other trips into town. But before she could read what it said, a quick glimpse of a familiar scene of chaos on the playground brought a wistful smile to her face.

Was it only a few weeks ago that she couldn't wait for the school year to end? Back in early June, she'd had it up to *here* with antsy kids with spring fever craning their necks to peer out the classroom window when she was trying to conduct the sopranos and the altos into some faint semblance of harmony for the spring concert. As for recess?

Recess duty was the bane of a teacher's existence, ranking only above cafeteria duty. There wasn't a teacher alive who didn't complain bitterly about it behind the closed doors of the lounge.

At the last possible minute she made a decision to swerve into the school's semicircular drive, and stared out through the windshield of the Jeep.

Never again would she have to shove her hands in her coat pockets and stamp her feet on the cold macadam for twenty minutes watching kids run and climb and scream when she would rather be prepping for the next class. Something in the dear awkwardness of these children brought Jamie to the startling revelation that—she was going to miss it.

A boy in a white T-shirt took a swing at his friend for tipping his hat off. With an arch of his pliable spine that would be the envy of any Cirque du Soleil performer, the offender dodged the swat and dashed away, resulting in an impromptu game of tag that had them tearing up, down, and under the slide and making Jamie catch her breath when the boy who was *it* leapt over a swing and sent it sailing, nearly catching his foot in the process.

Instead of children, from now on her days would be filled with endless meetings and curriculum planning and making sure her school was in compliance with all the latest legislation.

Sighing, she turned her head away, glimpsing the sign.

NOW HIRING: MUSIC TEACHER, MATH TEACHER, TEACHING ASSISTANTS. APPLY IN PERSON.

Apply in person? *How quaint.*

Jamie stared at it while she thought of the courage it had taken to move from the small farming community where she'd been raised to a metropolis where she didn't know anyone. But after sending out a dozen applications, that was where she had been hired. She still recalled how frightened she'd been those first few nights as she lay in bed behind her triple-locked door, unable to sleep because of the sounds that wafted up from the streets.

Every first teaching assignment was tough, but it was even tougher in a culture that you weren't used to. Philly might as well have been a foreign country. And gifted kids presented yet another challenge.

Back over on the playground, one girl braided the hair of another while a deceptively scrawny boy swung easily from rung to rung across the horizontal ladder. A couple more alternated up and down on the seesaw.

Not only had she adjusted to her new job, she'd succeeded beyond her expectations—and in record time. She'd been singled out for the quality of her work. Who in their right mind would turn down this promotion? Many teachers took endless continuing ed courses and worked for years based on the slim hope that one day, if they were lucky, they might be promoted out of the classroom.

And now she was considering asking to go backward. Not merely asking, but plowing through page upon page of forms . . . maybe even facing recertification if Oregon didn't accept her out-of-state credentials.

She grabbed her phone and typed in a query, then sat there staring at the answer.

The following states have reciprocity with Oregon: Alabama, Arizona, Arkansas . . . Impatiently she skimmed down the list till she came to the Ps. *Pennsylvania.*

Well. She dropped her phone onto the passenger seat and put her hands back on the wheel at nine and three. She didn't have to decide right now.

But why not now? She was here. Maybe it was a sign.

I must be crazy, she thought, getting out of the car and walking up to the school's tall double doors.

The universal school smells of crayons, musty library books, and newly waxed and buffed floors drove home to her what it was she was about to do.

Behind the glass sat a receptionist, and behind her stood a middle-aged woman with a friendly face in a loose white tank top.

"I was driving by and I saw the sign out front," said Jamie. "I'd like to talk to someone about the music teacher position."

"Er—" The receptionist glanced over her shoulder at her coworker and then back at Jamie. "You'll have to make an appointment."

Relief flowed through Jamie. Now she could simply go through the motions of setting up an interview and then call and cancel it.

The woman in white paused and looked at Jamie. A smile came over her face. Then she said something to the receptionist and disappeared.

"Actually, Dr. Keller happens to have time right now, if that works for you."

"Oh. Well, as you can see," Jamie said, humiliated to have been caught completely unprepared, "I don't have my résumé or anything."

At least she didn't have to worry about coming back. Her fate was sealed. Now all she wanted was to get out of there as fast as she could.

Jamie heard a door open.

"I'm Dr. Keller," said the woman in white. "Would you like to come back to my office?"

"Well, I, ah . . . It was just a spur-of-the-moment idea . . . obviously I didn't give it much thought or I would have called first and come prepared."

"C'mon back," she said lightly. "We'll just chat. If it comes to it, you can send me your stuff later."

Chatting with Michelle Keller was like picking up the thread of a conversation with an old friend she hadn't seen for a while. She told Jamie more about the job opening and then invited Jamie to tell her about herself.

First Jamie talked about her teaching experience. Then she explained what she was doing in the Willamette Valley.

"You came out here for a vacation, and you ended up going to work for the winery you're staying at?"

Jamie nodded.

"Which one? I probably know of it."

"The Sweet Spot."

"I see. I guess it's fair to say we've established that you're a little impulsive—"

"On the contrary. That's the funny thing about this whole summer. Normally, I weigh all the options before I make a move."

"And yet . . . here we are."

Jamie shook her head slowly. "I was just driving by and I saw the kids."

"You mean, the sign."

"No," said Jamie, realization dawning on her only as the words left her mouth. "The kids, playing on the swings."

Dr. Keller waited patiently.

"I was drawn to them. It was like the car was pulled over by a magnet."

"It sounds to me like you may be having second thoughts about your new position."

Hearing someone else say that was like turning on a faucet. "I don't know if it's just *my* kids or any kids that I'm going to miss. After all, I *do* happen to have the best students anywhere. I know gifted kids get a bad rap in some quarters for daydreaming and questioning the purpose of assignments that seem arbitrary to them at first, but when it comes right down to it, they're just like other kids, only more creative. All they need is a little understanding and for someone to point the way so they can find their own path, not make them march lockstep."

"They sound very special."

"They *are.*"

"What about the kids on the playground today? Without seeing them, I don't know their names, but I can tell you that only ten percent of our student body at Newberry is made up of exceptional kids. So, given that, what was your impression of them?"

She took a deep breath. If this were any other interview she would have endeavored to come up with the best answer to guarantee her the job.

But Dr. Keller had been forthright with her. She deserved honesty in return.

"I have to think about that."

The superintendent smiled. "Yes. You do."

As she drove back to the Sweet Spot, she wondered what Hank would think about her moving to Newberry. She again heard his voice when she was struggling to find a handhold on Raven's Rock. *Sometimes what looks like the obvious solution won't be. You have to stretch. Use new muscles you're not used to using.*

When Jamie got back to the inn, she found Hank at Ellie's computer. She tossed her jean jacket across a chair and hung the keys to the Jeep on the keyboard.

Hank turned around. "How's Ellie doing?"

"Still not speaking. But she seemed to enjoy my playing. She wrote her name. I admit she had a lot of help from the nurse. See?" she asked, handing him the note.

"That's progress," he said, looking up at her with hope in his eyes that struck a chord in her.

"I told her you'd be in to see her tomorrow."

The image of a small plane filling the computer screen caught her eye.

"What's that?" She leaned over the table where he sat and he spun his chair back around to face the laptop.

"I promised you a flight over the vineyards."

Jamie was taken aback. She hadn't been sure he was serious about flying her over the Sweet Spot the day he'd brought it up, the very first time she'd been with him in his tasting room. By now, she thought he'd simply forgotten. With all that had happened since then, she could hardly blame him.

"The airport's just down on Dopp Road. I pointed it out to you on the way to town, remember? How's Tuesday, bright and early? The sooner I call, the more likely we are to get the date and time we want."

"But what about everything that needs doing around here?"

"We'll be back before the guests are finished with breakfast. Nobody will even notice we were gone. Besides, nobody can work twenty-four-seven. It's like you said when I met you. If you want something badly enough, you find a way to make it happen. He clicked the mouse. "Here's what the plane looks like inside."

She bent closer to the screen. There was barely room for a pilot and two passengers. In that tiny space, there would be no avoiding each other.

"Looks great, huh?"

She nodded enthusiastically.

"You're a fan of Erath, right?" he said when she hesitated. "And Montinore's Riesling?

"You know I am."

"We'll fly over them, too. It'll be amazing. As a matter of fact, that's a good idea. Make me a list of all your favorite Willamette Valley wineries and I'll have the pilot tailor the flight to it."

He looked up at where she leaned over his shoulder with hopeful eyes.

"Really?" She stood up then. "Awesome."

He scooted his chair in and began pecking the number of the airport from the website into his phone.

Chapter Twenty-two

Hank followed Bryce out to the center of Block Six, wary of what he might find there.

He inspected the vines carefully as they went, here and there fondling a greenish-purple cluster. Despite more rain than he would have liked early in the season, so far the ripening process seemed to be going well.

And then Bryce stopped and cupped a cluster that was brown and shriveled in the middle.

"See what I'm talking about?"

Bunch rot.

The botrytis fungus was always there. All it took was a little too much rain and a gash from a bird's beak or rough handling by a field hand during pruning to start an infection that could wipe out a whole harvest.

"If the humidity is high toward the end of the season, it's gonna spread like the devil."

"Let's get going and increase leaf removal to get the air moving between the bunches," said Hank.

"That's not going to do the trick," argued Bryce. "We pull too many leaves at this stage, we're going to run into a problem with sunburn. If you don't want to lose the whole block, we should spray."

"You know the drill. The key time to spray is at bloom. If we were going to go that route we should have already started."

"I'm telling you, it could still work."

"We're not spraying. You know as well as I do that those fungicides are at risk of developing resistance, the same as antibiotics. You go fast and easy with them, come the time you really need them they're not going to work. Besides, spraying goes against biodynamic principles."

"Nothing wrong with copper sulfur, as far as I'm concerned."

"Copper sulfur only works for powdery mildew. Not only that, I don't want to risk damaging fruit finish."

"I still say we need to spray."

"Just try it my way and we'll keep a close eye on it."

Bryce threw up his hands and stalked off, leaving Hank frowning at the shriveled grape cluster in his hand.

Chapter Twenty-three

If you don't love me, love whom you please
Put your arms round me, give my heart ease.
—"Down in the Valley," old American folk song

Hank stood behind the circle of benches surrounding the campfire with his arms folded. Jamie's impossibly delicate vibrato mingled with the wood smoke from the flickering orange flames and dispersed into the black night.

Along the benches, parents nursing adult beverages leaned on each other's shoulders while under the ancient oak tree, a scant handful of tireless children played themselves out chasing moths.

He used to forgo the sing-alongs. But this summer they'd become his favorite time of the day.

And tomorrow was going to be amazing. He'd stayed up late last night planning his and Jamie's flight down to the last detail, even called and talked to the pilot personally.

"Give my heart ease, love, give my heart ease
Put your arms round me, give my heart ease . . ."

The song was interrupted by the whoosh of rubber on a dirt road. Hank glanced toward the back porch where Ellie's empty rocker sat and was hit by a twinge of sadness. No matter how bucolic the setting, it wasn't the same without her.

There it was again. Definitely a car coming.

Please, he thought. *Not another Realtor. Not this time of night.*

Discreetly, he left the gathering to head around to the front of the inn.

There, he stood in the driveway with his hands on his hips and squinted into the headlights.

Looked like the airport van.

What the hell was that doing here? What had he missed? He and Jamie were doing their level best, but he wouldn't be surprised if a reservation had slipped through the cracks. He was going to have to start triple checking everything.

The van pulled under the porte cochere, the door opened, and a high-heeled foot emerged.

"Hank!" Delilah exclaimed, throwing her arms wide. But instead of the intended hug her mouth opened in an O and she flailed to keep herself upright.

Hank's hand shot out to steady her. Looking down, he saw her high heel sunk into the soft dirt.

The driver opened the back of the van and pulled out a bag big enough to hold Hank's entire wardrobe.

"How long are you planning on staying?"

"As soon as you told me about Ellie, I went to work rearranging my schedule. I thought you could use my help. I wanted to get here sooner, but this was the best I could do. I have to catch the next flight back to Denver tomorrow afternoon. Tell me, how is she?"

The driver with the long-suffering face cleared his throat.

"Tip the man, could you?" said Delilah without a backward glance. "I figured taking the limo was better than bothering you for a ride."

Hank reached for his wallet, tipped the driver, then carried her bags inside and set them by the door.

"Am I too late for the campfire? The plane food was inedible. All I've been thinking about is how good a s'more would taste."

Hank hesitated. Jamie was out there. She and Delilah couldn't be less alike. He couldn't imagine them together . . . especially with him in the middle.

He and Jamie weren't a couple. Were they? What made two people a couple, anyway? Proclaiming your feelings out loud? A ring? Sleeping together?

They had done none of that.

But quirks of fate kept throwing them together.

He asked himself what it was that attracted him to Jamie—aside from the obvious—the high-voltage current arcing between them that made him want to ravage her whenever she hovered too near; her restrained, controlled singing voice that hinted of fire smoldering just below the surface.

He appreciated the way she was always ready to lend a hand—holding out hope even when things looked hopeless, like her horrible fried chicken. And of course he was inexpressibly grateful for her unswerving loyalty to his grandmother.

Those were the obvious things. There were other, less obvious examples, too, facets of her personality that were still unfolding.

And even though she had drawn a line in the sand that she wouldn't cross that night at the Peak, he knew in his heart of hearts that the attraction was mutual. There were subtle signs everywhere he looked. He knew it by the way he caught her eyes lingering over at him in the midst of an everyday chore, and how, when he was struggling to cope, she teased him into a better mood.

Whatever the special bond between them was called, he was acutely aware of how fragile, how fleeting it was, and that one day soon it would be over.

He took Delilah's arm and led her away from the windows overlooking the fire circle and the pond. "Why don't we go in the kitchen and I'll make you something"—What? What could he tempt her with?—"green. A vegetable. I know—a salad. Or something." If he could just keep Delilah and Jamie apart until the morning, he could think through how to handle them together in the same place.

"No," she said, pulling her elbow out of his hand, drifting toward the window where the flickering flames had caught her eye. "It's a s'more or nothing."

Numbly, he followed her out the back door and down the steps.

Jamie had heard the vehicle, seen Hank fade into the night to investigate.

She considered interrupting her song to help him out. Who could it be? An unexpected guest who had been overlooked?

She racked her brain, trying to visualize the week's reservation sheet. Surely, a night arrival would've stuck out like a sore thumb.

Where were they going to put these newcomers? All the cabins were already occupied.

Her concern mounted.

"All set?" Bill asked with a meaningful glance around the benches. The talking and fidgeting among the guests were signs that they were losing their audience.

Jamie repositioned her guitar on her knee when the back-porch door opened and out came Hank with an unfamiliar woman. An elegant, fine-boned woman whose heels necessitated using Hank's arm as a crutch to navigate the porch steps leading down to the yard where they all sat.

At Jamie's feet, Homer lifted his head and growled.

She had doe eyes, anvil-shaped cheekbones, and the kind of svelte figure Jamie had grown up seeing in those iconic images of brides being carried over the threshold. But as Jamie's womanly curves had developed, it became more and more evident that that fantasy of one day being swept off her feet was only that—a fantasy. And no amount of dieting would do the trick. The Martels didn't have those kinds of genes.

Maybe the woman was lost. Maybe she was on her way to a party at one of the many other nearby wineries and had stumbled upon the Sweet Spot by mistake.

So much had happened since Jamie had arrived at the Sweet Spot. She knew every winding trail. Could describe the house-wine blends, right down to the percentages of each varietal in them. She thought she knew Hank, too. Camping at the Peak, they'd found a common bond in their love for the land. And then Ellie's stroke had forced them even closer together, and things had fallen easily into place, as if meant to be. She'd almost forgotten she'd only known Hank for a matter of weeks. Maybe there was more to him than she thought.

"Now, you hush, Homer." Bill kept a wary eye on Hank and the newcomer as he patted the dog's head.

"Who's that?" asked Jamie, thinking aloud.

"I remember her. Calls herself a destination specialist. She was here last spring on a look-see."

"Look-see?"

"That's when they come to a resort and stay for a couple days to they can talk it up to their clients better. That one's slipperier than a lemon seed."

"What does that mean?"

Bill thought for a minute. "Means you have nothing to worry about with her as far as Hank goes."

She gave him a puzzled look.

"Do you think we're blind—me and Ellie and all the rest of the people who run this place? You're one of us. You belong here. She doesn't. She's an outsider, and she'll always be an outsider."

Two of the guests sitting directly opposite Jamie and Bill made a place for Hank and the latest arrival.

Hank got one of the peeled sticks leaning

against a tree and sat down beside her. Someone passed him the bag of marshmallows. He threaded one onto a stick and held it over the fire to brown at the same moment that the woman looked over and caught Jamie staring at them through the flames.

The woman kept staring at her as she whispered something into Hank's ear.

"'Summer Time.'" Bill's nudge brought her back to the present.

The crowd quieted in expectation.

Jamie marshaled her strength, dropped her jaw, and attacked the first note in her head register.

"I met a brown-eyed boy that summer
Between the meadow and the vine
Never intending to be lovers
Then came the taste of sweet red wine."

She envisioned the notes flying from her throat, pushing the limit of the song's dynamics.

"Now in the moonshine in my wineglass
I swear I see his face
And though it wasn't meant to be
Still in my mind I see
That summer time, that summer place."

She could hear Mrs. Anderson's voice in her head, admonishing her not to belt. But for once, she didn't care.

"What's the occasion?" Hank asked Delilah bluntly. He saw no need to stand on ceremony when someone showed up out of the clear blue expecting to be accommodated.

Delilah shot him a hurt look. "Concern for you and your grandmother, of course."

"You could have just called."

"I fly for free, remember? One of the perks of being a flight attendant. And I love coming to the Sweet Spot. It's just for one night. I hope I'm not imposing."

"Long as you don't mind staying in my grandmother's room. Afraid all the cabins are full."

"All I need is a corner somewhere."

"I think we can do you better than that." Even under the most trying circumstances, Ellie would never treat a guest less than hospitably.

"There's something else."

Hank looked up.

"Stew's offer on your land?"

"That's all over. Didn't he tell you? I turned it down." He stared down at his loosely clasped hands between his knees. He didn't like to admit it, even to himself, but since then there'd been moments when he'd wondered if he'd done the right thing. But that train had left the station. There was no looking back.

"Do you remember that other offer that Stew had pending? I thought you'd want to know that it fell through."

Something stirred inside him on hearing the news. "What does that mean to me?"

"It means that Stew asked me to tell you that he has a new offer for you."

His thoughts swirled. *Imagine—no more worrying about bunch rot and his stubborn vineyard manager.*

"Hank," she said with a nod toward the marshmallow he was toasting for her.

He brought the tip of the stick to his lips, blew out the flames and regarded the black shell.

"I'll make you another," he said, reaching for the bag.

With a flick of her fingers she said, "Don't bother. And this time, his client wants to talk to you himself. They're going to be together tomorrow morning at Stew's office at eight—that's nine, mountain time—and they asked me to set up a conference call."

"I already have plans for tomorrow morning." He had promised Jamie a flight over the vineyards while she was in the valley. And he always kept his promises.

"His client is headed out of the country tomorrow afternoon. That's the only time he'll be available for the next month. Hank"—Delilah laid a hand on his arm—"it's unusual for a Realtor to put a seller and a buyer together in the earliest stages of a transaction. Do you know what this means? It means they're willing to negotiate. You know what they say. Aim for the stars and you might just get the moon."

He swallowed.

He could postpone the sightseeing flight with Jamie. They still had a few weeks before she went back to Philadelphia.

"You have nothing to lose by talking."

He nodded.

"Great," said Delilah. "Where's a quiet place we can meet in the morning?"

"You're going to be on the call, too?" he asked.

"If it's okay with you."

He shrugged. Hadn't Delilah proven she was a shrewd businesswoman with her travel agency start-up and now that she was studying for her real estate license?

Around ten, the singing came to an end. Bill packed up and left. Some in attendance stood and stretched, while others lingered on the benches, talking, in no hurry to end the pleasant night.

Hank stood and with one hand hovering over Delilah's back, swept the area for Jamie, but she was deeply involved in coaching Brynn with her guitar.

Hank carried Delilah's bags up to Ellie's suite.

Then he went directly to Jamie's suite and knocked, but there was no answer.

A girl Brynn's age had to have a curfew. He got ready for bed. A half hour later, at eleven, he padded across the hall in his bare feet.

But there was still no answer.

"Jamie." He knocked again, louder, glancing warily down the hall to Ellie's room, where he'd left Delilah.

Where could she be?

He returned to his room and sat on the edge of his bed and thought. What could he do? Slip a note under her door? He couldn't wait until morning to tell her that he was canceling their flight over the vineyards.

He found her name in his list of contacts and called her, only to have the call go to voice mail.

"Jamie? This is Hank." He stood up and paced

the carpet. He'd never left her a phone message before. Whenever he needed her, she was right there. "I tried knocking on your door but you didn't answer. The reason I'm calling is"—he winced—"I have to postpone tomorrow's flight."

Chapter Twenty-four

Stewart Baker's client was Nick Rossi, a real estate agent on the staff of Countrywide Liquor Distributors, headquartered in Denver.

Stew prompted Nick and Hank to speak directly without his interference.

Nick began. "Hank, tell me what the stumbling block was on our earlier offer."

"There was more than one. But my main concern was taking my grandmother out of the only home she's ever known."

Nick thought about that. "Supposing we acquired only the vineyards and winery?"

"Go on," said Hank.

"You and your grandmother can keep the house and the acre of land that it sits on. You can even continue to run your inn if you want. As a matter of fact, to the casual observer there will be no sign that anything has changed. The biggest difference will be for you, in your workload. Let me ask you something. What is it that you've always wanted to do, but never had time?"

"I've always wanted to fly."

"Once my firm assumes the management of the vineyards and the winery, you'll be free as a bird. Hell, you can fly every day of the week if you want."

When the call was over, Hank told Delilah that he had some chores that couldn't be put off. He poured two cups of coffee and headed toward the barn.

In warm weather the horses stayed out all night. Now he paused at the peaceful sight of them grazing in grass covered in dew, their breath steaming in the early light.

He heard Jamie singing along with the radio before he saw her.

Dancer whickered a warning, and Jamie stopped currying his hindquarters and looked up expectantly. "Morning."

Hank stared at legs bared by skimpy cut-offs.

"I said, good morning." She followed his gaze. "If I'd known I was going to be spending the whole summer here, I'd have packed more jeans. This pair was on its last legs. No pun intended."

He cleared his throat. "Thought I'd find you out here. Brought you some coffee."

"Just set it over there on the ledge." She commenced with grooming.

Hank reached out to pat Dancer, but the horse threw back his head as far as his cross-ties would let him and showed him the whites of his eyes.

"You got my phone message?"

With a nod, she pitched the brush into a basket

along the wall and disappeared into the tack room, reappearing with a hoof pick.

"Been out already?"

"Dancer and I went for a good, hard ride, bareback, didn't we, boy?" She ran her hand over his foreleg. "Lift." The normally temperamental animal responded to her touch, docile as a kitten, and she began picking out the packed dirt.

Hank exhaled and shifted his weight, resting his hands on his hips while he tried to conjure up visions of forest fires . . . ice storms . . . anything but the vision of Jamie astride the Arabian in those short shorts, galloping across the meadows surrounding the vineyards.

"Putty in your hands, isn't he?"

"Well, that makes one." She laughed with irony as she moved on to Dancer's hindquarters, the tension thick between them.

"Where were you last night?"

"Are you keeping tabs on me now?"

"I knocked on your door before I called you. I wanted to tell you in person about canceling our plane ride over the vineyards."

"I took Ellie's rocking chair for a little spin. I didn't think she'd mind."

"I know she wouldn't."

"She's got a good view of the Big Dipper from up there on the porch this time of year. By the way. Couple of dead gophers in Block Nine."

Hank shook his head. "I'll be sure to check on that this afternoon. I'm sorry about the plane ride. I didn't know I was getting company."

"What did she want?"

"Who? Delilah?"

"Is that her name?"

"She wanted to tell me about another offer to buy the Sweet Spot."

Jamie forgot about currying Dancer. She stood up to her full height.

"With this new offer, I can sell just the ground and keep the house. That way, Ellie wouldn't have to move. And it wouldn't have to happen overnight. It would be early next year before the deal closed."

She thought about that for a moment, then resumed brushing Dancer harder than ever. "What about the horses?"

The horses.

"You said you could never get rid of the horses as long as Ellie was around. Or do you get to keep the paddock and the barn as part of the package?"

The meager one-acre allotment they'd be left with wasn't nearly enough ground to support the animals. Needless to say, Countrywide wasn't in the business of stabling pleasure horses. Their one priority was squeezing maximum productivity out of each acre. That meant bulldozing all of the outbuildings and planting them in vines. Dancer and Blitzer and the rest of the stock would have to be sold or boarded somewhere else.

Hank thought of Ellie gazing out the window of the inn to see nothing but vineyards coming right up to the foundation.

"Losing the horses would detract from the value of the inn, too," she said, the effort she was putting into brushing Dancer making her sound slightly out of breath.

Funny. That was what Delilah had told him on

her first visit to the Sweet Spot. More and more travelers were after experiences rather than things.

Dancer has never been cleaner, he thought.

"And the sheep?"

It pained him to admit it. "Without shelter, they would have to go, too."

"What will they use to keep down the weeds and fertilize the soil?"

How had it not occurred to him? Once the big boys—people who were more interested in quantity than quality—got ahold of his ground, there was a chance that all that effort by his grandfather, tearing out all those old trees and replacing them with vines, and then his dad, trying to rid the soil of contaminants, would have been for nothing.

Hank scratched the back of his neck. "About that flight. Rain check?"

"Rain check." She sighed, with a final pat to Dancer's neck. She unclipped his halter from the cross-ties and headed in the direction of his stall, but Hank stood in the way.

"Excuse me," she said.

He didn't budge. "Why don't you go in? Get some rest. I'll get Bill to take out the morning ride."

"I'll rest later. Right now I'm on a roll."

"Suit yourself," he said, stepping aside. "But you don't have to do all this. You know that."

"Got a lot of excess energy to burn off."

He watched her lead Dancer away until she was out of sight, wondering exactly when it was that he'd started caring about the opinion of the stranger he'd brought home from the airport in June.

* * *

Hank told Theresa that he'd be in the tasting room if Delilah was looking for him before the van took her back to the airport.

It was almost noon when she came in to say good-bye.

"I wanted to ask you about Ellie before I go. What's her prognosis?"

"Still touch and go," said Hank from behind the counter, where he was stocking bottles of Riesling.

Delilah slid onto a bar stool across from him, carefully considering her next words. "After Stew's initial offer, you said that Ellie was the biggest impediment to you selling. If worse comes to worst and she dies—"

Hank whirled to face her, thumping two bottles down on the counter, his knuckles white. "She's not going to die!"

"God forbid," replied Delilah calmly. "But you just said the doctors said it was touch and go."

"My grandmother is not going to die. It won't be long before she comes out of it. A little physical therapy and she'll be back home, good as new, where she belongs, and everything'll be back the way it used to be."

"Of course it will," she replied in a voice designed to soothe. "But wouldn't it be wise to have a contingency plan, just in case?"

Chapter Twenty-five

Hank and Jamie continued to take turns visiting Ellie and managing the Sweet Spot as best they could. One afternoon Jamie drove home trying to recall the contents of the fridge, hoping there was something she could make into a passable meal for Hank and her.

When she opened the fridge she saw a covered dish with a note on top.

Reheat at 350 for forty-five minutes.

Jamie frowned and peeked under the foil, but all she could see was an even layer of shredded orange cheese.

She couldn't tell what was hiding under that cheese, but whatever it was, it was going to be dinner.

She slipped it into the oven and turned on the heat.

An hour later, when Hank came in from work,

the nicely browned casserole was sitting on top of the stove, waiting.

"Something smells good," said Hank, hopefully spooning a giant portion onto his plate. "What is it?"

Jamie hesitated. "It's a surprise."

She served herself, then sat down across from him and watched as he tried it.

He looked up at her. "Tuna noodle casserole. It's great."

The biggest problem with cooking was that you had to do it every day. Not just cook, but come up with a menu, then a list of ingredients, then shop for those ingredients.

The next day Jamie again put off the daunting task of putting together dinner until the last possible minute.

She opened the fridge again. There was another dish accompanied by simple finishing instructions.

This time it was lasagna.

"Your cooking has come a long way," said Hank appreciatively, helping himself to seconds.

Jamie thought about who had access to the kitchen. It couldn't have been the teens. The only logical suspects were Joan or Theresa.

The following week, she walked into the kitchen after the trail ride ended early and caught Theresa penning what looked suspiciously like one of the notes on the phantom dishes.

"Ha! Caught you red-handed. I wondered who it was that's been making me look good."

"Those are my go-to dishes. I know them by heart. Don't even need to read the recipe anymore."

"Don't be so modest. You had to purchase the ingredients."

"I picked them up along with the regular shopping for the guests' meals."

"Those suppers have been a lifesaver. How did you even know I was struggling?"

"Your repertoire of songs may be impressive, but when I kept finding empty boxes in the trash in the mornings, I realized you could use a little help. I was here anyway."

"What can I do to thank you?"

"You helping Brynn is all the thanks I need. Those guitar lessons have made all the difference. She's gaining confidence. She's been having friends over, going out more."

"You're giving me way too much credit. All I did was show her a few tricks. It was more encouragement not to hide her talent, if anything."

"Whatever it was, I'll be forever grateful."

Chapter Twenty-six

At a small table in the tasting room sat Hank and Rob Stickler.

Hank poured Rob a small glass of pinot, slid it in front of him, and waited, observing Rob's face carefully as he drank.

Rob smacked his tongue against the roof of his mouth. "Discernible tannins." He swirled his glass, noting the color with a critical eye. "Was it made using the whole cluster technique?"

Hank nodded. "Impressive."

The interview to replace Ellie had been going on for the past half hour. So far Hank had determined that Stickler's knowledge of wine was certainly up to par.

Stickler set his glass down on the table, which was empty except for the bottle and two glasses. "I have to ask. Isn't there some sort of application?"

"We're not that formal around here. I figure when I meet the right person for the job, I'll know it."

"No application? Then how will you know about my education? Track my employment history?"

Hank spread his hands. "I thought I'd just ask you."

Stickler frowned. "But what about references? Background check?"

"Have you ever been arrested?"

"No."

"Well, then. That's out of the way."

Rob shifted his weight. "Say I take the job. You'll give me a complete, detailed list of my responsibilities along with your expectations, so that when the time comes for my review, I'll know if I'm meeting my employment goals." He looked at Hank expectantly.

"There's no list."

How could there be, when every day was different? Some days Ellie might be running the tasting room. The next she could be whipping up dinner for a crowd, and the next on the phone with the vet about a lame horse or a lamb that had come down with a virus.

Rob wrung his hands in his lap. "No list."

"'Fraid not."

Hank rose and extended his hand. "Thanks for stopping by. I'll let you know when we've made a decision."

Hank walked Stickler out of the tasting room and stood with his hands on his hips, watching as Stickler used his cuff to rub away a smudge on the already spotless windshield of his Volkswagen Rabbit.

Stickler was the fourth candidate that week he'd

interviewed to replace Ellie. The first had accepted a lengthy personal phone call and then demanded a salary that was twice what he could justify. The next had all the right skills, but her personality was so abrasive Hank was afraid she'd offend the guests. The third had been a no-show. Hank had relented after the man called and apologized profusely, and granted him a second chance. But the guy was twenty minutes late.

Stew had given him a considerably longer window of time to decide about his latest offer. It might have been designed to make Stew look bighearted, but Hank knew it was a strategic move. Stew was banking that Hank was simply skittish and that given enough time, the idea would take root.

Whatever the reason, Hank had to admit—it was working.

When Hank walked through the front door of the inn after the Stickler interview, the tinkling of Ellie's baby grand stopped him in his tracks. It had been years since he'd heard Ellie play.

He followed the music into the great room, where Jamie concentrated intently on the sheet music lying open against the music rack.

Without disturbing her, he sank into the leather couch, let his head fall back, and closed his eyes.

When she was finished, she slipped the front piece of music to the back and leaned in to study the next one in the thin stack.

"Oh," Jamie said, making room when Hank sat

down beside her on the bench. "I didn't hear you come in."

"What was that?"

"Schumann's Opus 54. It's one I'm familiar with."

"I remember when Grandma used to play."

He saw compassion in her soft smile. "How did the interview go?"

Hank pulled off his cap and ran a hand through his hair. "This isn't going to work."

She twisted to face him. "What do you mean?"

"I don't think I was cut out to do this."

"I take it Stickler isn't your man."

"If Bill had been there, he'd say Stickler was wound up tighter than a banjo string. It's not just Ellie's job that needs to be filled. I've taken a good, hard look at the staffing situation. There's been a steady uptick in the number of visitors in the past year. We could use another housekeeper and tasting-room docent, too."

"Those positions are more defined. Hopefully those searches will go more smoothly," said Jamie.

"What if they don't? Joan and Theresa have been a godsend, but they have to leave when school starts. And so do . . ." His voice trailed off.

In her mind, Jamie finished Hank's sentence. Very soon, she would be leaving, too.

She had sent her résumé to Dr. Keller. She was going to tell Hank about her interview during their plane ride. Moving to Newberry would open up a world of possibilities, not just for her career, but for Hank and her.

But that was before that woman had shown up.

Even after Hank canceled their plane ride, she still considered telling him. And then he told her about the new offer to buy his land.

If Hank left the Willamette Valley, would she still want to move here?

"You'll do it the same way your parents did it, and Ellie and all the people that came before them, by pouring your heart and soul into it. Their strength and resolve runs through your blood."

Hank looked around at the room filled with mementos. "I've been giving more thought to that offer."

Jamie jumped up from the piano bench. "Let's take a walk."

"I want to check on the sugar."

"I'll walk out to the winery with you to get the refractometer."

As they walked along the bank of the pond, she gazed out at the rolling blue hills in the distance.

"This looks an awful lot like the countryside around my old farm. I'll never forget the night I found out I was going to lose it. Spring break of my junior year in college . . ."

She'd whipped up a batch of macaroni and cheese—the good kind, the kind that comes in the blue box—to go with the traditional Easter ham. Thankfully that was a cinch to make. All you had to do was warm it up.

After supper, her sister and her sister's boyfriend slipped away for a while.

Jamie was sitting on the back stoop of the limestone farmhouse while Dad put the cows to bed.

Easter had come late that year. The days were growing longer. Purple crocuses fringed the steps. A barn cat zigzagged through the yard, leaping at unseen bugs.

The promise of spring was all around her. Her eye landed on the clothesline pole, and she remembered when she and Sally used to twirl around it when they were kids.

That's what she was doing when Dad ambled out from the barn, sank onto the stoop, and without preamble, broke the news.

"I'm gonna sell the farm, Jamie."

She'd stopped mid-twirl and stared at him in disbelief.

"The developers have been after me for years. I held out for as long as I could, but I think it's time. This farm is an island in a sea of housing developments. The market is strong. I might never get as good a price."

Sell the farm? Jamie struggled to wrap her head around it. That farm was the only home she had ever known. It had been built by her great-grandfather. She and Sally were the fourth generation to live there. The farm represented security in a world that seemed to be getting shakier with every report of breaking news.

Dad looked down at his vein-roped hands. "I know it's going to take you some getting used to. But it's been four years that your mom's been gone. With the price of milk being decided by the politicians nowadays, it's harder than ever to make a living as a dairy farmer."

She looked at his shoulders, wondering when they had begun to sag the way they did. For a long moment the only sound was the distant hum of a car passing down the valley road.

"I sold the herd to Jake. He's coming for them this week."

Jamie's cousin, who farmed in Chester County.

"I asked him to wait till after your Easter break from school, so I could tell you in person."

"Have you told Sally?"

His head bobbed up and down as he stared at his feet.

Jamie, being the younger of the two, was the last to know.

"What about you?" All her dad had ever done was farm. "What will you do? Where will you go?"

"I'm looking at a town house over in Allendale. With the price they're giving me, I can pay off your and your sister's college loans and still have enough to live on. Maybe even leave you something, when that day comes. That's more than my father could do for me."

"Your father left you this," she said, gesturing toward the fields blanketed in spring green. "I'd rather have the house and pay back my loans myself." She sounded like a petulant child, but she couldn't help it.

"It's for the best. You and Sally'll be able to start your lives without being saddled by debt; I'll be able to pay off my bills and buy a little place to grow old in."

* * *

They paused outside the winery.

"How'd that make you feel?" asked Hank.

"Like the ground was crumbling beneath my feet."

Hank pictured her there, coming to grips with her loss.

"Dad gave me money out of the house sale to pay for this vacation. I guess that's why he encouraged me to come, even after Kimmie backed out. He said it was a belated graduation gift, but it was really a consolation prize."

Hank got the tool he needed and Jamie followed him into the vineyard, where he selected a handful of individual grapes from several different vines.

"Here, I'll show you how to do it. Squeeze a drop of juice into the tube."

She did as he told her, popping what was left of the grape into her mouth.

"It's like a thermometer, only instead of temperature the reading tells you how much sugar's in the grapes. What's it say?"

"Fifteen."

"Now we'll test these other ones and average the results. That'll give us a good idea of how the whole block is progressing. On the day the reading, or Brix, averages twenty-five, that's when we'll pick."

"That very day?"

Hank nodded. "When the time gets closer, we check the Brix three times a day. Usually we pick at night."

"Seriously? How can you see?"

"The pickers show up around midnight wearing

headlamps. From a distance they look like human fireflies hovering over the vineyards. A few hours later, they're on to the next place. It's as if they had never been here."

She savored the sweet-tart taste of another crushed grape. "It's a miracle that something like this could come from a stick in the ground."

"It's not random chance that makes these grapes taste the way they do. It's terroir. Basalt on top of lava on top of ancient ocean floor. That and the maritime climate is what makes Sweet Spot wines so special."

Jamie laughed.

"What's so funny?"

"I'm just wondering who it is you're trying to convince of the unique quality of your land. Me? Or yourself?"

Another week passed.

Hank left his journals lying open on his desk and took his refractometer out to check sugar levels.

As he did every time he walked through the rows, he examined the clusters, checking for ripeness, color, and signs of disease. The grapes felt warm and voluptuous in his hand. He bent and inhaled their sweetness.

Then he stood up again, awash in a good feeling. He had been right about removing extra leaves to offset higher humidity. He was glad he had stood his ground and not allowed Bryce to cow him into spraying.

This time he picked random grapes from an assortment of vines, squeezed them into a cup, mixed the juice with his finger, and put a drop into the device.

Twenty. The same level of sugar the grapes had had last year on today's date, according to the journal. That boded well for another good vintage.

Hank closed his eyes and exhaled a breath he didn't know he'd been holding. At least *something* was going as planned.

Maybe Jamie was right. Maybe he could make a go of this.

Chapter Twenty-seven

Jamie's hair whipped out behind her as she navigated the red ragtop into Newberry one last time.

It had been a week of "lasts." The last trail ride. Singing around the last campfire, toasting one last marshmallow with the very stick that Hank had whittled for her back on a June evening when all this had been new to her, when her feet had been clad in sneakers. Now the routine of the Sweet Spot felt as familiar as her broken-in Noconas.

Her flight left tomorrow. But she couldn't leave Oregon without telling Ellie good-bye. There was so much she longed to ask her. If only she could talk back. Maybe she could give her some answers.

Never again would she see the way the afternoon sunlight glinted off the snow-capped Mt. Hood, across a middle ground of forest-green firs and filtered through the leaves on the corduroy rows of vines.

Never again would she walk into a room lit up

by Hank's easy grin. Or watch his brow furrow with concern over his spreadsheets.

After parking at the rehab hospital, she looked into the rearview mirror, dabbed her eyes with a tissue, and cleared her throat.

She needn't have bothered. She found Ellie looking the same as she had since she'd first taken ill a month earlier. The little-used notepad still lay forlornly on the blanket.

Jamie sat down on the bed at Ellie's side, took her hand, and began making small talk, as usual.

But tonight Jamie had more to talk about than her herb garden.

"I'm expected back at school soon. I found a new apartment. And guess what? It's got a bathtub! It looks real pretty from the pictures online. It's on the second floor instead of the fourth, like my old place was. Still safer than being on the first floor, but without as many stairs to climb. I'm looking forward to seeing my dad. I want to spend a few days with my sister and brother-in-law and my niece and nephew, too, before I get back to the grind."

Jamie paused, searching Ellie's face. She'd been so hoping Ellie would be better by the time she had to go. But she was still stuck inside herself, powerless to get out.

Though her eyes were open, there was no sign that she'd heard a thing Jamie said. Not a blink, not a twitch of a muscle.

Gently, she released Ellie's limp fingers and picked up her guitar.

She played Ellie's favorites. Then she sang the song she'd composed up on the Peak.

She was on the last line of the chorus when her voice cracked.

She took Ellie's hand again and squeezed it. "Miss Ellie, they say you can hear. Listen to me. You have to get better. Hank needs you."

Through her tears, she thought she saw something move on the bed.

It was Ellie's finger, inching toward the notepad.

"Ellie?"

For the first time since her stroke, Ellie was plainly looking at her.

"Ellie!" gasped Jamie. Chills tingled through her. "What is it? What do you want?"

Quickly Jamie set her guitar aside and stood hovering over Ellie, not knowing what to do. "Do you want to write?" She wrapped Ellie's fingers around the pen, positioning the notepad under it.

Her eyes softly closed, the pen sagging in her weathered hand.

Maybe it was only wishful thinking. Maybe she had only imagined Ellie's eyes looking into hers with comprehension.

She kept hold of her hand for a while longer, stroking the thin skin with her thumb. But the hands on the big clock on the wall advanced until it was time to say good-bye.

"I have to go now, Miss Ellie. I need to go back to work. My real work." She smoothed Ellie's hair from her forehead.

Maybe she should call somebody to make sure Ellie was all right. She got up and stuck her head out into the hall, but it was empty and quiet.

She went back to the bed. Ellie's chest rose and fell. She looked to be sleeping calmly.

Jamie put her guitar back into its case and slung it over her shoulder. Then she bent and kissed Ellie's soft hair.

Goodnight, Miss Ellie," she whispered. "Thanks for everything."

It was growing dark when Jamie got back to the inn.

She called Hank the moment she got to her car, and again when she was halfway to the inn, anxious to tell him that Ellie might have shown a sign of improvement. A faint sign maybe, but anything was better than nothing.

But he didn't pick up.

"Hank." She jogged into the inn, calling out his name.

There were a handful of guests in the great room, but no Hank.

Homer padded up to her, wagging his entire rear end. There was always worry in his eyes these days. She crouched down to scratch his neck. "Poor guy. You've been lost without her, too, haven't you?"

"Hank," she called, pushing open the door to the kitchen.

Not there, either. She hung up the keys to the Jeep and wondered where to look next.

Then she heard the heavy steps on the back porch.

Hank came through the door with a stricken look on his face, flanked by Nelson and Bill.

Jamie frowned, confused. What were they doing all together at this time of night in their hats and jackets, as if they were going out somewhere? "I'll drive you into the rehab," said Nelson to Hank.

"I'll call Joe Bear. I know she'd want him to do the services," said Bill, punching a number into his phone.

Bill spotted Jamie staring. "Hold on, Joe," he said into his phone. He swept off his hat and clapped it to his breast.

"The hospital called. Miz Ellie passed."

Chapter Twenty-eight

Not thirty-six hours later the airport van pulled into the inn at the Sweet Spot, right on schedule, to deliver the first wave of guests anxious to begin their wine country vacations.

Those departing with early flights home would board the van for the trip back to Portland. Passengers booked on that night's red-eye who would prefer to spend their remaining precious hours of vacation time sipping pinot noir on a patio overlooking the valley rather than in the airport would linger a few hours until the second shuttle arrived.

Among the luggage in a corner of the great room waiting to be loaded onto the "late" van were Jamie's suitcases and guitar case.

The staff smiled to the faces of the guests. But behind the scenes, they went about their duties sad-eyed.

Jamie cleaned the Sunflower Suite thoroughly and stood in the doorway looking around at it for a long moment, trying to memorize every last detail, before closing it with a quiet click.

She couldn't bear to sit in there and think while she waited for the afternoon shuttle. She'd rather work through her grief by doing the same thing she'd done all summer, helping out in any way she could.

Every time she caught a glimpse of Hank, her heart went into her throat. She wanted to talk to him, to offer her condolences. But now, in addition to his work, he had Ellie's wake to plan. He was always either surrounded by people, on his cell phone, or both.

On the front porch, a housekeeper was doing her best to check in new arrivals, but the line was backed up and she was clearly becoming flustered.

"You look like you could use a hand," said Jamie.

"But, this is your last day . . ."

Wordlessly, Jamie smiled and relieved the housekeeper of the electronic tablet, to her obvious relief.

As the next guest stepped up, Jamie peered down at the list of names. "Welcome to the Sweet Spot. And you are?"

"Delilah Arnold."

Jamie's gaze slid from her tablet to ten brightly painted toes, high-heeled sandals, then upward along slender calves, shapely knees, an expensive handbag in the crook of a well-creamed elbow, and finally, cat eyes in an unnatural shade of green.

Somehow Jamie managed to choke back the

nausea roiling through her. "I'm sorry. I can't seem to find your name on our guest list."

"This trip wasn't planned."

Jamie's heart beat double time. "I'll have to check our availability to see if we can accommodate you. Without a reservation . . ."

The woman inched forward so slightly. Not enough to be noticed by the others standing around chatting, but enough to make Jamie uncomfortable at the invasion of her personal space.

"Where's Hank?"

"I'm afraid he's tied up right now. I know how to handle check-ins."

"Hank will understand. I'm a close, personal friend of—*Hank!*" Delilah waved wildly and ran past her so close that Jamie could smell her sultry, oriental perfume.

Jamie looked over her shoulder to see Hank striding purposefully toward them with his sights set on the tasting room across the drive. When he spotted Delilah, he broke stride, obviously taken aback.

"Hank," said Delilah, throwing her arms around his neck. "I came as soon as I heard. I'm here to help in any way I can."

Hank blinked. "I'm on my way to check on the guys cleaning up around the pond for the wake tomorrow, and to make sure we've rented enough chairs."

Delilah tucked her arm into his. "I'll go with you," she said firmly, pulling him onward.

Jamie was used to performing in front of an audience, but maintaining her cool while checking in the rest of the guests pushed her acting skills to the limit. The minute she was finished, she headed for the one place where she had never had to hide her emotions.

Early that morning Joan and Theresa had appeared unbidden and set to work preparing for tomorrow's wake. Now a bewildering array of dishes spread from the kitchen counters onto the antique sideboard. But there was no sign of either woman, just Homer lying in his usual spot, still waiting faithfully yet forlornly for his mistress to come back.

Fond as Jamie was of Joan and Theresa, she was grateful for a moment alone in which to recover from the sight of Delilah's arms around Hank's neck.

She pulled out her usual chair, but before she could sit down, Homer growled long and low in his throat.

Between missing Ellie, neighboring vintners and growers dropping off gifts of food and wine, and the people involved in planning the wake, no wonder poor Homer was confused. It could be anyone he was growling at.

Still, for once Jamie didn't feel like making small talk or fielding yet another guest's question.

She slipped behind the pantry door.

"Hello? Anybody here?"

Delilah.

Inside the pantry, Jamie cringed. Through the crack in the door she saw Homer stand up and bark.

The screen door screeched. "Homer!" Theresa scolded. "Stop that. I'm surprised at you. Shoo! Get out."

Jamie heard the click of Homer's toenails on the floor, followed by the slamming of the door.

"Sorry! It's been mayhem around here today. Between that and losing Ellie, poor dog doesn't know what to think."

"You are . . . ?" Delilah inquired.

In the pantry, the ice in Delilah's voice sent a shiver through Jamie.

"Oh. Theresa. I've been filling in since Ellie got sick."

Light footsteps came and were gone.

"That's my daughter, Brynn," said Theresa. "She works for Miss Ellie in the summers, bussing tables. When Ellie got sick, they recruited a couple of us moms to help out."

"I see."

"Well, if you'll excuse me, Hank wants me to make a certain recipe of Ellie's for the wake tomorrow. Let's see here, where was I? Stir in one cup grated . . ."

Jamie leaned her head back against shelves of canned goods and closed her eyes, willing Delilah to go away.

"Is there something I can do for you?" Theresa's voice sounded strained. "You'll find some cold beverages out at the bar."

"Actually, there is." There was a pause and deliberate footsteps. "My name is Delilah Arnold."

"Pleased to meet you, Delilah. And now—"

"I prefer Ms. Arnold. I just spoke with Mr. Friestatt. There are going to be some changes around here. Now that Ellie's gone, I'm the woman in charge of this place."

In the pantry, Jamie's head came forward and her eyes popped open in her head.

"Is that right? Since when? Until I hear it from Hank, I answer to no one but him or Jamie Martel. She isn't even gone yet, and already here you are, thinking you're going to fill her shoes?"

"Jamie is nothing but a spare hand."

"Is that what you think? Well, I beg to differ. And it's not just me. You can ask Brynn. She said Jamie and Hank—"

"Jamie and Hank what?"

Jamie strained her ears to listen, but before Theresa could answer, Delilah jumped back in.

"Forget that. What I'd like is a little picnic basket made up. I'm not fussy—just some sandwiches, a vegetable plate, maybe something sweet. Do you have any desserts, Theresa?"

"Desserts?" asked Theresa incredulously. "Well . . . er . . ."

Theresa had sprung gallantly to Jamie's defense, but the fact was that Jamie was on her way out. Theresa had Brynn's college tuition to save for. She needed to work.

"Those are all the dishes people brought special for tomorrow. I guess it wouldn't hurt anything to cut you a little piece of pie."

Jamie heard footsteps going toward the sideboard.

"What kind do you want? There's blueberry, here's a cherry one . . ."

"Surprise me. Put the pie and the sandwiches in that basket. I'll be back for it in twenty minutes."

With that, Delilah left.

Jamie exhaled and thought of falling onto Hank

from Raven's Rock . . . long, sweet kisses in the moonlight up on the Peak . . . clinking glasses with him in the tasting room.

She thought she knew Hank. From day one, she had treated the Sweet Spot as if it were her own, giving willingly of her time and efforts without a second thought.

In his grief, had he really caved to Delilah's whim?

Now, instead of rolling up her shirtsleeves yet again, she slipped out of the kitchen when Theresa's back was turned.

She ran to the cool shade of the stables and sat down in the straw next to Dancer until she knew the driver of the late van would be looking for her.

And then she was packed into the van with the others, driving under the iron-link chain that held the weather-beaten sign that said WELCOME TO THE SWEET SPOT for the last time, and she felt like the heart with the bull's-eye pierced by an arrow was a reflection of her own.

"I brought you something to eat."

Hank looked up bleary-eyed from his laptop, uncomprehending. Food was the last thing on his mind.

"Hank," said Delilah. "You're exhausted."

"These emails can't wait."

She reached over and, with a crimson fingertip, gently pressed down on the lid.

"Hey. What—"

"You need a break from all of that."

He must have been out of it, because the next

thing he knew he was allowing himself to be led out of the tasting room.

When he saw his Jeep idling outside, he stopped. "Where'd you get the keys?"

"On the keyboard in the kitchen. It was easy. The hooks are labeled."

He followed Delilah to the Jeep and climbed into the passenger seat. "That way," he said numbly, pointing down the private dirt road toward a random spot with a view.

Minutes later they got out and he watched hesitatingly as Delilah spread Ellie's old quilt on the rough ground.

"Could've just eaten in the Jeep."

"Don't be silly," she said, sitting down cross-legged, patting the empty space in front of her. "What's a picnic without a blanket?"

He lowered himself in front of her and took the sandwich she offered him.

"I know you've got a lot on your mind, but before we get into all that, there's something I wanted to be sure I mentioned," she said between bites. "Guess who I called? That top-notch aviation school in Colorado you were looking at right after college. They have a package that includes three ground lessons, two flight lessons, basic supplies, and a video training course. I couldn't wait to tell you about it."

"Did you think I didn't know? I learned that when I took my discovery flight back when I was still in school."

After that, they finished eating in silence. Afterward he sat with his elbows resting on his knees, resting his eyes on the scenery.

Delilah lay down next to him, gazing into the azure sky.

"How are you doing?" she asked.

She seemed to sense that he needed to vent.

"Overwhelmed. Since the minute she passed, it's been nothing but people asking me nonstop questions about what I want to do about this and that. Did I want her buried or cremated? What should they dress her in? Who should do the service?

"The number of people we're expecting keeps growing. My cousin, Jack Friestatt, his wife, Jack's parents, Don and Melinda, all my second and third cousins and their families. All the local growers and vintners knew and loved Ellie. Add to that the townspeople and the employees, past and present . . ."

"Have you had time yet to think about the bigger picture? What you're going to do, down the road?"

"My grandmother's body is barely cold. There'll be plenty of time to think about that when all the fuss is over."

Delilah sat up suddenly. "Hank."

With a hand she gently turned his head to meet her eyes. "Look at me. Can't you see it written all over my face? *I love you.* I think I've always loved you, even back when we were in school."

Hank blinked uncomprehendingly.

"You feel it, too. I know you do. I can see it in your eyes."

Hank shook his head slowly, comprehension dawning on him. "I barely know you."

She shifted to sit directly in front of him, her face inches from his. "How can you say that," she pleaded, "when we've known each other for years? You're distraught, that's all. I admit, now's not the best timing, but I couldn't hide it any longer. Now that Ellie's gone, there's nothing tying you to the Sweet Spot. Come back to Denver with me."

"Now?"

"As soon as the funeral is over. We'll get married! There's nothing left for you here. Walk away." She laid a hand on his arm. "Don't overthink it. It's that simple. Just walk away. We'll start a whole new life together."

Married? Hank yanked his arm out of her grasp, leapt to his feet, and headed back to the Jeep, ignoring the remnants of their picnic.

"Am I moving too fast?" Delilah hurried after him, catching his arm. "We can dial it back. I've become somewhat of an expert in boutique resorts. Once I transform this place, you won't even recognize it. Hot tubs, a spa, an Olympic-sized pool . . ." She turned him around. "It'll require an injection of capital, but we could end up with a net gain when we do sell."

Hank evaluated the woman before him the way he evaluated a wine, noting every aspect. She was beautiful, savvy, and ambitious.

"Why me?" he asked.

There were men who would beg for a wife like her.

Men like Ryan Rowling.

Following the gala, he'd never given Rowling another thought. Why now, with all the things crowding his mind?

What were Rowling's last words to him? *Keep one hand on your wallet.*

Of course.

Delilah opened her mouth to reply, but Hank held up a halting hand. "So you can share in the profits?"

"Hank, I—"

"That's why you invited me to Denver in the first place, wasn't it? Not because you're my friend. You stood to get a cut of Stew's sales commission. Come to think of it, that's probably what inspired you to get your real estate license."

"You don't understand."

"And now you're thinking *if he can't be persuaded to sell yet, I'll marry him, improve the property to get even more from it, and then divorce him and split the proceeds fifty-fifty.*"

He stuck out his hand. "Where are the keys?"

"Hold on," she pleaded. "We're not finished talking."

"Give. Them. To. Me."

When she finally relinquished them, he wasted no time making his way to the Jeep, leaving the food behind on the blanket.

"Where are you going?"

"Back to the inn. You can ride or walk. Your choice."

She had barely scrambled in beside him when he shoved the gear stick into drive and the Jeep jerked forward.

"I want you out of my sight."

She dropped all pretense. She sounded like a stranger when she said, "The late van has come and gone."

"Rent a car. Call a cab. I don't care how you do it, but I want you out of here now, today. I don't want you here when I lay my grandmother to rest."

Hank strode into the great room, a man on a mission. Then he spotted the baby grand and pulled up short and looked around.

"Jamie!"

But there was nothing but the ticking of the grandfather clock.

He went to the kitchen. "Jamie!" he hollered, knowing in his heart of hearts that it was futile.

Theresa looked up from the cutting board where she sliced tomatoes.

With a sinking feeling, he checked the time. "Where's the late van?"

Pausing her knife, she said, "Been here and gone."

That couldn't be. That meant that Jamie had gone and he hadn't said good-bye to her.

He breezed past Theresa without speaking and out the back door, letting it slam behind him, not knowing where he was headed.

Jamie had been trying to get his attention since Ellie died. But like a fool, he had put other things ahead of her, as if they had all the time in the world.

Now she was gone, just like that? Impossible! He began walking in circles.

Not that she would have known where to find him if she'd looked, out picnicking with Delilah when he should have been planning his grandmother's funeral.

He stopped at the paddock fence and called Jamie's phone, but when it went straight to voice mail he hung up quickly. What would he say?

Briefly he considered racing to the airport to try to catch her before she boarded her flight.

And then what? he thought, halfway to his vehicle. Take her in his arms? Ask her to give up her teaching career and come back to the Sweet Spot on a whim? That was hardly rational, or fair.

Head bowed low, he turned around and trudged back to the inn.

Just when he'd lost Ellie, now Jamie was gone, too.

He tore off his cap as he walked. How was he going to get through tomorrow's wake without her?

And what about after that? He'd gotten used to her being there, from their first cup of coffee of the day, to helping him with any problem that arose, to hearing her singing the last thing at night before he hauled his work-weary body up to bed.

He dragged a hand down his face, distorting his features. How could he live without her?

He heard the screen door open and looked up to see Theresa standing there with a worried look on her face, wringing her hands.

"Are you okay?" she asked him.

She was obviously distraught.

But though he was dying inside, he had to get a grip. He was the only one left holding this place together.

He straightened his spine. "I'm fine."

"I have to talk to you."

Hank wrapped his arm around Theresa's shoulder—surprised at what he could do when he set his mind to it—and led her around the inn onto the back porch.

"Have a seat. There, in Miss Ellie's rocker."

"I wouldn't feel right sitting there, so close to . . ."

Right. Bad idea. "Okay. Well, do you want to take a walk?"

In answer, she descended the back steps and headed toward the pond.

"Spare hand, my foot," muttered Theresa, looking over her shoulder, once they were safely out of earshot of the inn. "I can't imagine what it'll be like when that woman moves in full time. Specially if Miss Ellie isn't here to mind things. I'm telling you right now, Hank, you're going to be losing people left and right."

"What are you talking about? Who's moving in?"

"Miss High-and-Mighty. She comes into my kitchen and starts ordering me around like I'm her personal servant or something. And when it's plain as day I'm trying to get ready for Miss Ellie's wake!"

"What did Delilah say to you?" Hank growled.

"That she's in charge from now on."

Inside, Hank seethed. But somehow, he kept his voice calm. "Well, you don't have to worry about Delilah. She's been, let's say, permanently banned from the Sweet Spot."

"Really?" Theresa's face relaxed, to his great relief.

"Really. And I'm sorry she upset you, and I hope it won't affect your working here. Because I value your work and I would hate to lose you any sooner than I have to, when you go back to your job at the cafeteria."

Her heart flew to her ample breast. "Oh, thank goodness."

Then she was sober again. "What about Jamie? Didn't you get to say good-bye to her?"

"I must've just missed her," he said around the hard lump in his throat.

Theresa turned down her lip.

"Did you?" He craved knowing something, anything about Jamie's final moments at the vineyards.

"No."

Strange. That didn't seem like Jamie.

"She is a good person," said Theresa with a sigh. "She'll be missed."

You have no idea, thought Hank, rubbing his jaw. *No freaking idea.*

Chapter Twenty-nine

Jamie stepped outside the airport in Philly and inhaled air as thick as pea soup. She'd forgotten how humid the Mid-Atlantic could be in August. Within minutes her hair frizzed up into a pyramid twice its normal size.

She hadn't seen her family all summer. Though retired from farming, Dad still got up before dawn every morning. He said it would be nothing for him to drive the hour and a half to the airport to meet her incoming red-eye and then take her back to Lancaster County. But in the time since she had booked her return flight in June, life had gone on. An organizational meeting had been scheduled at her school. If she rented a car, she would have just enough time to pop by and see the apartment her sister had found for her before showing up for the meeting, and then head home that afternoon.

Philly's rush hour streets were in a state of chaos. Wherever she looked she saw tall buildings in some stage of construction or deconstruction. She felt hemmed in by a mass of cars, trucks, and buses, all alternating between speeding and jerking to a stop a hairsbreadth from the bumper in front of them.

Great. Now she was stuck behind a lovely trash truck. The smell had her holding her shirt over her nose to breathe. And now there was a siren wailing behind her. In her rearview, the column of vehicles inched toward the right, but she was stuck in the middle lane with no place to go. Somehow the ambulance threaded the needle until it was directly behind her, red lights flashing, the driver gesturing angrily at her.

She rolled down her window, the humidity immediately making her skin stick to the seat of her rental car, and threw her hands in the air. "What am I supposed to do? I can't move!" she yelled into her mirror.

Eventually, the cars to her left found a way to edge over enough to let the ambulance pass.

She'd already seen pictures of the apartment, so there were no real surprises there. The best thing that could be said about it was that it had a bathtub. Not that she could have upgraded if she wanted to. Even an administrator's salary only stretched so far.

She had managed to snatch a few hours of restless sleep on the flight, but by the time she arrived at school, she was feeling the effects of trying to squeeze too many commitments into a limited amount of time.

The meeting of department heads was in a second-floor classroom. Jamie sat next to a window with a view of postage-stamp-sized macadam wedged between the school and the graffiti'd brick wall of another commercial building. Halfway through the meeting she heard shouting and looked down to see a boy in a white T-shirt take a swing at his friend and miss, resulting in a chasing match that had them zigzagging back and forth within the chain-link enclosure until one tagged the other, and then they changed direction.

"Jamie?"

"Hm?"

"Parent volunteers," said the superintendent. "Would you be willing to coordinate that committee?"

"Those students . . ." Jamie said with a nod toward the window. "Are they ours?"

Her school had a policy of opening up their playground to the neighborhood kids during the summer.

Her superintendent strolled over and looked outside. "I'm not sure. I don't interact with individual students enough to get to know them."

"They look familiar, but then I teach—er, *used* to teach—every student in the school, so I'm not sure," said Jamie.

"Let me have a look." The young, athletic language-arts chair seized the chance to climb out of his cramped seat. "This is only my third year out of the classroom. I might recognize them." He leaned over the window. "Yes." A smile lit up his face and he knocked on the glass and waved. "That's Malcolm Levon and Kwame Jackson."

The boys looked up and started yelling and waving their arms at their former English teacher.

"I thought I recognized them," said Jamie with a small wave of her own.

Her heart started to pound. What was she going to do, now that she wouldn't be around them every day, guiding them, nurturing their budding talent, watching them grow?

But the school year was about to start. Too late now to call up Dr. Keller. Newberry's new music teacher would already have been hired. At this moment, he or she was no doubt in a meeting of her own, or readying the music room for the year's new crop of eager young faces.

"The volunteers," said her superintendent.

Jamie blinked. "Yes," she said, jotting a note of it with a trembling hand.

"Is everything all right?"

"A little jet-lagged. Would it be possible to turn up the air conditioning?"

The other administrators exchanged glances.

"It's already freezing in here," said the science chair, pulling her sweater closed.

Then why was Jamie suddenly burning up, but her hands were so cold she could barely control her pen?

Somehow she managed to make it through the meeting.

When it was over, she walked down the hall to her new office. On her desk was the box of books and files she'd requested to be delivered there. Last spring, when she'd carefully packed them up, they had seemed indispensable. Now, when she pulled them out one at a time, they seemed to belong to someone else.

She sat down in her black vinyl chair and practiced rolling it in and out, only to find there wasn't enough room between her desk and the wall and she kept bumping into it. She'd have to be careful of that.

When she was driving down I-76, halfway to Lancaster County, it occurred to her that she hadn't put away any of her books. Why not? There was certainly no shortage of shelves, given all the wall space afforded by the lack of windows.

She stared through the windshield and thought. With a new apartment and an important new position, she should be raring to go. Instead, she felt vaguely let down.

Maybe she was coming down with something.

It was probably just nerves. The start of a new school year was always bittersweet. Exchanging those precious weeks of freedom—despite popular opinion, teachers didn't really have three whole months off, what with wrapping up loose ends in June, mandatory continuing ed classes, and planning for the next year—for the promise of a fresh start.

Reality was slowly sinking in.

Change was never easy, but she had no choice.

She was going to supervise her school's music department.

And the Sweet Spot was being sold.

It might be months before it was official. Hank had told her that himself, back when he was considering the first offer. She had tried to stop him time and again with her songs and her stories, but he hadn't listened. Hank was throwing away his roots. She'd heard it with her own ears. And for what? Some abstract notion of freedom.

Lancaster County, Pennsylvania

"What time's the mailman come?" Jamie asked her sister.

She'd been home for three days. Now she was on her computer in Sally's homey kitchen, printing out her new lease so that she could return a signed copy to the landlord.

"Around four. Better hurry if you want to mail something."

Jamie licked and sealed the flap of the long envelope and walked woodenly out to the gray metal mailbox by the road. She pulled down the door latch. But something kept her from taking that irreversible step. Why was she hesitant? She would finally have her own place with a big bathtub. Wasn't this exactly what she had worked so hard for?

Brushing away her reservations, she deposited the envelope in the box and raised the tiny red flag.

Now she was committed.

As she walked back to Sally's house, her phone rang.

"Hank?"

"Jamie." It was one p.m. in Oregon. From his post behind the bar at the tasting room Hank could still see his last customers climbing into their cars. He closed his eyes and braced himself against the wall and sucked in what felt like his first complete breath in ages. *God, it is good to hear her voice.*

Three days had passed since he'd buried Ellie.

The day after the wake was spent cleaning up from the hundreds of guests that had come from all over the Willamette Valley to pay their respects. But someone was missing. Someone Hank had taken for granted until it was too late.

He clutched the phone like a lifeline. "How are you?"

"I'm fine. I'm so sorry about Ellie."

"Your music was one of the last things she heard. I'll always be grateful for that."

"I thought she was showing signs of improving. What happened?"

"Doctor said she had a blood clot that broke off and went to her brain. The first stroke was only a precursor. There was nothing anyone could have done."

"I'm sorry I didn't get to say good-bye. But I couldn't postpone my flight. I had things to do to get ready for the school year."

"How about you? Glad to be home?"

Jamie had seen the missed calls from Hank while her plane was en route to the East Coast. She'd thought about calling him back a dozen times. But she didn't want to know the details about the Sweet Spot being sold.

Now, hearing her name on Hank's lips had her pulse racing.

She had a million questions. How had the funeral gone? How was the staff adjusting? What happened next in the sale of the property?

She didn't ask any of them. It was easier to pretend that everything was all right.

She looked out across the cornfields next to Sally's house, through the Mid-Atlantic haze toward the low purple hills. Oddly, the mountains seemed to have shrunk a little while she'd been gone.

"It was great to see my family and friends. I'm outside at my sister's house right now. She's been a real gem. Arranging family dinners. Letting me sleep on her couch until my lease starts in a couple weeks. I can't believe the summer's almost over. Can you hear the locusts singing?"

There was a pause while he listened.

"I think so."

"I've always thought of that as my back-to-school song. The song of a season coming to an end."

Like their one, sparkling summer.

"Well"—he cleared his throat—"I wanted to be sure to thank you for everything you did. For me, and for Ellie. All those visits to the hospital. The trail rides, the tasting room, teaching Bill some new songs." He laughed, but she knew him well enough to know it was forced. "Especially that."

Jamie bit her lip and looked down at her feet as she paced.

She stopped in the shade of an ornamental pear and fingered the tip of a low branch. "Thank you for—"

"Hey, Jamie? Hold on a sec. Bryce is jumping up and down, waving the refractometer."

She waited for the inevitable.

"It's time," said Hank.

Across three thousand miles, the edge of excitement in his voice came through loud and clear. "Time for the crush."

A thrill shot through Jamie. She imagined the

scramble to get everything underway. Hank would get the pickers in there that very night to avoid picking in tomorrow's heat. Then came the sorting, the de-stemming, and the crushing. All that before fermentation commenced.

She longed to be there. To see the buzz of activity, hear the shouts of the workers in the fields. To be a part of harvest time, the dramatic conclusion of all Hank's hard work.

But she was no longer part of that scene. It would be October before Hank had time to breathe again—let alone brood over a former hired hand.

Out of sight, out of mind.

"You're going to have your hands full. Good luck with the harvest."

"Great hearing your voice."

She knew he had to go. Still, she was overcome with disappointment that their call had to end so soon. What had she been expecting—a lengthy heart-to-heart?

"Give Homer a hug for me."

"Think of me when you wear those Noconas."

And then there was nothing but silence.

Jamie whisked away a stray teardrop, slid her phone into her back pocket, and staggered toward the house.

Two things she was grateful for: keeping her passion in check, and never telling him about the job in Newberry that she'd applied for on a foolish whim.

Meanwhile, the cornfields shimmered in the late-day heat and the locusts sang their hypnotic song.

But somehow, it sounded flat.

When Jamie got back inside, Sally's youngest

was propped on her mother's hip eating Cheerios one by one from a plastic cup.

"Let's see your pictures of your new office," Sally said.

But before Jamie could bring up the photos on her computer, the subject line of a new email grabbed her attention. She shrieked and her hand flew to her mouth.

She tore out the front door as the mail truck pulled in front of the house. The carrier had already pushed down the red flag and was reaching into the box when she cried, "Stop!"

Just in time, she reached into the box and yanked out her lease before it went into the mail truck.

Sally, with her baby still glued to her hip, and her toddler with his thumb in his mouth, stared at her from the screen door as she came skipping back.

"What on earth is going on?"

"I got the job!"

"What are you talking about? What job?"

"The job in Oregon!" Jamie replied breathlessly, sliding back down in front of the computer to read Dr. Keller's letter again.

I'm writing to inform you that at the eleventh hour, the individual initially chosen to fill the music teacher opening at Newberry has changed her mind and taken a position in Portland instead. Your application is the next in line. Have you found the answer to the question we discussed in your interview? And if so, are you still interested in the job?

"What job in Oregon? Will you please tell me what's going on?"

"Never in a million years did I think I'd get it. Let's see." She leapt up and began to pace. "I have to resign my department-head job. Notify the landlord that I won't be taking the apartment. Figure out how to get all my stuff shipped across country . . ."

"Let me see that." Sally deposited the baby in his high chair, dumped more Cheerios into his cup, and slid the laptop around to where she could read it. She skimmed over the letter, then turned to Jamie.

"You just got home and now you're going to turn right around and go back out there? What about your job back here? Your big-time promotion?"

"When I saw the kids playing on the macadam, that's when I knew. I don't want to be department head."

Sally shook her head. "But you'd be the youngest department head the school's ever had."

"Who cares, if it's not what I want? All I want to do is teach."

"But, why Oregon?"

How could she describe to Sally the Willamette Valley's lush vineyards, the acres of wildflower meadows, the carefully tended farms? The hard-working, high-spirited people who lived there? The Willamette still had a frontier quality about it . . . a sense that anything was possible.

"Because . . . it feels like home to me."

Chapter Thirty

September

At the Sweet Spot, the grape harvest was in.

Hank walked the vineyards endlessly, thinking of changes he'd like to make, like altering drains and slopes for the next time he was plagued with a wet spring. Compared with the prime summer months when he could practically watch the grapes growing before his eyes, now the vineyards appeared peaceful. But they were far from dormant. The leaves continued to bask in the weakening autumn sun, storing up starch. Beneath the soil, the vines were sending out new roots; tiny hairs sought out crucial nutrients. Together, these processes were what would allow the vines to survive during the coming winter. Without that critical four- to six-week period between harvest and the first frost, the vines would freeze and die.

He filled up the long evenings reading back

through his collection of vineyard journals, sticking bookmarks in pages. And he continued to keep careful notes in the current year's journal.

He kept careful watch on the racked wine, periodically withdrawing samples from the tanks and barrels for quality control and blending trials.

He decided to start making his own compost from vine prunings, grass clippings, and sheep manure.

Jamie moved into a town house in a complex within walking distance to Newberry Elementary School.

Her colleagues gave her a warm reception. Her dad sold her car for her and she used the money to buy another one.

And she scrambled to ready her new classroom.

She still had to pinch herself now and then to make herself believe that she had actually done this. Moved all the way across the country.

She joined the choir at Friends Church and bought a bed and some living room furniture. In Oregon, her teacher's salary went much further than it had in Philadelphia.

Whenever people asked her what had attracted her to the Willamette Valley, she joked that wineaux like her were few and far between in Pennsylvania, but here in the Willamette Valley, she was in her element. She could barely make a move without stepping on one.

That seemed to satisfy them. So far, nobody had associated her with the young woman who'd worked as a hired hand at the Sweet Spot last summer.

Aaron Beekman, her mentor, called to tell her he had accepted the department chairmanship in her stead, and to thank her for the complimentary things she'd said about him when she called to tender her resignation.

She kept herself so busy she hardly had time to miss Hank. But often, late at night, especially when she heard an owl outside her window, she thought of all that could have been.

On a day of gray skies that sent yellow aspen leaves skittering by her living room window, she opened up her email as she ate her solitary supper.

Jamie,

Out here in the Willamette, it looks like fall. It's quieter now that the tourists are gone, and without Ellie here. The weather's been dry but getting cooler. The oak out by the pond is turning shades of orange and red.

Yesterday I rode up to the Peak and something happened that made me think of you. I heard a loud clacking sound. It was two big bull elk in the rut, clashing antlers over a herd of cows. I thought about how much you loved the sky up there, how bright the stars were. The sounds of a summer night in the wilderness. Remember when you played your guitar and the coyotes sang along with us? I'll never forget it.

You're probably pretty busy with the new school year, back East. I hope the new job is everything you thought it would be.

Guess what? I started taking flying lessons.

Hope this letter finds you safe and well.

Hank

P.S. By the way, I tried calling you again, but it seems you have a new number. It's clear you've moved on. If you ever do feel like talking, I'm here.

Jamie read his words over and over until she could recite the letter by heart.

But tempted as she was to write back, it was far better to start fresh, as Hank was going to do early next year, as soon as the sale of the Sweet Spot became final. His decision to resume flying lessons proved that he was already preparing for the move.

From her very first class, she loved teaching music at Newberry Elementary. How could she have been so arrogant as to think no other students could measure up to the gifted kids back in Philly? Her new pupils were every bit as bright and curious and eager.

With every week that passed, she grew more certain that teaching and living in a rural setting was what she was meant to do. Following a few false steps, she now knew which coffee shop served her favorite brew and which deli carried the best takeout . . . which streets were one-way only and the shortcut to get onto the highway that ran alongside the town.

She was alive with the excitement of discovery.

There was only one drawback. She had no one to share it with.

She found herself having long conversations with Hank in her head at night. Relating something funny a student had said or done that day. How the chorus was progressing toward the holiday concert. The fact that while he believed she was three thousand miles away, she was only ten miles down the road.

Maybe it was sheer loneliness, or maybe the glass of pinot she'd had with supper, but one night she began spontaneously tapping out a letter.

Dearest Hank,

I miss you like crazy. Every morning, before I even open my eyes, I'm already thinking of you from my dreams. I picture you waking up in your suite at the vineyard, imagine you having your coffee alone in the kitchen, pouring a flight of pinot for thirsty tourists excited to drink Sweet Spot wine on the actual premises.

I remember your crooked smile, and the way you looked at me with those melting brown eyes. The warmth of your arms the few times you held me, the soft insistence of your lips.

And then I try to lose myself in my responsibilities, only to return to you again at the end of the day.

Hank, if you only knew the thoughts of you I take to bed each night. You're in everything I do. Everyplace I go. Every breath I take.

Jamie reread her words, hit delete, and began anew.

Hank,

I know I haven't written up until now, but as you know, this school year has entailed a lot of changes. Most of my free time is taken up decorating my new apartment and getting to know my new neighborhood, which, thankfully, is much quieter than the one I used to live in.

Needless to say I haven't ridden lately, but whenever I notice my Noconas in my closet I think of Dancer. I'll bet he likes the cool weather. I can just picture him, kicking up his heels in the cool morning mist. Feed him an apple or two for me.

All the best,

Jamie

Before she could change her mind, she pressed send.

Chapter Thirty-one

October

Jamie's letter resulted in a flurry of return correspondence. All of Hank's letters were platonic in tone. And he was careful to skirt the one, glaring issue that had always come between them. He talked about the people they knew, the vineyards, and the animals, as if nothing were amiss. As if he wasn't making plans to either sell the stock or find another place to keep them, to divest himself of generations' worth of furnishings and musical instruments and other precious stuff—stuff, like his grandmother's flowered dishes, or, as she herself had once callously called them, "crap"—that made a house a home.

It took all Jamie had not to respond immediately and at length to each of them. But if she were to ever get over Hank Friestatt, she couldn't be his pen pal. It was way too risky for her heart.

Yet she couldn't go so far as to delete his emails. Every word was committed to memory, every letter filed in a special folder under his initial.

Crisp leaves of gold and orange drifted around her shoulders as she walked to and from school, pulling her wheeled backpack behind her.

She had survived trial by fire in the tough city schools back East and a cross-country move to a rural district that truly valued education. For the first time, she enjoyed the full support of the parents and the administration. Kids came to school ready to learn, and classes were of a reasonable size. She was able to focus more on teaching music, and less on classroom management.

She was becoming friendly with two other music educators who had formed a band called T-Bone that played classic country ballads and some crossover rock. It was a time-honored way for music teachers to pick up a few extra dollars on the side.

One day, Tony, who played rhythm guitar, invited her to come and hear them play.

"I'd love to. Where?"

"Every Friday night. The Turning Point. On Main."

The tavern where she and Hank had first danced.

"Something wrong?" Tony chuckled. "You look like you saw a ghost."

She brushed away his concern. "What could possibly be wrong?"

She'd spent every evening by herself for weeks. Was it worth risking running into Hank to stop by for a drink with coworkers and to hear them play?

That first Friday night when she walked into the Turning Point, she held her breath, scanning the heads of the patrons for a certain ball cap with TEXTRON AVIATION on the front, breathing a sigh of relief when she didn't see it.

That night turned out to be the most fun she'd had since moving to Oregon.

She went back the next Friday, and the next.

The wives, teachers, and other followers of the band accepted her into their group.

Gradually, she stopped looking for Hank there.

"Maybe sometime we'll get you behind the mic and see what you can do," said Tony one day when they shared lunch duty in the cafeteria.

"I'm not sure about that." She chuckled nervously. It was one thing to sit in the audience, and quite another to draw attention to herself.

"Don't be so modest. I've walked past your room and heard you sing."

Let Tony believe it was modesty. Better than telling him that she didn't dare put herself in a position where certain people might see her and be bound to talk. She just needed to lie low until the New Year. After Hank was gone, the coast would be clear.

One morning close to Halloween, Jamie woke up to a world covered in white. The snow didn't amount to much. The road to her school was clear by the time she pulled onto it from her development.

After the three o'clock bell, Jamie routinely checked her email.

Dear Jamie,

This has been a strange year. To add to the weirdness, last night we had our first snowfall, much earlier than usual. I wish you could see how the vineyards look covered in white.

The cold makes the horses frisky. I got up early before it melted, saddled Blitzer, and rode him up to the Peak to see the view.

I sat there and watched the sun come up in the East, where you are. I've been doing that a lot lately.

By now the summer must seem like it was a long time ago. But I hope there are some things about it you'll never forget.

Hank

Hank looked for Jamie's reply to his email, but as usual, there was none.

The last time he'd heard her voice was back in August when she was still at her sister's place. When he called her again a week later and got a recording saying that her number was no longer in service, he'd tried twice more, not wanting to accept that she had changed it without telling him the new one.

No doubt things were back to normal in her life in Philly by now. Maybe there was even someone wining and dining her. Someone who wore suits to work and always had clean fingernails. Whoever he was, Hank hated him with a passion.

Chapter Thirty-two

November

On one of his daily walks through the vineyards, Hank noticed something lying hidden among the vines. He squatted to get a better look and saw that it was yet another dead gopher.

Separating the cover crop of clover with his hands, he located his burrow. And sprinkled around it, grains of Molex.

He stood up and yelled, "Bryce!" at the top of his lungs, even though he knew he was the only person within a hundred yards.

He yanked his cell phone out of his back pocket. "Bryce? Block Nine. Get over here. Now."

"What the hell is this?" Hank said when Bryce came tramping up.

"You think you can just ask those gophers pretty please to scram and they're going to disappear," said Bryce. "It doesn't work that way. We've tried it.

Only one way to get rid of them for good and that's Molex."

"How could you take it upon yourself to go against the whole philosophy of this vineyard? You knew my father. You knew how much it meant to him to go green. How much it means to the quality of the wine. To our image. Our brand. I've been busting my ass trying to get biodynamic certification. We're almost there. All I need is for the regulators to come out here and find this Molex and it'll set us back who knows how long.

"You're fired."

Bryce didn't bat an eye. "You can't fire me. Your daddy promised me a job as long as I wanted one. Everyone in Ribbon Ridge knows he was a man of his word."

Bryce had known Hank since he was a teenager. He knew where to stick the knife to inflict the most damage.

Hank only hesitated a moment. "Dad's gone, and so is my grandmother. I'm in charge now. The Sweet Spot is mine to run, my way."

"Without me, who's going to tell you when to pick the crop?"

Historically, the final decision on when to pick had always been Bryce's.

"Not your problem anymore. Get your gear and get out."

"Good luck with that." Bryce turned and stalked away, leaving Hank standing among his vines with shaking hands—and a growing self-confidence.

* * *

The next morning he and Nelson were working on winterizing the irrigation system.

"Ever hear from that Miz Martel?" Nelson asked casually as he forced compressed air into a line to remove the water.

At the mention of Jamie's name, Hank's nerves went on high alert. No one knew he'd written to Jamie once, let alone a dozen times.

Without looking up, he shook the last drops out of the line. "Why'd you ask?"

"Strangest thing. Seth Thompson said someone saw her down at the Turning Point last Friday night. Said she was there with some people watching the band."

"Seth Thompson likes to stir up trouble," snapped Hank. "Hand me that end cover, will you?"

As Hank capped the line, he asked, "How's Seth even know Jamie?"

"How should I know?" Nelson rose unsteadily from where he'd been squatting and went over to disconnect the compressor from the other end of the line.

And then Hank remembered. After Ellie's stroke, Jamie had made numerous trips to the post office.

"You been ornery as a redneck fool ever since that woman left, back in August."

Hank made his way to the next line that needed checking. "I might be ornery, but you're the one who's taking Seth's gossip seriously. You must've watched too many of them soap operas back when you were laid up."

"Now why'd you have to go and remind me?"

They laughed, their squabble over.

But as they finished blowing out the irrigation

system, Hank couldn't get past the rumor. He'd been avoiding the Turning Point all autumn. It brought up too many memories about a pair of new Noconas and an impromptu dance.

It was after one a.m. on a frosty Friday night when Hank and his friend and fellow vintner, Roy, finally shuffled into the Turning Point. They had already tossed back a few at a Newberry brewpub. Hank didn't dare let himself believe that he'd actually find Jamie there tonight. If he did, he wouldn't have wasted any time after his conversation with Nelson. So then why had he been priming himself, screwing up his nerve with the help of some liquid courage?

Now that cold weather was here to stay, the social season was heating up. Winter was the time when everyone from the most renowned winemaker to the lowliest field hand came in from the outlying areas to party, and the townspeople were more than eager to renew existing friendships and expand their circle of acquaintances.

The tightly packed throng stood three-deep at the bar. While Hank waited with Roy for their turn to order, an exotic, dark-eyed woman caught his eye and smiled. He had seen her somewhere before, on the periphery of his circle of friends who didn't eat, drink, and breathe the wine industry. There was a time when he might have bought her a beer and worked his way over to her. Not anymore. Not tonight.

From the opposite side of the long, narrow room came the sharp twang of a guitar. Hank looked behind him, but tall as he was, it was impossible to see the band's faces through the crowd.

"Good timing," Roy yelled over his shoulder. "The band's still playing."

Before Hank knew it, a guitar intro transported him back in time to a private performance before a crackling fire under a half moon up at the Peak.

The skin on his arms puckered up. His hands grew moist. His pulse pounded in his head. And when the intro was over, he heard again that honeyed voice.

"If I could turn back time
Take you there with me
Maybe then you'd see
Into my past."

He had to see her for himself, to prove to himself that he hadn't lost his mind.

He clawed his way through the throng like a madman. How many long autumn nights had he lain awake, the memory of that voice sabotaging his sleep? Seeing again her hair blowing out behind her as she galloped Dancer through the meadow behind the vineyard? Her strong yet graceful hands clinging to Raven's Rock?

Now, here was Jamie, standing right in front of him, not thirty feet away.

Her hair was full and flowing. Her arms were covered by a jacket, but she wore a skirt that cleared her knees with room to spare. If he lived to be a hundred, Hank would never forget the first time he'd seen those legs emerging from a voluminous white skirt, when all he'd ever seen her in before that was the jeans she'd brought in her suitcase for a two-week stay in wine country.

On her feet were a pair of beat-up Noconas.

> *"If you'd just take my hand*
> *Walk a mile with me*
> *Baby then you'd see*
> *The best things are those that last."*

With the spotlights trained on her, she couldn't possibly see him standing in the shadows.

His mind raced. Had she never left Oregon? He'd never actually seen her leave. But that made no sense. He couldn't believe she'd concoct an elaborate lie and stick to it all summer.

So, assuming she had left, when had she come back?

"What's with you? You took off like a shot," said Roy at his shoulder. "Here. You forgot your beer."

Hank's hand curved around the cold bottle, his eyes never leaving the stage.

Roy joined him in his rapt attention for a moment before nodding toward Jamie in admiration. "If that's not whatcha call a flatliner, I don't know what is."

Considering that Hank's heart was about to pound through his chest, Roy's description was right on the money.

He could hardly wait to rush the stage the second she was finished, to take hold of her and study her face at close range and get the answers to all his questions.

But—what if she wasn't here alone?

Hank searched the front row for likely suspects. There was no one obvious, as far as he could see.

The ballad ended and Jamie slipped her guitar strap over her head and set her instrument upright in its stand back by the drum set, then whispered something to the rhythm guitarist.

"Last call," came from somewhere far away.

What should he do then?

Think. But his brain didn't work. His thoughts were all tangled up with his emotions.

Now Jamie was returning to center stage, enfolding the mic head in her hands. "Thank you so much," she said to ongoing applause.

Heads bobbed left and right for a better view as they listened eagerly, not ready for the night to end.

"Thank you."

She waited for the applause to ebb and the voices to quiet before continuing. "This past year has brought a lot of changes to my life. It hasn't always been easy. But somewhere along the road I learned that to get what you want, sometimes you have to take off the armor . . ." Her jacket slid off her arms to the floor, revealing two thin red shoulder straps connected to whatever was hidden beneath her black halter top. ". . . and go out on a limb."

The crowd clapped and howled its approval.

"And so for my last number"—she smiled mischievously—"I'm gonna go a little sideways."

Whistles and fists pumps punctuated the close air as the well-oiled audience all but mobbed the stage in hungry anticipation, while Jamie carried the mic stand to the very edge of the low platform, planted her feet in a wide-legged stance, and with a nod to her guitarist, launched into a fierce rendition of a bad-girl chart-topper.

She flipped her hair . . . cocked her hand on her hip, and flirted shamelessly.

By the time she built up to the chorus, the whole room was rocking.

The second verse allowed for a collective breath, but when Jamie picked the mic stand clean off the floor, leaned into it at an acute angle, curled her lip and belted out the second chorus, the Turning Point was in a state of pandemonium. Arms had breached the edge of the stage and she was forced to step back, out of the reach of grasping hands.

It was a side of Jamie that Hank had never even dreamed existed.

His body was covered with goose bumps. He couldn't look away, even as the band took their bows, thanked the wildly appreciative crowd, and said their good-nights.

It took a while until the applause finally tapered off and people began to filter out of the tavern into the night.

"You ready to head out?" asked Roy. Both of their cars were parked within walking distance. Roy followed Hank's line of sight to where the musicians gathered their equipment. "C'mon. I'll walk out with you."

Hank didn't budge. "You go ahead. I'll catch up with you later. There's something I've got to do."

"Suit yourself." Roy regarded Hank with apparent confusion. Then, his eyes lit up in a mistaken realization and he grinned and swatted Hank on the arm. "Good luck."

Onstage, the guitarist handed Jamie a bottle of water and tossed an arm loosely around her shoulders. Hank stared intently at the man's face. He thought he knew everybody within twenty miles of the Sweet Spot, but he couldn't place this guy.

Reluctant as he was to let Jamie out of his sight again, he had calmed down enough to come up with a plan. He went out to his SUV near the bar's rear exit and watched for her to come out.

The guy who'd given her the water made a couple of trips out to a minivan, loading it with instruments and amps. At last, a bundled-up Jamie emerged from the bar, deposited her guitar case in the back, and hopped into the passenger seat. When they pulled out, Hank followed at a discreet distance.

He followed the van across town into a new town-house complex behind Newberry Elementary, where he maneuvered into a space in the parking lot that afforded him a view of the unit whose door Jamie was opening with a key dug from her purse.

Must be her place. Or . . . *theirs.*

Through semi-open blinds he saw a light flick on inside the town house.

Minutes ticked by while Hank watched the two converse. Occasionally the man gesticulated. Hank would've killed to hear what he was saying.

Then his heart sank to his feet as Jamie opened her arms and the man stepped into them. They embraced—for how long, he never knew—because the next moment, Hank shoved the gearshift into drive and spun out of the parking lot, stone-cold sober despite the number of beers he'd drunk.

At that pre-dawn hour, his was the only car on the road.

Until tonight, he had been clinging to a scrap of hope.

But now that hope was gone.

No wonder Jamie hadn't responded to his calls and letters.

She had found someone else.

Inside Jamie's town house, Tony poured out his troubles to Jamie.

"It's all my fault," he moaned. "I promised Tracy I'd cut back on gigs to spend more nights at home with her and the kids. But we didn't have anyone else who could sing. Besides, the money's good. That's why I'm so grateful you were willing to front the band tonight. I need to start spending more evenings at home, helping her with the kids and all," Tony explained. "The extra income's nice. But lately, being pregnant again, she needs me more than she needs the money."

"I'm sure this is just a little lover's spat," Jamie assured him. "You'll see. She'll be waiting up for you when you get home."

"I hope you're right," Tony said.

Jamie hugged her coworker sympathetically.

The squeal of tires in the parking lot distracted them only briefly.

"I'm sure I am, and I'll be happy to fill in for you whenever you need me."

After all, thought Jamie, *it's not as if anyone else cares where I am on Friday nights . . . or any night, for that matter.*

"Now," she said, placing her hand lightly on Tony's back and pressing him toward the door.

"It's late. Go on home and tell your wife how much you love her."

"Thanks for listening," Tony said, slipping into his thick gloves. "I needed a female perspective. Tracy's the only woman I've ever loved."

"That's what friends are for. Thank you for letting me make my big Newberry 'debut,'" said Jamie, drawing air quotes.

Tony left then.

She lifted a slat in the blinds to watch his minivan drive off to his pregnant wife and his children, wondering if she would ever be so lucky.

The image of Jamie and her lover's silhouettes embracing tortured Hank.

Seth was right. All these weeks longing for Jamie, believing that she was gone for good, and the whole time she'd been only a few miles down the road.

With hindsight, it was a good thing he hadn't known. If he had, there'd have been more than one night when he might have caved to temptation and run to her, only to be crushed when she politely but firmly shut the door in his face.

He went back and reread the sole letter she'd written him, to see if he'd missed something. It said she had new students and a new place.

Was Newberry Townhomes the new place?

And if so, was she teaching in Newberry, too?

Frantically he pulled up the school website and scrolled down the list of teachers' names, clicking on the M's. There she was. *Jamie Martel, Music. Newberry Elementary.*

She was teaching at Hank's old school.

Why hadn't she told him?

So much had changed since she'd gone. There was so much he wanted to tell her. Like how he'd fired Bryce and recommitted himself to the long-range plan to get biodynamic certification. How he was coming into his own, seeing the Sweet Spot in a whole new light.

But Jamie Martel didn't belong to him. She never had. She was as free as a bird to do whatever she chose, with whomever she chose.

He had paid her to do a service for a specific length of time. She had faithfully performed the work she was hired to do.

She owed him nothing. And she deserved to be left alone to live her life.

Early on the morning of Thanksgiving Day, Hank and Roy perched on a vinyl swivel stool at the counter at the Main Street Café, plowing through a half-dozen cinnamon donuts.

"First year without your grandma's gotta be tough. Where you eating dinner?" Roy asked Hank.

"My cousin Jack's house. You?"

"Sister's place in Tigard. Hoping I get to sit at the kid's table. One of the advantages of still being single."

Hank chuckled.

"Hey." Roy elbowed him. "Last Friday night at the Turning Point . . ."

Hank flashed Roy a wary glance.

". . . you end up getting lucky?"

Hank went back to carefully studying the mug cradled between his hands. "Naw."

"Almost seemed like you knew her," Roy said, whisking some crumbs off his flannel shirt.

"Used to."

"Past tense?" Roy picked up his third donut and examined the colored sprinkles.

Hank sipped his coffee. "We were short a hand in the tasting room last summer. She filled in for a spell."

"That it?"

"That's it." Not a word about how moist her plump lips were. How soft her skin. How she smelled like an irresistible blend of sugar cookies and Ellie's cutting garden in August.

"You wouldn't be the first one to mix business with pleasure," said Roy, as if he had read Hank's mind. "I'm not one to judge."

"Nothing to judge," Hank replied tersely.

When it was time to leave for his cousin's place for dinner, Hank stalked back to his SUV, yanking his collar up against a stiff west wind blowing down his neck.

Why had Roy had to go and bring up Jamie?

He shivered. This was his first Thanksgiving without Ellie. He was going to miss her stuffing.

But he was blessed with extended family, the strength to work hard, and a few good friends. And he was beyond thankful that he still had the Sweet Spot. Even if it might get lonesome at times with no one to share it with, some people would call that having it all.

Chapter Thirty-three

December

Jamie's oatmeal-colored carpet was littered with scraps of the colored paper that she was using to construct a new bulletin board for the hallway outside her classroom. While she sat cross-legged on the floor performing the mindless task, her mind was free to wander.

She still ached inside with missing Hank. But it had been weeks since he'd emailed her.

I guess he finally gave up, she thought.

The next day, as she and Tony were wrangling their students onto the bleachers set up on the auditorium stage for the Christmas concert, he asked her to sing with T-Bone again during the coming weekend.

"I got a ton of positive feedback from your first appearance. If you could fill in for me full-time, I can stay home with my family at night until the baby's born."

She'd agreed, and during a break between sets, a stranger with a sandy-colored mustache handed Jamie a glass of red wine.

"I guessed pinot. How'd I do?"

She looked blankly at the glass, momentarily flustered. "Thank you," she finally said, looking up into kind green eyes. "That is, yes, I do happen to like pinot noir."

"Whew. That's a relief. My name's Roy Matthews, and I grew the grapes that went into this wine. Mind if I sit down?"

Outside of her school, he was the first person Jamie had met since she'd returned to Oregon.

Roy stayed at her table and watched her sing the rest of her repertoire.

And when he asked for her number at the end of the night, she caved and gave it to him.

When Jamie mentioned Roy's name to one of her coworkers in the lounge the following Monday, she confirmed that he was the never-married owner of a small winery near Dayton.

The following Saturday, Roy took Jamie to dinner at Cuvée.

It didn't escape her that he'd gone to the trouble of getting a haircut and had on a chestnut leather coat that appeared to be new. It had been a long time since anyone had cared enough to impress her.

Over a bottle of wine and burgers, Jamie told

him about her eastern upbringing and her infatuation with Willamette Valley pinot. But she edited out the part about working last summer at Hank's place.

Roy entertained her with stories of winemaking, his first love—his kindergarten teacher, back when he was a student at Newberry Elementary—and his large, close-knit family.

After dinner, Roy drove Jamie back to her town house and walked her to her door. When he leaned down to kiss her, she let him.

The kiss was pleasant, if a little dry.

But the date hadn't been wasted. She felt like she'd made a new friend.

Two days later, Jamie's phone rang.

"I'm packing to go skiing in Utah with relatives, for Christmas," said Roy. "I know it's a little last-minute to make a date for New Year's Eve, and if you're not into celebrating the most festive night of the year with someone you barely know, I get it. But there's a formal party at the Newberry Inn. No expectations. Just a chance to get dressed up, dance, and have a good time."

Jamie stalled. But then she pictured the alternative—spending New Year's Eve all alone, far from family and old friends.

"That sounds fun."

"Pick you up at seven."

Jamie owned one long dress—black velvet with four spaghetti straps leading up from the straight neckline to a choker collar—purchased at a boutique in Manayunk to wear once a year for her annual winter holiday concerts. It never failed to bring her luck, and so she had managed to squeeze it into her crammed suitcase in its plastic garment bag before flying back to Oregon.

Maybe it would work its magic yet again.

The grapevines stuck out of the picture-perfect blanket of snow like naked, brown sticks. To the casual observer they appeared almost dead. But Hank knew they were only resting. Just beneath the surface was a great deal of hidden activity. The tiny new roots that had grown after the crush were little by little allowing precisely the right amount of snowmelt into the vine to keep it alive during its dormancy and prepare it for the coming spring.

One frosty December morning on his way out to do maintenance on the tractor, a glimpse of his passing reflection in the grandfather clock stopped him cold. His hand went to his new beard. When he stroked it, the hollows in his cheeks almost made him look like a hibernating bear.

After a moment, he continued on his way out to the barn, thinking that just like his vines, on some level he was still reflecting on all that had happened in the past months, in hopes of making sense of it.

He yanked out the level plug above the clutch pedal to check the transmission fluid. Not far away in the horse stalls, Dancer wickered, and he saw again in his mind's eye Jamie astride his back, laughing as she pounded down the valley toward Raven's Rock, surrounded by green foliage, her red-gold hair flying out behind her.

He wondered what she was doing this winter season. That is, when she wasn't with *him*.

Surely right now, at 10:25 on this weekday morning, she was at school. But Christmas was fast approaching. Soon she would be on winter break. And the school event that always preceded that was the holiday concert.

If she wanted to be left alone, he thought, checking the fuel filter with freezing fingers for accumulated water, then he would respect that, even if the knowledge that she was never more than a few miles away from him was slowly eating him up inside.

But did that mean he couldn't go to the annual holiday concert? Why not? Newberry Elementary was his very own alma mater. There was a time when he used to sing in those winter concerts. And it was open to the public. Besides, he told himself, he could use a little injection of Christmas spirit. It was in short supply this year.

After he finished vacuuming the radiator grill, he wiped his hands on his bandana and pulled out his phone. The concert was that night. If not for Dancer, he might have missed it.

He strode around the corner to the horse stalls, hearing them stamp and stir at his approach.

Grabbing an apple from the box on the wall, he pulled out his pocketknife, cut it in half, and fed it to Dancer while he rubbed his forelock.

"This is from Jamie," he murmured, watching him chew. And then he added, "Good boy," for giving him a plan.

Hank got to the school early, but he didn't want to go in yet. Instead he sat in his SUV and watched the citizens of Newberry trickle into the school, obsessively checking the time. When the ushers closed the doors and only one minute remained before starting time, he sneaked into the darkened auditorium and slipped into the first seat in the back row.

It had been a dozen years since he'd last set foot in the building, but the lingering smells of that day's cafeteria lunch and pink rubber erasers made it seem like just yesterday. Surrounding him in the semidarkness were the loud voices of children and the shushing of parents, who then proceeded to converse with other adults at the same decibel level, only to be interrupted by their children and shush them again.

This went on for what seemed like forever. How could he have forgotten? These things never started on time. Fragments of his own concert days came back in broken bits and pieces. What came first? Orchestra or chorus? Was there a Christmas play? Damned if he could remember.

It occurred to him too late that in waiting till the last minute, he hadn't procured a program. And that in years past, there had always been a problem with them running out. No doubt something to do with their meager paper budget. Now he wouldn't even know when Jamie would come on stage. He would just have to wait and wonder.

At last the curtains opened to the principal, who after a prolonged welcome announced that tonight's program was called "Home for Christmas."

And who should come out next to lead the orchestral ensemble in "We Jazzy Kings" in his pressed gingham shirt, knit tie, and khakis, but Jamie's new boyfriend.

Hank's plan had turned out to be a disaster. He slouched down in his seat and clenched his jaw, willing himself not to stare at the man introduced as Mr. Anthony Harwood while praying to Jesus for a speedy end to the song, but he was unable to tear his eyes away. What did Jamie see in him? Okay. Objectively speaking, he was perky and fit-looking. He'd give him that. Clean-shaven, too, he thought, self-consciously rubbing his hand over his beard.

The next number, appropriately, Hank thought, was "In the Bleak Midwinter."

He breathed a sigh of relief when Harwood left the stage, only to be replaced with a Charlie Brown skit.

This is ridiculous, he thought, trying to get comfortable in the squeaky auditorium seat. What did he think he was doing here? He ought to just slip out the same way he'd come in, like one of those sneaky vineyard gophers.

And then the principal returned and the next thing Hank knew, she was announcing the kindergarten, first- and second-grade chorus conducted by Ms. Jamie Martel, singing "Away in a Manger," and he sat up to his full height and stared unblinking at a vision in black velvet.

She turned her back on the audience, but from his seat at stage left Hank could still see her smiling profile encouraging her students, singing along with them, emphasizing each syllable. Hungrily, he took in every minute detail, from her crowning glory flowing down her back to the four-inch heels he didn't know how anyone could even stand upright in, let alone glide in like she did.

Seemingly only seconds later, he was surprised by applause. He was so transfixed watching Jamie, he hadn't heard a note of the song.

Next came the third-, fourth-, and fifth-grade choir, and finally all grades in the finale.

All the participating teachers came out and took a bow together. And then Mr. Harwood took it upon himself to grab the mic and extend a special thanks to Ms. Martel, Newberry's newest music teacher, for the exceptional job she had done.

That was all Hank needed to see. He got up and with a shove of the heel of his palm to the wooden door, he strode briskly out into the night.

It was bitter cold inside his SUV. On his drive back to the Sweet Spot, in the quiet, snow began to fall.

Behind the heavy stage curtains at Newberry Elementary, a celebratory mood prevailed.

Tony's wife, Tracy, lumbered back, holding the hand of her toddler, to congratulate the teachers.

"Killer dress," she said to Jamie with undisguised envy. "I can't wait until I can fit into something like that again."

"Thanks. It's my good-luck dress."

"Well, it worked for you tonight. You and your kids were great. By the way, what are you doing for Christmas?" she asked, absentmindedly rubbing her free hand in slow circles over her protruding stomach.

"Singing at the eleven o'clock service at Friends

Church," Jamie replied breathlessly, still nursing a post-performance high.

"What about after that?"

Was she really doing this? Forcing Jamie to admit that she was spending Christmas alone?

She pasted on a grin. "Oh, I have things to keep me busy."

Tracy frowned. "Like what? What kind of things?"

Jamie sighed and gave her an exasperated look. "Okay! If you must know, work on a new word wall."

"Work? On Christmas." She rolled her eyes. "No. You're having Christmas dinner with us."

"I couldn't," said Jamie. "You and Tony have already gone out of your way to make me feel welcome. Christmas is for families."

"Are you kidding? After your taking over the mic for the band, we're the ones who owe you. One o'clock. I hope you like ham, because that's what we're having, and I don't have the energy to go out and buy something else at this point."

Jamie laughed. "As long as you don't mind my store-bought cookies."

On Christmas Eve, the streets of Newberry were strung with multicolored lights. Jamie shuffled through the snow in her Noconas to Christmas Eve services.

"There's Ms. Martel!"

She looked up. By now, every child in town knew her name.

"Mommy, look! It's Ms. Martel," they called out again and again. Of course, their parents wanted to get a close-up look at the new music teacher they'd only seen from afar at the holiday concert.

Inside, the tiny church was hung with greens and red bows and packed with worshippers. Singing "Silent Night" a cappella as she lit her candle and passed it down the pew from neighbor to neighbor, for a brief moment she felt a sense of community, like she belonged.

The hour was late on the East Coast when services ended. Jamie and her family video-chatted while they unwrapped the presents they'd sent one another.

The next morning, she awoke with a smile to church bells. But when she remembered that there was no one to get up and sit around the tree in her pajamas and open presents with, she closed her eyes, snuggled deeper in the covers, and rolled over to try to go back to sleep until it was time for her to go back to church to sing with the choir.

Standing in the chancel looking out on the newly familiar faces of students and their parents as she shared the gift of her voice, a warmth suffused her veins, and she felt blessed. Truly, giving was better than receiving.

Afterward she stuffed herself with cookies at Tony and Tracy's house and played with their adorable kids until it was time to go back out into the dark, and her empty town house.

Chapter Thirty-four

New Year's Eve

It was snowing again on the afternoon when Roy stopped by the post office for the mail held for him while he'd been away.

"How was your Christmas?" asked Seth.

"Fine and dandy. Yours?"

Roy was in no mood for Seth's usual long-winded banter. He'd been gone for over a week. First he had winery business to attend to, and then he had to get decked out for the party he was taking Jamie to that night, and he still hadn't unearthed his tuxedo from the nether reaches of his closet.

"Santy Claus came for the kids, that's the important thing," Seth reported. And then he added, "Say, how's your friend Hank doing since his grandmother died?"

"He's hanging in." Roy sorted through myriad

envelopes without looking up. Seth was more full of news than the *Newberry Herald*. He was always looking for grist for the mill.

"Hate to think of him rattling around in that old inn all by himself. For a while there last summer I thought maybe he and that girl who worked for him had a chance."

He had Roy's full attention now. "Who's that?"

Seth sighed dramatically. "The one from back East. You know, that tall blond gal. The one that got a job teachin' over at the elementary."

"Jamie?"

"That's it! Jamie. Jamie Martel."

"What about her and Hank?"

"Well now, don't quote me. All I know is, they were seen dancin' awful close at the wine fest back in July."

"That so?" Roy replied.

As he left the post office, he was already pulling up Hank's number. Hank agreed to meet up at the café.

Roy checked the time before stashing his phone in a back pocket, then swore under his breath. He really didn't have time for this. He looked up at the pewter sky. The gritty flakes stung his face. This was the kind of snow that stuck. It was going to make for tricky driving later.

Still, he had to talk to Hank before tonight. Why had he denied that there was anything going on between him and Jamie? And why had Jamie neglected to mention the fact that she'd ever worked at the Sweet Spot?

* * *

"Happy New Year." Roy closed one hand around Hank's while the other grasped his arm just above the elbow.

"Happy New Year," Hank grumbled.

"Don't recall as you were ever one to grow a buck beard," Roy joked as they climbed onto their counter stools. "When was the last time you went deer hunting?"

Hank rubbed his jaw without smiling. "Just haven't felt like shaving lately."

When the server came over, Roy ordered two coffees.

"I'll take a double shot of whiskey in mine," Hank added.

"Before I forget," Roy said, "I got a message for you from a woman named Margarita. She was up at the bar at the Turning Point the last time we were there." He pulled up a photo and showed it to Hank. "Remember her?"

Hank shrugged. "Maybe."

"Ran into her again at the White Horse. She told me next time I saw you to tell you she's dying to meet you."

Hank nodded politely.

"What's the matter, man?" Roy demanded.

"Nothing's the matter."

His friend raised a brow in doubt. "How're things going out at the Sweet Spot?"

"Fine." Hank brightened a little. "Matter of fact, better than fine. This fall I've had a lot of time to think, and I've made some decisions for the coming year. Got a head start by getting rid of some dead wood. Come hiring time next spring, I'm completely overhauling the staffing structure. And the chardonnay grapes my dad planted aren't living up to their potential. I've been thinking about it, and I'm going to rip them out and replace them with pinot gris."

Roy nodded in frank admiration. "Three years ago you were wrenched back to the Willamette Valley kicking and screaming. There was even talk that after seven generations, the Friestatt dynasty might finally be coming to an end."

At that, Hank looked up. He hadn't known his waffling had been so obvious, let alone the subject of scuttlebutt.

"Small town," said Roy with a hint of apology. "Just keeping it real, between friends. I'm glad to hear you're finally coming into your own. What was it that turned you around?"

Hank thought for a while. "I was too bullheaded to see what was right in front of me. Took losing almost everything I had to see what I have left."

Roy laughed and slapped Hank on the back. "Along with the vineyards, you inherited the Friestatt stubborn streak. What'd you do for the holiday?"

"Wasn't feeling particularly festive this year."

"Can't say as I blame you for that. You're still getting over losing Ellie. But you had to do something. Who you got working out there this time of year?"

"Inn's closed for the season. The wines are tanked and barreled. Just a skeleton crew of field hands giving me a hand with trellis repair and maintenance. I'm mostly just selling."

Roy shook his head. "No good spending Christmas alone."

"What's past is past. No sense looking backward. Enough about me. How 'bout you? How was Alta?"

"The powder was waist deep, man. And so dry you could blow it off your glove. Come along with us next year."

"Intrude on your family vacation?" Hank huffed and shook his head. *Had it come to that?*

Roy peered into his coffee cup and weighed his next words.

"What is it?" asked Hank. "You didn't call me down here the minute you got back to get caught up with the latest gossip. And on New Year's Eve. You must have plans. Big date."

Roy spread his palms. "I already brought it up once. Don't want to hound you. But—"

Hank tried to mitigate his sinking feeling with a fortifying swig of Irish coffee.

"Straight up now, between friends. Did you—*do* you and Jamie Martel have some kind of thing?"

Hank spoke carefully. "She's a great girl. Like I told you before, she filled in for Nelson when he was out with his broken leg."

"That it?"

"What's it to you?" he growled. Just thinking about Jamie dredged up pain he'd rather forget.

"When I went to the post office this morning to pick up my mail, I heard something from Seth Thompson."

Hank's whole body tensed up.

"He said you and Jamie were seen dancing close last summer at the Turning Point. Any truth to that rumor?"

Hank hesitated. He hadn't told a soul his version of what happened last summer. "She came out here on vacation about the same time Nelson broke his leg and Bailey took off." Once he started talking about Jamie, he couldn't seem to stop. "It was Ellie's idea to hire her. Couldn't believe she said yes. Must've been meant to be, because it wasn't long after that that Ellie took sick, and Jamie was right there by my side every minute, juggling reservations, hiring extra help to keep the kitchen going . . . she just knew what to do, as if by instinct. All the while running to the hospital to see that Ellie had her own hairbrush and pajamas. Taking her flowers from her own garden. No way could I have gotten through last summer without her."

Roy smoothed his napkin on the table. "It's no fun losing a good employee. But it's not enough to make a man stop shaving, snub his nose at a fox like Margarita for no good reason, and start lacing his morning coffee with whiskey." He looked up at Hank expectantly.

"There might have been more to it than that."

Roy nodded. "Now we're getting somewhere. So. You gonna tell me, or are you going to waste another half hour of my day playing twenty questions?"

"Then she was gone." Hank's hands went palms up. Then he propped his forehead in his hand. "I thought she went back to her job, back East. At least, that's where she told me she was going. Till the night you and I saw her at the Turning Point."

"Jeesh," said Roy. "No wonder you were spooked."

"I've never been so happy to see someone in my life," he blurted. Losing Ellie had been hard, but losing Jamie at the same time had been almost unbearable. After trying to bury his grief for four months, it was such a relief to finally admit it.

"And now?"

"Now she's seeing the rhythm guitar player in that band she's with," he said, miserably.

"Who, Tony Harwood?"

"That's him. They teach together. And from what I can tell, that's not all they do."

Roy looked at Hank incredulously. "Tony and Tracy Harwood are one of the tightest couples I know. I met them soon after they moved here from California, a couple of years ago. What makes you think he and Jamie have something going on, just because she's in his band?"

"I saw them with my own two eyes! Followed her back to her place that night after the Turning Point." Hank described the scene he'd witnessed through Jamie's living room window.

"You followed her back to her place, but there was nothing between the two of you except that she worked for you?"

Hank scrubbed his hand through his hair. "It's not like it sounds," he explained with a pained expression. "Like I tried to tell you, we had 'something.' What are you supposed to do when your heart starts going berserk and your hands start sweating every minute you're around a woman? And she felt the same way. I know she did, but . . ."

"Why did she lie then, and tell you she was going away?"

Hank couldn't speak around the painful lump in his throat. But no words were necessary. Wasn't it obvious? She just wasn't that into him.

Roy gave a snort. "You must've read it all wrong, that night you went a-spying. I just saw Tony and Tracy, Christmas shopping with their toddler. Tracy looked to be about nine months pregnant. Everything seemed fine to me."

With the faintest spark of hope, Hank searched Roy's face.

"I got to be straight with you, though, man. I took Jamie out for dinner a couple of times."

At Hank's reflexive reaction, Roy reared back and raised his palms in self-defense. "Can you blame me? She's the best thing to hit this town in a while. I thought I cleared it with you. Nothing happened. She's as nice as she is pretty, but there's just no . . . what'd you call it? 'Something?' No 'something' between us."

Hank relaxed, but only a bit. "You sure she feels the same way?"

"If she didn't, I think I'd know. There's nothing between us but a peck on the cheek. Truth is, she seems kind of lonely. Doesn't know anybody except the teachers she works with down at the school." Roy paused. "One more thing you oughtta know. I asked her to go to the big New Year's dance at the hotel tonight. But I got an idea. Why don't *you*—"

But Hank was already out of his chair, sweeping his ball cap and sheepskin coat from the wall hook, and headed toward the exit.

"Hold up!" Roy threw some bills on the counter, grabbed his own coat, and chased after Hank.

It was snowing harder now. The air was thick with swirling white flakes from a charcoal-colored sky.

"Hold up, man." Roy jogged down the sidewalk

in the yellow glow of the café lights. "Where're you headed?"

"Where do you think?" Hank shouted over his shoulder, thrusting his arms into his coat sleeves against the rising storm.

At the end of the walk, Roy halted. "Got it," he said with a salute, though Hank's retreating shape was already fading into a blur. "Okay. No problem. Just—tell—Jamie I'll . . ."

But his words blew away in the wind.

Jamie had been monitoring the forecast on and off all day. She wasn't sure what to expect with regard to tonight's festivities; whether the party would go on in spite of the storm or be canceled due to inclement weather.

She hadn't heard from Roy, so she'd gone ahead and bathed and dressed.

Now she turned the TV station back to the weather channel yet again.

"A rare holiday snow storm is pounding the Willamette Valley. Snow is expected to accumulate another five inches. Winter storm warnings have been posted for the northern and western Cascades . . ."

Restless, she went around the room she had already cleaned, rearranging curios and straightening rugs. She stopped pacing, propped her hands on her hips, and surveyed the blue sofa accented with cream throw pillows that she had carefully selected from the mall in Tigard.

Something was missing. And then it hit her. All her furnishings and knickknacks were brand-new. Unlike her grandmother's flowered dishes and the collection of objects at the Sweet Spot, they had no provenance to give them meaning.

She went to the mirror and ran her hands down the column of black velvet that smoothed out her curves. She had worn it only a couple of weeks ago to conduct the holiday pageant. It was the only thing she had left that had a history.

Dark had fallen outside her window, and it was still snowing so hard she couldn't see a few feet past the glass. Shivering, she turned up the gas fireplace until she had a lively blaze.

Hank was used to driving in wet weather, but snowstorms weren't a common occurrence in the Willamette. In the short distance from the café to Jamie's town-house complex, he had to stop twice to reach out his window and flip snow off his wiper blades. Even four-wheel drive didn't keep the SUV from sliding all over. Thank God most people had the sense not to be out on a night like this. His was practically the only car on the road.

He set his jaw. In a matter of minutes he was going to see Jamie again. That was all that mattered.

The white lines that let him know what lane he was in were invisible in the snow. He leaned harder into the windshield, fighting against the wind to keep the vehicle out of the ditch he knew from experience ran parallel to the road.

The town houses should be coming up soon. Though he couldn't bear to waste even another second, his foot eased off the gas as he pivoted his entire upper body in search of the sign.

It didn't register that the radio was even turned

on until a song came on that he hadn't heard since the day he picked up Jamie at the airport.

> *"When I find your house, I'm gonna rip that door off its hinges . . ."*

At last he skidded to a stop in her parking lot, narrowly missing a parked car. He forced the truck door open, the bottom of it scraping through white stuff, and bounded with giant leaps up the steps to that same door he'd seen Jamie enter that November night, with the guy from the band.

Shaking with cold, exertion, and nerves, Hank pounded on Jamie's door, rubbing his frozen hands together in an attempt to stave off the cold.

Guess the party's still on, Jamie thought when she heard the knock, wishing she felt more enthusiastic. She hurried to admit Roy in out of the storm.

But when she opened the door, it wasn't Roy, but Hank standing on her stoop in that bulky shearling coat, snow piling up across his broad shoulders.

It had been four long months since she'd been this close to him. He looked decidedly different.

His nose and ears were pink with the cold. He'd grown a beard, and it was sprinkled with snowflakes. But the biggest difference was in his eyes. Gone was the frown in his forehead, the clouded look of indecision. His brow was smooth, and his eyes shone with clarity.

The wind howled. Hank's breath came out in visible whooshes.

Jamie stood there motionless, heedless of the snow already accumulating on the floor.

"Hank? What are you doing here?" She looked around his six-foot-three frame. "Where's Roy?"

"Roy's not coming," Hank replied huskily, edging past her into the room.

She stepped back, still stunned, while he slammed the door shut and pulled off his gloves, laying one on top of the other on her kitchen counter in an absurd attempt at neatness.

It was quieter now with the storm shut out. They stood and stared at each other, each unsure of what to do next, how to act.

"I must look like hell." Hank chuckled, brushing the snow from his hair.

His nervousness touched her.

"No"—she shook her head slowly—"you look . . . amazing."

Jamie was the epitome of East Coast elegance in that form-fitting gown she was poured into. Her lashes, darkened for the special occasion, accented the blue of her irises, and tonight the ponytail was gone, in its place flowing amber waves caressing her bare shoulders. And there was her scent that he'd despaired of ever smelling again, the smell of summer in the dead of winter.

He took a step toward her, reverently taking her bare shoulders in his ice-cold hands.

She sucked in a breath.

Pulling her into him, he studied her face and tilted his head to kiss her, chucking his cap when the bill got in the way.

His greatcoat followed, scattering more snow across her floor. He wrapped his left arm around her waist and pulled her close; with his right he cupped the side of her face. He thumbed the plump center of her lower lip, gently opening her mouth, and then he kissed her.

Jamie met his mouth with equal ardor.

He reveled in her curves, maneuvering his body to maximize their points of contact. Coming up for air, his eyes fell to the subtle shadow of cleavage above her bodice where her chest rose and fell. Resting his forehead on the crown of her head, he reached around to undo the tiny button at her nape that held up the velvet choker-collar encrusted with crystals. It fell, taking her bodice down with it, baring the crest of her breasts. He paused, fixated on the sight. Then he slowly raised his hands to cup them in wonder.

He raised his head and looked into limpid eyes, then bent it again to kiss the twin swells, peeling her bodice lower as he did, exposing her nipples, feeling them harden beneath his fingers. Then he suckled her and her head fell back, her eyes closed, and a whimper came from her throat.

At their feet, the snow from his boots was melting into puddles on the tiled foyer.

Hank yanked off his boots and hopped deeper into the room in his stocking feet, never taking his eyes off Jamie. At last, his terrible longing was going to be satisfied.

He clasped her wrist and quickly surveyed his surroundings. Through a doorway, his gaze landed on the bed, and he pulled her toward it with an almost savage intensity.

In the bedroom, he gathered her to him again, pressing her exposed chest against his old blue chambray shirt.

"God, I've missed you, Jamie," he whispered into her hair. "I couldn't breathe without you. Couldn't think. I thought I'd lost you forever. You never left my mind. Never left my heart, not for a minute. I don't want anyone but you . . . ever."

He kissed her again, relishing her mouth, claiming her for his own.

His fingers fumbled for her zipper and when they found it, drew it down smoothly. The gown fell another stage to drape about her hips, exposing her creamy belly. Hank sat down at the foot of her bed and pulled her between his legs, covering the newly bared flesh with kisses, luxuriating in the decadence of his desire.

Deliberately, he eased the soft, heavy fabric lower, still lower until the gown pooled around her feet, leaving her standing before him in only her satin panties and heels. Hank leaned back on the bed.

"Look at you," he breathed.

Jamie bit her lip, suddenly shy. She shivered in the cool air of the bedroom.

"Cold?" Hank immediately stood and enfolded her naked body against his fully clothed one. He caressed her thoroughly, roving his hands over her exposed skin, kissing her neck beneath her ear, under her chin, and then again on the opposite side. He spread his fingers wide against her backside and urged her hips into his.

"Is this really happening?" he half whispered into her neck.

"Please," she begged, opening his shirt, snap by snap. "It's been way too long coming."

A corner of her mind swirled with questions, wondering how he'd found her, what his intentions were, and why she was reacting the way she was, not only giving in to his apparent sudden whim but madly urging him on. But those eyes told her all she needed to know. The details could wait.

Impatiently, Hank ripped his remaining snaps apart and shimmied out of his shirt, revealing his firm, muscled chest. Then he enveloped her in his arms again, savoring the feeling of warm skin against skin.

Jamie melted into his embrace. "These, too," Jamie said, fingering the top button of his faded Levi's.

"Yes, ma'am," replied Hank enthusiastically. "I aim to please." He took over the job and had them off in a flash—underwear, too.

She kicked off her heels and together they tumbled onto her duvet, smiling into each other's eyes in the firelight that filtered in from the living room.

He was magnificent. Long and strong and firm. For endless minutes, their hands explored each other, touching. Stroking. Loving.

When he sensed the time was right, Hank reached between her thighs.

Jamie was drowning in desire. It was as if they'd been unexpectedly launched on some wild, foreign sea and were being carried away on a magical current.

"I've wanted this for so long," Hank whispered as he rhythmically stroked her again and again.

Nothing in the world mattered anymore except his hand, driving her inhibitions away, taking her somewhere wondrous, up over the edge of that enchanted ocean. She rose up, up, up, clinging to him for dear life.

"I've got you. Let go," he whispered in her ear, "I've got you right here, right in the palm of my hand. Let go. Let me catch you. I'll always be there to catch you when you fall . . ."

From somewhere far away she heard a voice cry out his name.

For a few shimmering moments she hovered high above her body. Then, gradually, she floated down, down from the heights to which he'd lifted her, until at last she came back to her senses and found herself safely tucked into the shelter of his arms.

It was just like in her dreams. But this time it was real. He was real, really there to fill her, wholly and completely.

Before she knew it, he climbed between her legs and took possession of her, and she wrapped her legs around his waist and matched his cadence with abandon.

Much later, Hank lay on his side watching Jamie, playing lazily with her hair.

"Something I've been meaning to ask you since forever. What color do you call this?"

She shrugged a shoulder. "I never really thought

about it," she murmured sleepily without opening her eyes.

And he'd thought everything was settled. Now he would have to keep studying it in all kinds of light as she accompanied him through his life, riding Dancer and Blitzer through the meadows at dawn, worrying over bunch rot in Oregon's infamous drizzle, and later, curled up together on the old leather couch, sipping wine by candlelight.

With a satisfied grin, he sighed and rolled onto his back, knowing he would sleep better that night than he had in ages.

Chapter Thirty-five

A New Year

For Hank and Jamie, that New Year's Day rang in more than a new year. It was the start of a whole new life.

At the end of Jamie's school day when her headlights streamed down the lane to the vineyards, the silver sky, behind the shaggy outlines of the horses' winter coats, was already streaked with gold.

Later, Hank would build a fire and they'd eat supper—a very simple supper—curled up on the leather couch, savoring the luxury of having the great room all to themselves in the off-season.

One evening deep in January, when Jamie handed Hank a plate with a grilled cheese sandwich on it for the third time that week, she sensed that he had something he'd been wanting to say but didn't know how.

"What is it?" she asked suspiciously.

"Nothing," he said, examining his sandwich.

"Tell me," she said, curling up next to him with her plate on her lap, taking a bite.

"What happened to those great casseroles you were starting to make at the end of the summer?"

She set her plate on the coffee table and helped the long string of cheese into her mouth, then licked her fingers.

She had known this day would come, but she still wasn't prepared.

"You're blushing," he said, amused.

"I have a confession to make."

"Don't tell me." He fell back onto his old leather couch with abandon, confident that this time, the back was high enough to catch his head.

She made a guilty face.

"Theresa," he said.

"I'm sorry." She hung her head. "When it comes to cooking, I'm afraid I'll always be hopeless."

"Come here," he said, gathering her into his arms.

He studied Jamie's face, glowing in the firelight. "We'll survive, living on love."

"And wine," she added, clinking her glass with his.

"I'll drink to that," he replied.

February through April, Hank fulfilled his occasional winter travel obligations while Jamie continued to teach.

The May concert was the highlight of the school's spring calendar and the culmination of months of work. At the conclusion of the final number, Jamie was thrilled to turn around from her podium to take her bow and see Hank lead the audience in a standing ovation.

One fine Saturday in early June, a crowd gathered around the pond in back of the inn. Jamie's family and Kimmie had flown out for the occasion. The entire staff of the Sweet Spot, from the head winemaker to every last field hand, had accepted their invitation. Jamie had even surprised the guests by delivering invitations to their cabins herself.

Some of the men carried the trestle table out into the yard and set it in the shade of the oak tree. Joan and Theresa had heaped it with fried chicken and all the fixings, prepared according to Ellie's recipe. And there was a case of pinot cooled to the perfect temperature, with corkscrews sitting at the ready.

When all the guests were seated, Jamie was about to conduct her chorus of Newberry schoolchildren, the boys freshly shorn and girls with flowers in their hair, when Bill rose and looked out at the road, where two men in dark shades were getting out of a black sedan.

"Realtors," said Bill. "I'll get rid of em."

"Wait," said Jamie. "Tell them to come in and join us."

Bill looked at Hank, who had come walking over. "You sure?"

"Why not?" said Hank. "We're immune to them now. At least for another generation."

Bill sighed and shook his head. "You say so."

A minute later, seats had been found for the confused men, and Jamie led her school children in singing Disney's "Part of Your World" while Sally, her sister, walked down the aisle to a flower-bedecked arbor that led to the vineyards beyond.

The song ended to appreciative murmurs and applause. Jamie pressed her hands together at her heart center and bowed to her kids, then walked the short distance to the bottom of the aisle formed by the guests' chairs, where her father waited.

At the other end stood Hank, grinning from ear to ear.

She smiled softly at him as she fingered the loose bouquet of flowers and herbs freshly picked from Ellie's garden.

The fiddlers drew their bows. Brynn strummed a chord, and a stylized wedding march filled the air, pricking up the ears of the horses grazing in the paddock.

The eyes of the Willamette Valley were on Jamie as she slowly walked down the grassy aisle on her father's arm.

When she reached Hank, she handed her bouquet to Sally and together she and Hank faced Joe Bear.

"Hank and Jamie, before you met, you were two halves, unjoined. The opposite wings of a bird. Two halves of a seashell. Slaves to searching.

"You were apart, yet connected—two lost spirits seeking a common ground.

"Now you have found one another, and today, before friends and family, you vow to share all of life's trials and blessings, knowing that, in binding yourselves together, you become free."

Hank turned to face Jamie, took her hands in

his, and brought them to his lips. "Jamie, thank you for your patience with me."

From the rear of the crowd where some men stood, there came an anonymous snort.

Properly chagrinned, Hank smiled, then went on. "From the time our paths first crossed, we were meant to be. Now, our joining is like a tree to earth, a cloud to sky." He slipped a simple gold band onto her finger and his lips met hers softly, firmly, without hurrying.

Over in the paddock, Dancer whickered.

"Jamie." Joe Bear nodded to her.

"Beloved partner," said Jamie. "Keeper of my heart. Love like ours conquers fear, removes doubt, and establishes an unshakeable foundation. It is from this foundation that we can maintain perspective in times of trouble and rise from the ashes of our mistakes. Let our love be always clothed in summer blossoms so the icy hand of winter never touches us."

Joe Bear placed his turquoise-ringed hand atop their clasped ones in conclusion of the simple rites. "Bless the union of these two spirits, so alike that the Creator has designed them for life's endless circle."

Hank and Jamie turned to face their loved ones to cheers and the merry sawing of fiddles.

Roy danced with Kimmie, and Theresa danced with Jamie's dad, and the field-workers lined up to dance with the Sweet Spot's new official first lady.

"How'd you know to send her my way?" Hank asked Jamie's dad as he watched her mingle among their guests, referring to the way he had encouraged her to vacation in wine country.

Charles Martel shoved his hand in his pocket and jingled his change.

"Girl needs wide-open spaces. Even when she was a little thing, she was more likely to be out in the fields while Sally was inside with her mother. That's all done with back where we're from. All built up now." He looked around. "Vineyard's a perfect fit for her."

Late that night, when the kitchen had been cleaned and the guests were secure in their cabins, Jamie and Hank sat on the back-porch steps, leaning into each other.

"It was a great wedding day," Jamie murmured.

Hank smiled up at the stars. "Ellie would've loved it," he replied.

"I feel like she's here with us," said Jamie.

All was quiet again, except for the call of an owl.

"Well," said Hank with a sparkle in his eye. "Only one thing left to do."

He stood and reached for her hand.

No sooner had she gained her feet than he swept her off of them again with a mighty grunt.

"Oh!" she gasped.

"Did you think I was going to let you cross the threshold yourself on your wedding night?" he panted, carrying her up the steps to the back porch, with his tongue out.

"Yes, actually, I did," she said, giggling. "But I should have known better."

They had been married less than a month when one afternoon Hank said to Jamie, "I believe I promised you a plane ride, Mrs. Friestatt."

He held out his hand and helped Jamie into the passenger seat of the Beechcraft Bonanza he'd bought upon earning his license to fly solo.

He got in and brought the engine to life.

"Nervous?" he asked Jamie through the headphone mic.

"In a good way." She smiled back.

"Hold on tight. Here we go."

They hurtled down the narrow runway at Ribbon Ridge Airport, Jamie's breath catching as she felt the ground fall away.

By the time they reached altitude, she was accustomed to the noise.

Hank had flown over the valley countless times while logging his required flight hours. He knew not only the viticultural areas; he could also point out the specific vineyards in each area, even the blocks within each vineyard.

"I couldn't have asked for a better tour guide," Jamie said.

"Wait and see," Hank said. "I saved the best for last."

A short time later he pointed down and asked, "Recognize that?"

She looked down at the irregularly shaped fields resembling corrugated cardboard.

"That's the Sweet Spot!" said Jamie. "That's ours."

He grinned. "I got some news a couple weeks back. I've been saving it for when I could finally take you up."

She turned to him. "Tell me! Don't keep me waiting."

"We got our certification. You're looking at Ribbon Ridge's newest biodynamic vineyard."

In the fullness of the moment, Hank's eyes found Jamie's. He reached over the controls and rested his hand on her growing belly.

The Sweet Spot wasn't a cross to be borne. It was an enduring gift to be opened again and again. When the time came, he would pass it on to his children, and they, in turn, to theirs.

He took several passes until he'd pointed out each individual block.

"Now, whenever you run on about a certain block, I'll be able to see it in my mind," she said.

For a while, they soared along without speaking.

Finally, he said, "It's getting late."

"It's still plenty light out."

"Tonight's the solstice. We have a long night ahead of us." Now that Ellie was gone, Jamie would step into her shoes to help Hank bury the cow horns in the annual ritual. "We're going to be up way past midnight."

He raised an eyebrow. "Ready?"

She nodded. "Theresa left supper in the oven."

Hank grinned. "Hiring her away from the school cafeteria was pure genius."

He turned the yoke and the plane rolled sideways and headed for home, the evening sun glinting off its wings.

Craving more wine and romance from
Heather Heyford?
Be sure to check out her
Napa Wine Valley and
Oregon Wine Country romances
Available now wherever ebooks are sold.
Keep reading for a sneak peek of
the first books in each series
A Taste of Chardonnay
and
The Crush

From *A Taste of Chardonnay*

Chapter One

Friday, June 13

"Are you my Realtor?"

Chardonnay St. Pierre tried to hide her wariness as she approached the man who'd just stepped out of his retro pickup truck. This wasn't the best section of Napa city.

Their vehicles sat skewed at odd angles in the lot of the concrete building with the AVAILABLE banner sagging along one side. Around the back, gorse and thistles grew waist-high through the cracks in the pavement.

A startlingly white grin spread below the man's aviators.

"Realtor? You waiting for one?"

For the past half hour. "He's late." Char went up on her tiptoes, craning her neck to peer down the street for the tenth time, but the avenue was still empty. She tsked under her breath. She should've taken time after her run to change out of her skimpy running shorts, she thought, reaching discreetly around to give the hems a yank down over her butt. And her Mercedes looked more than a little conspicuous in this neighborhood.

Where was he? She pulled her cell out of her bag to call the Realtor back. But something about the imposing stranger was distracting her, demanding another look. "Have we met?" She squinted, lowering her own shades an inch.

He turned sideways without answering and examined the nondescript building, and when he did, his profile gave him dead away.

Oh my god. Char's breath caught, but he didn't notice. His whole focus was on the real estate. She'd just seen that face smiling out from the *People* magazine at the market over on Solano when she'd picked up some last-minute items for tonight's party.

"What have you got planned for the place?" he asked, totally unselfconsciously.

Then she recovered. To the rest of the world, he was Hollywood's latest It Man. But to Char, he was just another actor. Who happened to have a really great dentist.

"I could ask you the same thing."

"I asked first."

Though she wasn't at all fond of actors, her shoulders relaxed a little. Obviously, she wasn't going to get raped out here in broad daylight by the star of *First Responder.* It was still in theaters, for heaven's sake. He couldn't afford the press.

Still. This building was perfect. And it'd been

sitting here empty for the past three years. Just her luck that another party would be interested, right when Char was finally in a position to inquire about it.

To Char's relief, a compact car with a real estate logo plastered from headlights to tailpipe pulled up and a guy in his early thirties bounded out with an abundance of nervous energy.

"This business is *insane*," he said by way of introduction. "Dude calls me from a drive-by and wants me to show it to him, like, *now*, right? So I drop everything, even though I'm swamped with this new development all the way over on Industrial Drive. And then he doesn't show up till quarter of—"

He caught himself, pasted on a proper smile, and extended his hand toward It Man.

"Bill Diamond. And you're Mister . . . ?"

"McBride." The actor shook his hand, then turned and sauntered back to the building with his hands on his hips and his eyes scrutinizing its roofline.

"Ryder McBride?" asked Diamond. "*The* Ryder McBride? Oh!" A smile overspread his face. "Cool! Very cool. Nice to meet you, man." He nodded once for emphasis.

Char stepped up, removing her sunglasses and slipping them over the deep V of her racer-back tee.

"Hi." She thrust out her arm. "I'm—"

The Realtor's eyes grew even wider, as his hand reached for hers.

"I know who you are . . . *Chardonnay St. Pierre, right?*"

He was still holding on when Char's phone vibrated in her other palm. One glance at the screen and she sighed.

"Excuse me."

But Diamond didn't let go.

"I've got to take this," she repeated, pronouncing each syllable slow and clear. She gave a little tug, and he came to, his fingers relaxing. "It's my little sister."

She ducked her chin and pressed answer.

"Where are you?" Meri's voice sounded tense.

"Downtown."

"You've got to come meet Savvy and me. Papa's in jail."

Bill Diamond was still gaping when Char dropped her phone into her shoulder bag.

"I'm so sorry. Something important's come up and I have to run."

Like a guy who'd come to expect disappointment at every turn, his face fell. "Oh."

Char felt a stab of empathy.

"Did you want to reschedule?" His brows shot up hopefully.

It was a given. But right now concern for her family eclipsed everything else. "I'll have to call you."

As she turned to go, Ryder spoke up.

"I'm staying. Mind showing me around?"

Char stopped in her tracks halfway to her car and glared back at him. She thought he'd barely noticed her. But she'd swear his broad grin was designed purely to tease.

"Excuse me? This is *my* Realtor."

"Ah, actually . . ." Bill cleared his throat, looked at the ground, and then back up at her. "I work for the seller."

"But *I'm* the one who called you to meet me here," she insisted.

He looked from Char to Ryder and back as he juggled his options, then shrugged. "But you're leaving."

Char's thoughts raced. She hated to leave those two here together, to cook up some deal to steal the building out from under her, but she had no choice. "Fine. Bill, I'll be in touch," she called, climbing into her car, then pulling out of the lot a little too fast.

She loved Papa. Truly, she did. But at times like these, she'd give anything for an ordinary, run-of-the-mill dad, in place of the notorious Xavier St. Pierre.

From *The Crush*

Chapter One

Rap rap rap!

Juniper Hart was agonizing over which of her wine business's creditors would luck out and get paid this month when she heard a loud knocking at the door of her tasting room.

Her head shot up from her bills. She scrambled out from behind her desk, heedless of the papers she set sailing. Inches short of the threshold, she skidded to a stop to smooth down her faded T-shirt emblazoned with WE ARE PINOT NOIR. From the other side of the door, she heard a familiar voice.

"Last I knew, Lieutenant, you had women in, let's see—Fort Bliss, Fort Belvoir, and New York City. And that's just stateside."

Though the words meant nothing to her, Junie recognized the timbre of her old friend Sam Owens's voice. Sam had racked up numerous awards for his military service before moving back to his hometown. These days, he made a living ferrying tourists around in his Clarkston Wine

Consortium van, introducing them to Willamette Valley wine. And now, from the sound of it, here he was, delivering eager wine enthusiasts right into the palm of Junie's hand.

She pasted on her best smile and threw wide the door. "Welcome to the pinot state!"

"Hey, Junie!" said Sam warmly. "Like the new greeting."

"Sounds way better than 'Welcome to Broken Hart Vineyards,' " deadpanned Keval, thumbing his cell phone without looking up.

Junie cringed at the innocuous-sounding nickname. Keval Patel might be the town of Clarkston's god of IT, but he could use some help in the tact department.

But wait—these weren't Junie's desperately needed new customers making a detour off the established wine trail. Despite their chins sporting some degree of hipster stubble, to her, these guys would always be the same fresh-faced, coltish boys they'd been back at Clarkston Middle School. Ever since her dad died and her brother left town, they were practically all the family she had left. All except the one with the Ivy League haircut, dressed more for a job interview at Brooks Brothers than a drive in the wine country.

"Thought you said Oregon was the *Beaver* State?" the stranger asked Sam, eyeing Junie up and down. "Because, *damn* . . ."

Heath Sinclair's burst of laughter was cut short by Sam's swift elbow to his ribs.

"Why else would I leave a city where women outnumber men to fly all the way across the country?"

"Thought it was to do a brother a favor, Lieutenant." Sam raised a weary brow. "Sorry, Junie. We've done two tastings already, and some of these bozos forgot how to spit."

"I had all good intentions of expectorating when we started out." Heath straightened, still clutching his side. "But I'm a beer drinker. Beer drinkers swallow. It's what we do." Heath should know—he was the founder of Clarkston Craft Ales.

"Juniper Hart"—Sam stretched out an arm toward the stranger—"this is Lieutenant Manolo Santos."

The lieutenant nodded in curt, military fashion. "Pleasure."

"Manolo's a construction guy from back east. Came out to give me some expert advice on the new consortium building."

Junie examined Manolo dubiously. Tall and broad shouldered with a flat belly, it was easy to imagine him in a sweat-stained work shirt, hefting a load of two-by-fours. But the quick gleam in his eye, the pride in his bearing, and his impeccable grooming pegged him as more than just your typical manual laborer.

"Construction guy?"

"Construction engineer, technically," he replied.

"What exactly does a construction engineer do?"

"The official U.S. Army definition?" He flashed her a blindingly white grin. "Someone who works a twelve-hour day/night shift seven days a week on a rotational basis in a remote location."

Sam gripped Manolo's shoulder affectionately. "What the lieutenant here does is solve problems.

Converts ideas into reality. Manny's helped design roads, schools, and hospitals from Arizona to Iraq."

"Is that so?"

Manolo shrugged off Sam's compliment like a too-tight shirt. "Think of me as kind of a combination Jason Bourne and Bob the Builder."

"You're forgetting horndog," added Sam, to backslaps and shrieks of mirth.

Junie dismissed Manolo and slanted her eyes at those she knew better. "You guys sure you can handle another one?"

They straightened their spines, trying their best to look contrite.

Keval tsked and gave her an incredulous look. "Are you *serious*?"

"C'mon, Junie. Let us in," pleaded Rory, whose family's apple orchard adjoined Junie's land.

"I'm designated driver." Sam jerked a thumb toward his log-splashed van parked out in the field, some distance away.

She propped her hand on her hip and pretended to consider her options. If not for Sam roping them in, no tourists would ever find their way off the main road to her boutique winery. Junie owed Sam big-time.

When she figured they'd suffered long enough, she broke out in a conciliatory smile. "C'mon," she said, stepping aside.

The men shuffled past Junie into the tasting room in single file, with Tall, Dark, and Sketchy bringing up the rear.

"After you, ma'am."

His baritone was soft and deep. Arrogant eyes

the rich brown of espresso made the back of her neck prickle. *A man who seems too good to be true usually is.* She brushed off her warning instinct, slipped behind the counter, and dealt out five generic white coasters. Those would have to do until the day she could afford to have them done right, custom-printed with her name.

Lieutenant Santos's head swiveled on his neck, absorbing every detail of Junie's humble tasting room . . . the unfinished ceiling, the plywood walls, the makeshift bar cobbled together from cast-off parts. The closer he looked, the more inadequate she felt. So what if it wasn't the Taj Mahal? She was doing the best she could.

She kept half an eye on him as he wandered over to the opposite side of the room, where a picture window would be someday, if she was lucky. His every movement was a study in controlled power. Wherever he went, the others followed, drawn to him like bees to a hive. He said something Junie couldn't quite decipher. Whatever it was, her friends found it highly entertaining.

Daryl Decaprio, Clarkston High's most notorious flirt. The resemblance was uncanny.

When the laughter finally died down, Daryl's twin drifted over to watch her work. The temporary bar served only four without crowding. But there was an eighteen-foot slab of live-edge white oak out in the barn just waiting for the right time to be installed.

"You wouldn't happen to have anything to eat back there, would you?"

"This is a wine-tasting room. If you're hungry, there're some restaurants in town."

He raised a palm. "Fair enough. No harm in asking."

She launched into her rehearsed pitch. "So, where're you from?"

"Born and raised in Hoboken, New Jersey. But I left there a long time ago."

Junie busied herself opening a two-year-old vintage. She felt the heat of his gaze travel over her hands, up her arms to her chest, her neck, and finally her face.

"What's a beauty like you doing hidden away in a place like this?"

Her hands paused where they struggled against the stubborn cork. Beauty? *Her?* He didn't just look like Daryl; he laid it on thick like him, too.

Stick to your script, Junie. What had they said at that free class for entrepreneurs at the Yamhill County Extension? She was the one who should be asking the questions. Marketing 101.

She gave the screw a vicious twist. The cork came out with a muted pop, and she began to pour the one-ounce servings used for sampling.

"How long will you be in the Willamette Valley?"

"Not long. I'm a traveling man. Just passing through."

Lieutenant Manolo Santos was a walking, talking cliché, thanks to his good looks and bad lines. *Be nice to everyone,* they said in the class. *You never know who might turn out to be an ally.* She clenched the bottle tighter in her moist palm, determined not to fumble under his penetrating glare, ally or not.

Sam hoisted his glass and the others followed

suit. But before he could make a toast, the stranger beat him to it.

"To the Beaver State," he said, eyes sparkling with mischief.

That brought more cautious chuckles, as her friends weighed their loyalty to her against the novelty of the suave newcomer in their midst.

Sam swirled his wineglass at eye level, checking for all the signs: color, viscosity, legs.

Rory downed his glass like cider and followed it with a satisfied belch.

Junie's heart sank. Heath was a brewer and Sam was in the wine business, like Junie. Keval was industry, too, if doing IT for the consortium counted. Was it too much to ask for them to appreciate what she was trying to do here? They'd tried her wine before. They knew word of mouth was everything. That's where sales came from. But they couldn't pass the word on about how great her pinot was if they persisted in chugging it like marathoners on Gatorade. Maybe they couldn't handle three tastings in one day, after all.

"Yummy." Keval licked his lips and picked up a battered copy of *Wine Spectator* from the bar. "Just think, Juniper. Maybe you'll be in here someday."

Yeah, right. She couldn't even afford to renew her subscription.

At least Sam had the decency to give his wine time to wander around his palate, letting it speak to his taste buds. "Your wine sings, Junie."

Junie swelled with pride. High praise, coming from Sam. But even he couldn't seem to find her a distributor, though he'd been looking for the past couple of years.

True to his word, he spat into the receptacle provided. "Now, how about that rosé?"

Junie poised the new bottle to pour, but there were only four empty glasses on the counter. She skimmed the room for the fifth, spotting it in the hand of Mr. New Jersey.

Thick, workingman's fingers cradled her fragile stemware. Dense lashes brushed against carved cheekbones as he lowered them to gaze at the ruby liquid. Then he glanced up over the rim, catching Junie staring. "Young, bright appearance."

He lowered his Roman nose into the bowl and sniffed, then looked up, his eyes landing in the vicinity of her chest. "Juicy plums." He swirled and sniffed again. "And some other fruit I don't think I've had the pleasure of tasting."

Junie forgot about the bottle she held poised, and it sank to the bar under its own weight. "Lingonberry. It's native to the Pacific Northwest."

Manolo drank then. But all the while he worked her wine around in his mouth, he didn't take his eyes off her.

The tasting room grew uncomfortably warm, despite the chilly April air. Lieutenant Manolo Santos had a politician's command of the room. Even the guys quit horsing around in anticipation of what he would say next.

"Soft and supple, yet structurally complex. I like that."

The breath Junie didn't know she'd been holding whooshed out through her broad grin. This vintage was her most ambitious effort to date, and that was exactly the response she had been going for!

"It's good in a wine, too."

While the guys cracked up, Junie's smile ebbed and her cheeks burned even hotter.

Manolo raised his glass. "To—Junie, was it?"

She glared daggers at him. He may have played her once, but she wouldn't let it happen again. Thanks to her experience with Daryl, she knew better than to trust guys like him.

"Could we, ah . . ." Sam motioned to the still-empty quartet of glasses.

Only then did she remember the bottle of rosé she still clenched by the neck.

After she set them up again, her usually level-headed, sweet friends surrounded Mr. Big Shot.

"To Junie!" he exclaimed, eyes aglow with a fire that disconcerted her, despite her resolve.

"To a promising future," said Sam, with a nod of appreciation for her skill as a winemaker.

The others echoed with woozy tributes of their own.

Testosterone-fueled shoulder bumps were followed by more enthusiastic clinks. "One more?" Heath asked, holding out his empty glass.

More laughter, more rowdy toasting.

Then Junie shrank at the sound of crystal shattering.

"I'll get the broom." She hurried back to her office, adding the cost of replacing the broken stemware to her long list of expenses.